Random Acts of Deceit

*Holly Anna Paladin Mysteries,
Book 2*

By Christy Barritt

Random Acts of Deceit

Random Acts of Deceit: A Novel
Copyright 2015 by Christy Barritt

Published by River Heights Press

Cover design by The Killion Group

This ebook is licensed for your personal enjoyment only. This ebook may not be re-sold or given away to other people. Thank you for respecting the hard work of this author.

The persons and events portrayed in this work are the creation of the author, and any resemblance to persons living or dead is purely coincidental.

All Scripture is taken from THE HOLY BIBLE, NEW INTERNATIONAL VERSION®, NIV® Copyright © 1973, 1978, 1984, 2011 by Biblica, Inc.® Used by permission. All rights reserved worldwide.

Other Books by Christy Barritt

Squeaky Clean Mysteries
#1 *Hazardous Duty*
#2 *Suspicious* Minds
#2.5 *It Came Upon a Midnight Crime*
#3 *Organized Grime*
#4 *Dirty Deeds*
#5 *The Scum of All Fears*
#6 *To Love, Honor, and Perish*
#7 *Mucky Streak*
#8 *Foul Play*
#9 *Broom and Gloom*
#10 *Dust and Obey*
#11 *Thrill Squeaker*
#12 *Cunning Attractions*
#13 *Clean Getaway*

The Sierra Files
#1 *Pounced*
#2 *Hunted*
#2.5 *Pranced* (a Christmas novella)
#3 *Rattled*

The Gabby St. Claire Diaries (a tween mystery series)
#1 *The Curtain Call Caper*
#2 *The Disappearing Dog Dilemma*
#3 *The Bungled Bike Burglaries*

Holly Anna Paladin Mysteries
#1 *Random Acts of Murder*
#2 *Random Acts of Deceit*
#3 *Random Acts of Malice*
#3.5 *Random Acts of Scrooge*
#4 *Random Acts of Greed*
#5 *Random Acts of Fraud*

The Worst Detective Ever
Ready to Fumble
Reign of Error
Safety in Blunders

Carolina Moon series
#1 *Home Before Dark*
#2 *Gone By Dark*
#3 *Wait Until Dark*
#3.5 *Light the Dark*
#4 *Taken by Dark*

Suburban Sleuth Mysteries
#1 *Death of the Couch Potato's Wife*

Standalone Romantic Suspense
Keeping Guard
The Last Target
Race Against Time
Ricochet
Key Witness
Lifeline
High-Stakes Holiday Reunion
Desperate Measures
Hidden Agenda
Mountain Hideout
Dark Harbor
Shadow of Suspicion

Standalone Romantic Mystery
The Good Girl

Suspense
Dubiosity
Disillusioned
Distorted
Imperfect

Christy Barritt

Dedication:

This book is dedicated to all those who grieve. I understand your pain. Prayers for comfort and peace to you.

Acknowledgements:

A special thanks to Deena Peterson and Mary Ann Hake for their help with this book.

Random Acts of Deceit

CHAPTER 1

My heart skipped a beat as Chase Dexter stared at me on my front porch.

Or maybe I stared at him? Which was probably against some kind of ladylike etiquette. In fact, I thought I'd read in one of my books on manners that I should play hard to get, but playing hard to get really wasn't my style.

No, Chase Dexter made me feel warm and fuzzy all over, despite the late-night chill around us. When he took my hand, pulled it to his lips, and softly pressed a kiss there, I felt like warm honey filled my chest cavity with its ooey-gooey goodness.

"As always, I had a great time tonight, Holly," he said.

"I had a pretty good time also," I told him.

He raised his eyebrows, his eyes dancing with mischief. "A *pretty* good time?"

I nodded, keeping my expression demure. "I don't want to give you an ego trip or anything."

He chuckled, the tone deep and low. The sound was almost more of a rumble that echoed from deep inside of him. I found it glorious and soothing. One day I really should record the gentle laughter because it could cheer me up on the grayest of days.

"You're one of a kind, Holly Anna Paladin."

I offered him a half shrug, trying to play it cool while

making it obvious that I was playing it cool. I was a confusing mess like that sometimes. "I take that as a compliment."

He shook his head, his eyes locked on mine as he swiped a stray hair behind my ear. "You just did it again, you know."

"I did what again?"

"That little thing you do."

"There's a little thing I do?" I had no idea what that thing was, but it sounded intriguing.

A smile played on his lips. "You tilt your head, pop your hip out, and get that coy I-have-a-lollipop-and-you-don't look in your eyes. You remind me of someone from the fifties doing a cover shoot."

"Interesting." Maybe I was better as this whole flirting thing than I thought, which was strange because I'd always considered myself a complete and absolute failure in that department. Then again, maybe Chase just brought out another side of me.

Chase stepped close, the look in his eyes moving from playful to smoldering. The look made my stomach flip forward, backward, and every other which way possible. "I'll see you tomorrow?"

I nibbled on my bottom lip as his gaze swept me away. So many endorphins were bursting inside my head that the moment should set some kind of record for warm fuzzies. "I'm looking forward to it."

His hand cupped my neck, and his thumb rubbed my jaw. He started to lean forward, to draw me closer, but then took an abrupt step back. We were supposed to be taking it slow. Very slow.

He seemed to remember that at the same time I did, and, instead, he took my hand and kissed it again.

With one last glance, he stepped away. "Good night, Holly."

"Good night, Chase." My voice sounded so dreamy and lovelorn that I almost wanted to smack myself. I'd never swooned over someone before. But every time I was around Chase, I definitely swooned so much that I could mentally hear Elvis singing "Can't Help Falling in Love" in the background.

With that, I stepped into my house, and the comforting scent of orange, rosemary, and vanilla filled my senses. This was actually my mom's house, but I was living with her for the time being. The situation was win-win for both of us.

Since Dad had passed away almost two years ago, I'd sensed that Mom needed someone. Plus, being a social worker didn't equate to earning great money, so I was saving all I could. I had confidence that when the time was right, I'd instinctively know I needed to find my own place. Until then, I was going to bloom where I was planted. Right now, that was my childhood home.

I flipped on the lights, and an empty house came into focus. A Tudor style with hardwood floors and immaculately stylish decorations, it was located on the outskirts of an area of town that used to be much sought after. However, through the years this part of the city had become only a shell of its former glory. My mom was one of the few who held on to the hope that the area could still be revitalized one day.

Mom was at a fund-raiser gala tonight. She attended at least one a week. She probably organized about one a month. That was my mom—a social butterfly and certified community mover and shaker. No cause was too big or too small for her to conquer.

I set my keys on the marble-topped table in the entry and hung my coat in the hall closet before hurrying upstairs to my room. I loved getting dressed up—the girlier the outfit, the better—but I also loved cuddling up in my favorite pair of comfy pajamas. I'd change out of my dress, come downstairs for a cup of Earl Grey, and listen to some of my favorite music—probably some Ella Fitzgerald tonight. Maybe "Someone to Watch Over Me." It had been running through my head all day.

It would be the perfect ending to the perfect evening. The perfect evening with Chase. We'd been officially dating for a couple of months now. Since then, I'd felt like I was walking on air and like nothing could possibly go wrong. I was having my moment in life, the one romantic movies liked to highlight, singers liked to sing about, and card companies made millions from. I was irrefutably in love.

I reached beyond my door to flip the light switch in my room. Though my fingers connected with the plastic lever, nothing happened. The space remained dark.

Strange.

Had my overhead light burned out? That seemed most likely.

I crossed the room, my haven with its shabby chic decorations of white and black base colors mixed with lace and floral accents. I had to reach the lamp on my nightstand. Five steps across the floor, I heard a movement and froze.

My throat instantly tightened, lodging a panicked scream.

Had I been hearing things? That had to be it. I mean, why would anyone be in my room? In the dark?

They wouldn't be, I told myself. I was hearing things. Of course.

I let out a nervous, airy laugh and took another step.

"Holly Anna Paladin," a deep voice said.

I gasped and twirled around. The voice had come from

the dark recesses of what was supposed to be my sanctuary.

Someone *was* in my room!

A stranger. Who had broken in. And people only broke into homes to do devious things, right? Or random acts of kindness, as I'd done in the not-so-distant past. But that was an exception, and a not-so-wise one at that, to the otherwise steadfast rule of stranger-in-the-bedroom danger.

I started to reach for the lamp, desperate to see with my own eyes whom I was up against. I hadn't recognized the voice. Nor was I expecting any late-night visitors. Especially not in my bedroom.

"Leave the light off." The man sounded authoritative. A certain hardness in his voice let me know, without a direct threat, that there would be consequences if I didn't do as he said.

My entire body tensed. My mind raced. My heart beat out of control.

I lowered my arm back to my side and turned fully toward the voice. "Who are you? How'd you get in here? What do you want?" As the words vomited from my mouth, my eyes flickered, desperate to adjust to the darkness. It was no use. Everything was still pitch black around me.

Based on his voice, I sensed the man was a few feet away, maybe near my window. The depth of his pitch indicated he could be large. The intensity and unwavering undertones made me think he was strong. The fact that he'd somehow gotten into my house let me know he was devious.

All in all, I realized I was in big trouble.

The man chuckled. Unlike Chase, though, the sound wasn't soothing. It was cold and methodical. "So inquisitive, aren't you, Ms. Paladin? What you don't realize is that you're not in a good place to ask questions."

Despite his warning, I asked, "What do you want?"

His chuckle faded fast. "I need you to listen closely and do exactly as I tell you. There's a man, and he's going to ask you out soon. You'll say yes."

Of all the threats I'd imagined he'd make, this was not one of them. "Someone's going to ask me out? I'm dating someone."

"You'll break up with Detective Chase Dexter."

My heart froze, and I almost laughed. Why in the world would I break up with Chase? That made no sense. We were perfect together. "I don't want to break up with Chase."

"Listen very carefully, Ms. Paladin." Agitation grew in his voice. "You don't have a choice. If you don't end things between the two of you, there will be serious consequences. You will need to be convincing in order to make this work."

My head swirled as I tried to process what the man was telling me. Serious consequences how? What exactly was this leverage the man thought he held over me? "What . . . what do you mean? I'm really not following this here."

"I mean that I'll kill your little lover boy if you don't do as I say."

I gasped as soon as the word *kill* hit my ears. He'd *kill* Chase? I needed to buy some time in order to process this. "Don't you think that seems a little extreme?"

"I repeat myself, Ms. Paladin. You're not in a good place to ask questions. You're just to do as I say or face my wrath. The latter won't be pretty."

I tried to think this through instead of allowing my emotions to dart up to Irrational Land, the place where my reactions got the best of me and panic ruled. There would be time for that later.

"So, break up with Chase and go out with a strange

man. That's it?" The words escaped my lips as if I'd just been given instructions about running an errand.

I had to think all of this through. There was a way out of this. There had to be. I'd simply tell Chase, and he'd handle this. End of story. It could be that easy . . . right?

"That's it."

"How many times do I have to go out with him?"

"You'll know when it's done."

"And then I can date Chase again?"

"In a manner of speaking. You think you can handle this?"

In a manner of speaking? What did *that* mean? Again, I'd have to think about that later. I had more immediate objectives that needed my attention.

"I repeat: Do you think you can handle this?"

"Since you threatened death, I suppose I'll have to," I mumbled, trying to placate the man.

I squinted. My eyes were adjusting to the darkness, and I could make out a faint silhouette near the window. But the man's features were darkened. He must have been wearing a ski mask or something.

"There's more," the man rumbled.

My heart lurched. How could there possibly be more? The man had dropped a major bombshell, one that was rocking my world. And it was going to get worse?

Dear Lord, what am I going to do? This has to be a joke, right?

"Chase Dexter lives at 1809 Bradshaw Avenue in the Clifton area of town. He awakes every day at 6:00 a.m. sharp. He eats a breakfast of bacon, eggs, and a protein shake before doing his morning workout in the basement. His knee has been hurting lately, but he hasn't wanted to tell anyone, since he's new to the police force here in Cincinnati, I assume."

"Really?" Chase had never told me that, but I had seen him rubbing his knee earlier tonight when we were at dinner. Why hadn't he mentioned anything to me?

"As far as I can ascertain, you're his one weakness," the man continued. "Although he *is* a recovering alcoholic, so drinking is like a phantom that is always lingering close just looking for the opportunity to gain its control. You make him want to be better."

His words only deepened the chill that pricked my skin, my body, and my heart. This man knew a lot about my boyfriend, things that a stranger shouldn't know. How had he found all this out? Was he a friend? A colleague on the police force? A neighbor?

"How do you know that information?" My voice cracked as fear pushed its way to the surface.

"I do my homework, Ms. Paladin. It's only wise in situations like these." He took a step closer. "That said, I should let you know that cameras are hidden in his house and yours. Maybe in other places also, but I wouldn't test me if I were you."

I shivered at his implications, at the feeling that my privacy and Chase's had totally been invaded. Even worse, I wasn't sure there was much I could do about it, and I deplored feeling helpless.

"There's also a bomb that's been placed in one of the air shafts in Chase's home. If I discover that you've told him about this conversation—and I *will* discover it—then Lover Boy will be blown to smithereens. Do I make myself clear?"

I stared at his silhouette, my heart pounding in my ears. This man was no joke. If I didn't listen to him, he was going to destroy my life. If I did listen to him, he was also going to

destroy my life.
    What was I supposed to do?

CHAPTER 2

The image of Chase dead, his body ruined with fire, his skin . . . I couldn't bear to picture any more. Each mental image made my heart feel like it had been pummeled with a hammer. Then placed in a blender until it was mush. Unmendable, irreparable mush.

"Do I make myself clear?" the man repeated.

"Yes," I whispered. My earlier assumptions that I'd figure a way out of this disappeared faster than my homemade cookies at the homeless shelter.

"What was that?"

I cleared my throat, trying to nudge my voice into action. "I said, 'Yes.'"

"Smart girl. Now, you're going to turn around and walk back into the hallway. I want you to go downstairs and check the locks on all your doors. A girl can never be too careful, especially living in the city as you are. It's a scary world out there, Ms. Paladin. Very scary."

"O . . . okay."

My knees trembled as I took my first step. *Don't give out on me now*, I prayed. I was almost to safety, to a place where I could run and escape. To a refuge where I might be able to think clearly.

Or was this a part of his evil plot? Was he waiting until my back was toward him in order to knock me out? To shoot me? To do some other terrible thing?

My footsteps quickened as I got nearer the door. When I was close enough to the hallway, I burst into a run. I didn't stop running until I reached the front door.

I started to pull it open but stopped myself. Instead, I leaned against the wood, my breaths coming in heavy gasps.

I couldn't run outside. I couldn't call Chase for help.

I couldn't talk to anyone.

My only choice was to stay here. I was alone and isolated from seeking help. Chase might have been my protector in the past, but now I was going to have to look out for him.

That's when reality hit and tears rushed to my eyes.

Break up with Chase?

I couldn't do it. I'd never told him, but I was in love with the man. I couldn't imagine not being with him. I couldn't call things off between us.

But what choice did I have?

I squeezed the skin between my eyes as an ache formed there.

Compose yourself, Holly. Get a grip. There's got to be a solution. There's always a solution. You just have to think outside the box. That's what Dad had always told me. Of course, that was usually in reference to some household project and not a threat on the life of someone I loved.

I drew in some deep breaths, knowing I couldn't remain frozen here at the front door until Mom came home. That would be too suspicious. She would ask too many questions, and then I might spill everything that had happened.

Of course, the man had only said not to tell *Chase*. I didn't want to take the chance, though. Not with Chase's life on the line.

Speaking of the man . . . where was he? Up in my bedroom still?

Moving quickly, I ran into the library and grabbed one of Dad's old guns. He'd purchased it after a string of home invasions had littered the area several years back. Gathering every ounce of courage I owned, I crept back up the stairs with the weapon in hand.

Did I really have the nerve to shoot this man? I didn't know. But I couldn't live with myself with all these questions hanging over my head. For all I knew, this intruder-slash-puppet-master could be setting up a bomb in my bedroom.

It was better to face things head-on sometimes. At least, that's what every Academy Award–winning movie I'd ever seen seemed to indicate.

By the time I reached the top of the stairs, my heart pounded so loudly in my ears that I was sure I wouldn't even hear an elephant sneak up on me. My hands trembled.

I supposed I was no GI Jane. I'd never really had aspirations to be. All I'd wanted was to help people, truth be told. And that was kind of a crazy realization considering that I was holding a gun right now and toying with the idea of maiming someone.

I paused outside my bedroom door. This was where I'd left the man. I hadn't heard him come down the stairs. Since my bedroom was on the second floor, it would be hard for him to escape out the window. By all indications, he was still inside.

I gripped the gun. After mentally counting to three, I pushed the door open.

My trembles deepened as I swung the revolver around the room. Where was he?

I hurried across my bedroom and flipped the lamp on.

An empty room stared back at me. The lacy coverlet on

my bed. The fake-fur rug. The whitewashed dresser.

But no man.

Where had he gone?

With more than a touch of trepidation, I opened my closet door. No one.

I searched under my bed. Nothing.

Had the man moved to another part of the house? He must have.

I crept down the hallway until I reached my mom's room. Still gripping the gun like I was one of Charlie's Angels, I slowly peered inside.

The curtains there fluttered in the breeze.

I ran to the open window.

The man must have escaped that way. Onto the roof of the sunroom and down the trellis. It was the only thing that made sense.

I sank to the floor as despair invaded me.

How was I ever going to get out of this?

All the optimism I was known for seemed to have vanished with the intruder.

***

The next day, nausea gurgled in my stomach, and it wasn't because it was Monday.

Only a couple of weeks ago, I'd started working as a constituent services aide for my brother, Ralph, an Ohio state senator. Prior to this, I'd been a social worker, but I took this new position in hopes of extending my reach. I could focus on the bigger picture here and maybe help with overall reform.

I was basically Ralph's eyes and ears in the community. I went to meetings, talked to people on the street, corresponded with concerned citizens, and advised my brother.

It was a change from working with people one-on-one, and there were times I really missed my old job. But I was happy to help Ralph. A former high school principal and school board member, he'd taken this position in a special election and was still adjusting to his new role.

Ralph's local office was located in downtown Cincinnati. We had about twelve staffers here, and right now most of us were sitting around the conference table talking about goals and objectives for this week.

I tried to focus on the meeting, but I couldn't. Last night kept replaying in my head. That's where my nausea came in.

When I'd awakened this morning after a few restless hours of sleep, I'd thought for sure this was all a nightmare. I tried to convince myself that my theory was true. I mean, what kind of person broke into someone's home and told them to break up with their boyfriend? Stuff like that didn't happen in real life.

But my fear was so real that I knew the encounter really had transpired. I had some serious choices to make.

"What do you think, Holly?"

My brother's voice pulled me from my thoughts. I snapped my head toward him. Right now I wasn't making a great first impression in a room full of cutthroat, career-oriented coworkers.

I cleared my throat and straightened, realizing everyone at the conference table was staring at me. "What do I think about what?"

Ralph eyeballed me. Hiring family was always tricky. I didn't want to let him down right now, as I was surrounded by some of the brightest minds in the area, including a few who questioned my placement here. They'd rightly concluded that I was on the job because of my connections instead of through fighting my way to the top. I needed more blood, sweat, and tears to earn their respect.

"I think it sounds like a great idea," Henry Tell said.

Saved by the Tell. That's what people around the office called him—partly because of his last name, and partly because he'd tell you exactly what was on his mind, whether you wanted to hear it or not. Sometimes he wouldn't stop telling you what he was thinking. Right now, the quality didn't seem that bad, since he'd taken people's attention off me.

The meeting continued around me. I tried to pay attention, but I couldn't wait until it was over. Twenty minutes later, it finally concluded.

I tried to escape back to my cubicle, but Ralph called to me first. "Could I have a minute, Holly?"

I sat back down and nodded. I went to grab my Styrofoam coffee cup and take a sip of the now-tepid drink. Maybe the usually comforting liquid would calm me. But, instead, I knocked the cup over. Brown liquid cascaded onto the table.

"Well, this is just peachy." I turned to grab some napkins from the condiment table behind me and collided with the Tell.

"Whoa, Tiger," he mumbled, gripping my arms and pushing us apart.

I quickly stepped back, becoming even more frazzled with how frazzled I was. I reached around him for the napkins, grabbed a stack, and mopped up the liquid I'd spilled.

I glanced up and saw Ralph staring at me, his eyes narrow behind his plastic-framed glasses. He knew I was rattled, but I had to keep the reasons why to myself.

Nerdy cute. That's how I'd heard people refer to him.

He was my brother, so he obviously wasn't cute *at all* to me with his sweater vests and strange affection for Sharpie markers. He was a widower who turned from a dedicated life as an educator to politics. Having a brother as a boss was interesting, to say the least.

I tossed the napkins into the trash just as everyone finished clearing out of the room—everyone but Ralph and me. My throat burned as I waited for his questions.

He was my older brother—by eight years—and since Dad had died, he'd taken it upon himself to watch out for me. It was sweet . . . and sometimes annoying. But I wouldn't trade him for anyone else. We'd been there for each other through thick and thin.

"What's going on, Holly?" He leaned against the conference table. Somehow, I felt like I'd been called into the principal's office.

I crossed my arms and reminded myself to look casual. But I couldn't decide whether to lean nonchalantly against the conference table like Ralph, or if I should sit in one of the padded chairs, or even if I should just stand tall. I bounced back and forth between all three options, which only made me appear more neurotic.

I finally stood and made the fatal mistake of touching my face. It was a surefire sign of my inner turmoil. Thank goodness, Ralph had never studied psychology, or he might have noticed.

"I just have a lot on my mind," I finally said, forcing my hands to remain at my sides and away from my face.

"Problems between you and Chase?"

"Problems?" I nearly snorted, but it wouldn't have been ladylike. "No, we're not having any problems. We—"

I stopped myself. If I was going to break up with Chase,

maybe I should sow some seeds to make it believable. One thing was very clear: I was a terrible liar. I considered it a gift because I really wasn't tempted to tell untruths with my inability to do so convincingly—and the fact that lying was wrong, of course.

But I didn't *want* to sow seeds of doubt about our relationship. I didn't want *any* of this. Couldn't I just have a little break from stress and grief and tragedy? Apparently not. Just as one set of problems rolled out of my life, another set rolled in. My life was practically Tornado Alley in the spring.

"We . . . what?" Ralph clarified, ever the good listener.

I shook my head, trying to pull myself from the dismal thoughts that had cloaked me all morning.

"We . . . may have a little disagreement," I finally said, choosing my words carefully. It was true. Chase and I *might* have a disagreement in the future when I tried to break up with him. Chase knew me pretty well already, and I wasn't sure I was going to be able to convince him we shouldn't be together. Or that I wanted to. I mean, we'd be going from bliss to doom. Our relationship wasn't bipolar like that.

This was all so confusing.

"What's going on, Hol?" Ralph sat fully on the table now, completely committed to our conversation. I had his full attention and his undivided focus.

In other words, this was the last thing I wanted.

"It's nothing really. Just some stuff that Chase and I have to work out."

"I hope you do work it out, because you and Chase seem good for each other. I haven't seen you this happy . . . well, maybe never."

His words were so bittersweet. I hadn't ever been this happy, but the disaster looming on the horizon twisted my heart.

"Thanks, Ralph. I appreciate it." I glanced at my watch. "Speaking of Chase, we're supposed to meet for lunch, so I should probably go."

He nodded and stood, as if his job was done. "I hope you two have a good time. I'll see you afterward."

A good time? That was hard to envision, especially since I had some serious choices to make: break my heart or save the man I loved.

CHAPTER 3

As I took the short jaunt from my car to the Chinese restaurant where Chase and I were meeting, I studied every man I passed. I stole a glance at the men in business suits hurrying past on their lunch break or talking on their Bluetooth headsets. I snuck glances at the meter maid who hovered by the cars parallel parked on the street, at two urban-looking teens, and at three college-age boys talking baseball.

Was some random stranger really going to ask me out? What was I going to say? And why? That was the thing: none of this made sense.

I didn't have enough information to fit together any of the pieces, how I played into this, or why someone might want to kill Chase.

Maybe it was someone Chase had encountered through his police work. Or someone from his past. Or . . . I really had no idea.

Whatever the reason, I had a feeling there was more to come. After all, if this had been just about hurting Chase through losing me, this threat would have ended after the breakup. But, instead, I was supposed to go out with someone else.

By the time I'd wandered down the sun-drenched street and reached the restaurant, I'd nearly convinced myself that this was all a joke.

There was no way someone could monitor everything I said. There was no way that man could possibly overhear a conversation between Chase and me at this restaurant. There were places I could go where Chase and I could talk privately and I could explain everything that was going on.

All I had to do was ask Chase to play along. Then I could spare hurting him, as well as breaking my own heart and possibly getting the man I loved killed.

Right?

I felt better by the time I sat down inside. Not great. Not giddy. I was still apprehensive and distracted. But I'd begun to justify my decisions. There was a way out of this. A simple way. I just had to find a place to speak with Chase privately.

Chase would know what to do next.

I'd almost married the man. He'd been my first kiss. Honestly, he'd been my first crush back when we knew each other in high school. We'd both had some growing to do before we were ready for each other. That's why, after almost ten years with no contact, we'd been placed back into each other's lives.

I'd seen my forever with the man, but we both knew he still had some demons from his past to work out before we could commit to each other. When Chase's brother had been killed, Chase had turned to alcohol. That one act had ruined his first marriage and his career. Chase was trying to rebuild now, and I'd been happy to help him in the process.

My heart lifted when I saw him enter the dimly lit restaurant. He wore a light-blue shirt, rolled up at the sleeves, and black slacks. If this moment had been a movie—an old, black-and-white movie would be my preference—stirring music would have been playing as a slow-motion sequence was cued. This was his entrance, the moment when the audience went wild because they'd been dying for the show's star to make an appearance again.

That's how I felt, at least.

If Chase had an Australian accent, he'd be a dead ringer for Chris Hemsworth of *Thor* fame. But it was more than Chase's looks that got to me—I loved the man's heart. His tough yet tender side. The way he made me feel so protected and safe and like a lady.

He kissed my cheek before sitting across from me. I caught a quick whiff of his leathery aftershave, just enough to make me want more.

"You look nice today," he said.

I looked down at my newly purchased vintage dress. It was olive green, but I'd paired it with a wide, black belt and a jean jacket. When I wasn't trying to restore people and families, I really liked repurposing clothes and accessories. "Thank you."

He glanced at the menu on the white tablecloth. "Did you order yet?"

"Not yet," I told him. Truth be told, I wasn't very hungry. My appetite had pretty much died a quick death after last night.

"I don't have much time because of a case I'm working on." He raised the menu. "But I'm glad we could meet."

"Me too."

I picked up the menu, but the print wouldn't come into focus. The next thing I knew, the waitress appeared at our table and Chase ordered something.

"And for you, ma'am?"

I swallowed hard, realizing I had to be more careful with my preoccupation. Chase would pick up on my unease too easily if I played it this way. "I'll have what he's having."

Chase gave me a strange look but said nothing. With

our menus gone, he leaned across the table toward me, and his hands covered mine. "Tell me about your day," he said.

I inhaled a deep breath, but it was uneven, like I was too eagerly sucking down air. I cut it off midway and forced a smile. "Nothing exciting. How about you?"

"Trying to put out fires. Tensions are high after what happened with Officer Mackenzie a couple of weeks ago. The police are Public Enemy Number One around some parts of town."

A local cop had shot a teen who pulled a gun on him. Upon further examination, officials found that the gun was actually a toy. The incident had incited outrage in certain groups in the area, who called the act unjust, especially since the teen who'd been shot and killed hadn't been doing anything wrong before the confrontation. Some said it was racial profiling. Others said the officer was simply trying to protect himself from a perceived threat.

I pressed my lips together in a frown. "I'm sorry to hear that. I hate all the tension and wish I could think of a way to fix it."

"And that's just one more thing to love about you, Holly Anna."

The depth of emotion in his eyes made me realize that I never wanted to let him go. Ever.

His hand slipped under the table, and I saw him rubbing his knee. My throat tightened. That man last night . . . he'd said that Chase's knee was hurting again. Could he be right?

"What's wrong?" I asked, trying not to ask any leading questions.

"Sometimes the old football injuries flare up again for no apparent reason."

My gut lurched with dread. The man had been right.

How had he known that? He really was keeping an eye on Chase, wasn't he? The cameras. The bomb. The private information he'd obtained.

This wasn't good.

"I'll be okay," Chase said.

Of course, he thought I was only worried about his knee. I wished that was my biggest worry.

Our food came a few minutes later, and I stared at the General Tso's chicken in front of me. I hated spicy food. No wonder Chase had given me a funny look.

"Feeling brave today?" Chase raised an eyebrow as a look of amusement fluttered through his gaze.

I frowned and nodded. "When you're afraid to try new things is when you start losing part of your youth. I need to hold on to as much as I can."

That seemed to appease him.

We said a quick prayer together, and afterward I began picking at my food while Chase heartily indulged. My mind traveled back to the man in my room last night.

Did Chase have any idea there were cameras in his house? Or a bomb in his heating shaft?

There was so much that could go wrong, and the stress of having this burden placed on my shoulders felt like too much to bear.

"Holly?"

I snapped my head toward him. "Yes?"

"You look like you have a lot on your mind."

My hand froze, fork in midair. "What? Do I?"

He tilted his head. I was toast, a goner, in trouble, and probably the worst person to have to pull off something like this.

Which was why I couldn't do it.

I was calling chicken. This man wouldn't pull me into his twisted game. I was putting my foot down.

"Are you sure there's nothing you want to talk about? Did you have another doctor appointment?" Concern etched his gaze.

I shook my head, needing to put that fear to rest. "Not since last week. I'm doing fine. The medication worked like a charm, and all my symptoms have cleared up."

A few months ago, doctors thought I had an incurable cancer. Instead, I had a unique form of panniculitis. Once physicians were able to treat the underlying cause, a bacterial infection, I went back to feeling like my old self. It was a gross misdiagnosis, but I was thankful to be healthy and to have the rest of my life ahead of me.

Suddenly, an idea hit me, and it was a brilliant one at that. I straightened as adrenaline zinged through me. "We should go away for a while."

He squinted, his head jutting forward ever so slightly. "What?"

I nodded, a little too excited for my own good. But I had a plan that could mean everything would work out, that could put the kibosh on my inner struggle. "Somewhere far away. Maybe the Bahamas. I'm not sure."

"Are you okay, Holly?"

I nodded again, another surge of adrenaline and self-identified brilliance making me feel giddy. Why hadn't I thought of this before? "I'm fine. More than fine. I think this is a great idea."

He leaned closer and lowered his voice. "You think you and me going on vacation together is a great idea?" He said the words slowly and in disbelief.

I brought my excitement level down a bit. "I know it

seems sudden. But wouldn't that be fun? Just getting away from everything for a while? Maybe go somewhere sunny. The beach. Yes, there definitely needs to be a beach. And there need to be smoothies. Some pineapple would be nice, also. Hawaii, maybe?"

"I can think of so many reasons I'd love to but even more reasons why we shouldn't." He rubbed his lips together before thoughtfully pausing. "Besides, even if it was a good idea, I just started at the department. I don't have that much vacation time."

He couldn't get out of this that easily. "Well, I can't think of a single reason why we shouldn't. Not even one."

"How about the fact that you just started working on your brother's staff? And it wouldn't be wise for either of us to use our savings on this. Not right now. Trips like that take planning and saving, and do you really think your family would approve of the two of us going on vacation alone?"

I frowned. He had some valid points, but he obviously wasn't seeing the whole picture here. If only he knew all the facts. "Don't you want to just throw caution to the wind sometimes?"

"You threw caution to the wind not long ago, and it almost got you killed. Do I need to remind you about all those details?" He raised an eyebrow as his tone remained warm.

I let out a sigh, and defeat dragged down my shoulders. Logically, I didn't expect him to say yes. But it would be such an easy solution if he did.

"What's going on, Holly? It isn't like you to talk like this."

I glanced around the restaurant. There were no cameras here. There was no way Shadow Man would know if I told Chase the truth while sitting here. Besides, the restaurant was noisy.

Silverware clattered, Zen-like overhead music whined, and lunchtime conversation rumbled. We were away from any windows. The man probably didn't even know we were here. Certainly, he had better things to do than track my every move.

I cleared my throat, knowing if I was going to say something, I had to do it before my nerves got the best of me. "Chase, I don't know how to say this."

"You can tell me anything, Holly. You know that." He sounded so stinkin' sincere.

"I know. I do." I shifted, trying to find the words. "It's just that—"

Before I could finish my sentence, an explosion sounded outside. The whole building shook. Windows shattered. Diners were thrown onto the floor. In an instant, Chase was on his feet.

"Stay there, Holly," he told me as he rushed toward the street.

Of course, I didn't stay where I was. I was too curious. I ran toward the broken windows, careful not to step on any of the patrons who lay on the floor with blood on their foreheads and cheeks. I'd help them in a moment.

I felt bile rise in my throat when I looked outside.

It was just as I feared: Chase's unmarked police sedan had been blown to smithereens.

CHAPTER 4

I knew the paramedics were on the way. Until they arrived, I helped to sort those injured into groups of critical and triage. Staying busy helped to keep my thoughts from going haywire.

That bomb wasn't a coincidence. But how had the man known I'd been about to blather everything? Was there a bug on me? Was someone listening to my every word?

I didn't know.

I'd have time to worry about that later. Right now I just needed to help the injured.

Thankfully, most people had only cuts and bruises. But one man appeared to have a broken arm, a college-age girl was having breathing problems, and another man had hit his head pretty hard. All in all, this could have been worse.

Were these people's injuries my fault? If I hadn't attempted to tell Chase what was going on, would that bomb have gone off?

I wanted to cry at the thought. Hurting other people was the last thing I wanted to do. That's what made all of this so difficult.

There was just no way to win.

I found a man moaning in the corner and shoved a small table off him. Blood gushed from his shoulder. Some shrapnel must have gotten him.

I knelt beside him. "It's going to be okay. Help is on the

way."

He only moaned in response.

I pulled off my jacket and pressed it over his wound, trying to stop the bleeding. My throat ached when I saw Chase step back into the restaurant. He'd been manning the scene on the street. Sirens wailed in the distance, and I knew help was close.

Our gazes connected. I remained where I was, trying to keep the injured man in front of me lucid until the EMTs arrived.

Chase and I didn't have to say anything to each other to communicate how we both felt: disgust. Disgust that this had happened and that people had been injured and that the crime had been so senseless.

He only stayed in the doorway a second before going back to the street and directing people away from the carnage that was left of his car, the surrounding vehicles, and several buildings.

That could have been his house.

He could be inside when the explosion occurred.

There would be no way anyone would survive something like that.

A small cry escaped from me as I thought about that scenario playing out. It seemed more real now than ever.

Thankfully, paramedics rushed in. I waved them over, and they took charge.

As they did, I dragged my feet back toward the table where I'd left my purse. My phone was buzzing.

As I pulled it out, I saw a text message there.

This is your fault. Heed my warning.

***

I felt like I could throw up when I stepped outside a few minutes later. I found Chase talking with a group of his colleagues near the epicenter of the explosion—his car. Immediately, he was by my side, squeezing my arm, and assessing me with his gaze. "You okay?"

I nodded, hoping I didn't puke on his shoes. That's how real it felt. "I think I've done all I can. Paramedics seem to have a good handle on everything inside. I'm going to get cleaned up and head back to work."

"I'm glad you're okay. That could have been much worse. If that blast had been just a little stronger . . ."

He didn't have to finish. He didn't need to because I knew. I knew it could have been devastating.

"Let me walk you to your car."

We started down the street, ducking under the police line and pushing through a crowd of onlookers.

What if that man was in the crowd? What if he was watching right now? Would *my* car explode next?

I forced myself to keep moving down the sidewalk. Shock seemed to be taking control of my body, though, and my head swam with sickening reality. There was a psycho toying with my life, the lives of the people I loved, and the citizens of the city I called home. None of this was cool.

"So the bomb was under your car?" I clarified, not sure I wanted to know.

Chase put his hand on my elbow. That's just how he was, always the gentleman. But I was so glad for his support right now because otherwise I might sink to the ground.

"That's how it appears," he said. "The bomb squad is investigating. We should know more by tomorrow."

"I'm so glad you weren't in the car when that

happened, Chase." *Don't throw up. Don't throw up.* Internal anguish had a tendency to make me want to vomit. It was one of my not-so-adorable qualities.

"Me too. Just one more thing to be grateful about."

We crossed the parking garage, climbed one set of stairs, and reached my car. I pulled the keys to my '64½ powder-blue Mustang from my purse.

"Be careful, okay?" My voice caught as my gut squeezed again.

You should break up with him. Right now. Just get it over with. Do what's best for everyone.

But I couldn't. The words wouldn't leave my lips, even after what had just happened. Was it my stubborn nature? Was I being selfish? Or was it simply fear that I'd lose the man I loved? I wasn't sure.

Chase kissed my cheek. "I'll call you later."

I nodded and watched him walk away. Then I climbed in my car. I waited until he was out of sight and then got out again. I knelt on the ground and looked under my car. I didn't know what I was looking for—blinking lights or unusual wires or a black box. I didn't see anything out of the ordinary.

Just to be safe, I also checked the engine. Again, I didn't see anything that looked out of the ordinary. But did that mean anything? I could be looking at a bomb and not know it. My bachelor's degree in social work hadn't exactly prepared me for this.

I sank back into the front seat. Eventually, I was going to have to crank the engine. I couldn't stay here in the parking garage all day. And I couldn't tell anyone that a homicidal maniac was blackmailing me and could have put a bomb in my car.

Why was everything so complicated? I didn't do

complicated. No, I was the girl who longed for simpler times. Who tried not to be consumed with busyness. Who desperately wanted peace and serenity.

My phone rang. I glanced at the screen and saw that it was my best friend, Jamie. Talking to my friend seemed like just the right medicine. In the least, it seemed like a way to delay the inevitable act of possibly discovering or detonating a bomb.

"Hey, girlfriend. What's up with you?" Jamie said, her voice tinged with urban undertones.

"Chase's car just exploded," I blurted.

She paused. "Come again?"

"We were having lunch, and his car literally exploded on the street by the restaurant."

"I just heard about an explosion downtown. You're telling me Chase's car was involved?"

"I wish that wasn't the truth, but it is." I closed my eyes as flashbacks rippled through my memory in aftershock-like trembles.

"Has the whole world gone mad?"

I leaned back in my seat. "Sometimes I think, yes, it has."

I longed to pour everything out to my friend and get her advice. I just couldn't think clearly. But I couldn't take that chance. Not when lives were on the line. Somehow that man must have known I'd been about to blurt everything to Chase.

"Not to change the subject from the horrific to the ordinary, but are we still on for dinner tonight?"

"Yes." My life had to continue on as normal, even if I felt anything but. What other choice did I have?

"Great. We'll catch up more then. In the meantime, stay out of trouble."

As soon as I hung up, I stepped out of my car again,

feeling like a nervous wreck. What was I going to do?

I kicked the tire in frustration, and immediately regretted it. My toe ached something fierce.

"Car problems?"

I twirled around at the voice behind me. A man in a business suit stood there and nodded at my car. The man was lean with an oversized head. His thick, brown hair, which was neither long nor short, emphasized the fact. It almost had a helmet effect. He was older than me, possibly by several years, but right now his eyes were as wide as a child's on Christmas morning.

I felt myself starting to stutter. "No. Well, yes. Kind of. I don't know."

"Beautiful car." He ran his finger across the hood. "They just don't make them like this anymore, do they?"

I let out a shaky, nervous laugh. "No, they sure don't."

"Is she having problems starting?"

"Yes . . . I suppose she is."

"Let me try for you."

Before I realized what was happening, he took the keys from my hand and slipped into the driver's seat.

"No, you don't want to do that—" I started.

Before I could finish, he cranked the engine. I held my breath and waited for the blast of fire I felt certain would come.

CHAPTER 5

I blanched, instinctively drawing away from the car. I held my breath, bracing myself, waiting, anticipating the blast.

"There you go. This baby is purring like a kitten," the man said.

I pulled one eye open, saw nothing had happened, and relaxed my shoulders. "Would you look at that?"

He ran his hand down the dash. "Whoever restored this did a great job. It's amazing. And the fluffy, pink dice are a nice touch." He tapped them and grinned.

"Um . . . yeah. My dad restored it. He liked to do things right."

His eyes narrowed. "Liked? Past tense?"

I licked my lips. "He passed away two years ago."

"I know how hard that can be to lose a loved one." He stepped out of my car and straightened his suit, suddenly appearing professional and businesslike again. The boy-like fascination left his gaze. "I probably shouldn't have jumped in your car like that. I guess I couldn't resist the chance. Sorry. I can be a little impulsive sometimes. My mom insists that it will be my downfall."

"I can't imagine why."

He glanced at his watch—a big, expensive-looking one. "I'm going to be late for my meeting. Take care and enjoy that car!"

With that, he was gone, disappearing into the stairway with his tie flapping over his shoulder.

I stood there, dumbfounded. I'd felt that way a lot within the past twenty-four hours. Surprises kept sweeping in and knocking me off balance.

On a positive note, at least I knew my car wouldn't explode when I started it.

But what a strange, strange encounter. A man had just hopped in my car and started it. Who did stuff like that?

I climbed into Sally—that's what I called my set of wheels—and started back to my house, still feeling dazed. I called Ralph and told him what had happened. There was no way I could go back to work looking like this. I had smut on my face and blood on my dress, and my hair was disheveled.

Speaking of which, that man hadn't even given my appearance a second glance. The realization was strange and disturbing. Most people would be taken off guard if they ran into someone who looked like they'd been through a war zone.

Not even Peggy Lee blaring "I Don't Know Enough About You" on my radio could make things better. The only thing that could possibly help would be erasing the past sixteen hours, and that was impossible.

Thankfully, Mom wasn't home when I arrived, because I didn't think I could handle seeing her. She'd take one look at me and go into a tizzy. I desperately feared experiencing a weak moment where I spilled everything.

With most secrets, the consequences weren't deadly. This one could be.

I paused in the entryway, replaying last night. I stopped only a minute into my mental movie. I didn't want to dwell on it. Replaying the man in my bedroom would do no good.

Yet, at the same time, my whole house felt like a not-so-safe place now. This morning before I'd left home, I'd searched everywhere for any hidden cameras. I didn't find any. If that man was telling the truth and there were devices hidden around my house, he'd done a masterful job concealing them.

And that really didn't make me feel better as I went to shower and change clothes. In fact, I felt like I was back in the girls' locker room in gym class, trying to keep everything covered at all times while still effectively cleaning myself.

I was finding it difficult to deal with an unseen foe with unknown motivation and unbearable possible consequences.

I had no idea what I was going to do. Had I mentioned that yet?

***

I sat at my desk at work and absently tapped my pencil against the desk while staring at the paper in front of me. I'd scribbled notes there, trying to sort out my thoughts, until it was time to leave.

Possible solutions:

Number one, convince Chase to get out of the country, with or without me. My first attempt at that hadn't worked.

Number two, go out with someone else, but don't tell Chase. Act like we broke up while never actually breaking up. It was two-faced and fake, and I didn't like either of those things.

Number three, break up, save his life, but crush both of our hearts. Was that really my only option?

I sighed. What was I missing here?

The clock finally hit five, and I put my pencil down. It was time to leave. I hadn't gotten much accomplished today anyway. I should have skipped going back to work because my mind was too far gone.

I drove to Jamie's favorite pizza place, a gluten-free joint where she could indulge in healthy food options and secretly squirt vinegar into her water because of all the "amazing health benefits it provided."

She'd lost one hundred pounds not long ago, and she'd had a different perspective on eating ever since. She was in love with coconut oil, made her own sprouted-grain bread, and had practically invested in one of her favorite almond-flour companies. I was happy to see her feeling so well about herself.

Jamie was already at the restaurant, simply named Joseph's, when I arrived. I slid across the glittery upholstery and into the booth across from her. The place smelled like fresh bread and gooey cheese, but the normally alluring scents had no impact on me now. My stomach was in too much upheaval.

In the middle of the Beastie Boys singing about fighting for the right to party, Jamie blurted, "You look like death."

Leave it to my BFF to get right to the point. "Thanks."

"You didn't decide to do extreme random acts of kindness again, did you?" She cocked a black eyebrow, her face full of expression as usual. I always said she looked like mocha-colored sunshine. Her curly hair sprang away from her face like rays flowing from the sun, and her countenance always looked bright and full of life.

We'd met freshman year of college and had been inseparable since then. I thought God sent her to me, and because of that I didn't take her friendship for granted. We'd been through a lot together and had always stood by each other.

Back to her question.

It was true that I'd gotten myself in a bit of trouble when I'd thrown caution to the wind and engaged in some extreme random acts of kindness not long ago. "No, I did not indulge in random acts of kindness again. I learned my lesson back in February, thank you very much. I now try to do purposeful and forthright acts of kindness instead."

She let out a sassy "um-huh" that indicated she didn't quite believe me. "So what's going on? Did that car bomb shake you up?"

I swallowed hard, knowing I had an honest excuse for my behavior. The fiasco outside the Chinese restaurant had shaken me, even though the issue went deeper than that. "Yes, it did."

She leaned toward me and lowered her voice. "Any idea who's behind it? You have the inside scoop?"

Even though Jamie was my best friend, I knew better than to say too much to this newspaper reporter. I didn't want to put her in a difficult situation, one where she had to choose between the story of her life and her friendship with me. Though I felt fairly certain she would choose me, I tried to avoid causing uncomfortable dilemmas whenever possible. It was the ladylike thing to do.

"Chase hasn't told me anything yet. It's too soon to speculate, I suppose."

"Oh, it's never too soon for speculation. Speculation is the fun part." She grinned, but the expression slipped quickly. "I wonder if it's related to the impending riots?"

"The impending riots?"

"That's the rumor after what happened with that police officer. Some people are calling for protests against the police."

What if that was what all of this was about? Maybe someone had retaliated against the police by planting that bomb.

But that wouldn't explain the text I'd received.

Just then, the pizza arrived. Jamie didn't have to ask me

what I wanted. We'd been here enough that she could order for us. I sacrificed my true preference in favor of her gluten-free pizza loaded with mushrooms, peppers, and onions. It actually didn't taste bad, all things considered.

Jamie began dishing out slices, melted cheese creating long strings between the pan and plate. "So, are you ready for your sister's wedding next Friday?"

I shrugged and snagged a wayward green pepper that had been browned in the oven. The brown ones were the best. "I guess. Speaking of which, I have to get everything done for her bachelorette party. Being the maid of honor is quite involved."

"I'm sure everything will be perfect. You're good at making things elegant and classy. It's your superpower." She widened her eyes dramatically.

"If only I actually had superpowers . . ." I muttered. Then I wouldn't be in the pickle I was in. Actually, *pickle* was too nice an expression. Unless it was a monstrous, flesh-eating pickle from a sci-fi movie.

Jamie twisted her head and narrowed her eyes. "Now what does that mean?"

I shook my head. "Nothing. Not really. I mean, don't we all wish we could snap our fingers sometimes and solve our problems. The world's problems, for that matter."

"I think you just gave me an idea for a new comic. Forget a career in journalism. I'll be the next Stan Lee instead. My character will be a beauty queen who gets her wish of world peace. The possibilities are endless."

We prayed over our food before digging in. Well, Jamie dug in, and I picked off some vegetables and munched on them.

"We've been friends for a long time, Holly. It's obvious something is on your mind. Is it just that car bomb, or is something else going on?" She pulled a tiny flask from her purse and poured it into her water.

"Are you spiking your drink?" I shrieked.

She gave me a "duh" face. "You know me better than that. It's vinegar. Turns out, you shouldn't leave it in plastic because the acidity can break it down. Then I found this aluminum flask, and I knew it was perfect."

"People are going to think you're a drunk."

She shrugged. "Let them think whatever they want."

I smiled. The girl was addicted to vinegar, but there were worse things to crave.

"So, what's on your mind?" She picked up exactly where she'd left off in our conversation.

How I longed to pour everything out to my friend. Jamie always had great advice, and I knew she could help me make sense of this mess. Was there any way I could cryptically tell her what was going on? I could speak in code or even pig latin, if I thought that would work. Maybe I could just be vague and somehow express the direness of the situation.

"Jamie, you wouldn't believe me. I know this sounds far-fetched, but the other night—"

"Hey, it's the Mustang girl!" someone said beside me.

I slowly turned my head toward the voice, knowing before my gaze connected with the person speaking who it was.

"You . . ." I muttered. Yes, it was the businessman who'd hopped into my Mustang and started it before I could stop him.

The man grinned. "I don't think I actually gave you my name. I'm Benjamin Radcliff." He extended his hand.

I stole a quick glance at Jamie before begrudgingly extending my hand in return. "Holly. This is my friend Jamie."

Benjamin shook hands with me, then Jamie. "Fancy

running into each other twice in one day, huh?"

I swallowed hard before explaining to Jamie, "We ran into each other earlier and had a long talk about my Mustang."

Jamie didn't look convinced. In fact, cynicism stained her gaze, and I had a feeling I'd be questioned later. "Interesting."

"You mind?" He pointed to the space beside me.

I started to make up an excuse as to why he couldn't join us, but, before I could vocalize it, he squeezed in beside me. Immediately, he looked at home, even if he was as unwelcome as a fever blister on your wedding day.

"I've heard great things about this place," he started, looking from Jamie to me like an overly friendly puppy dog. "Do you two come here often?"

Jamie and I exchanged a glance. No way was I telling him we came here every week. Based on our previous track record—however brief it was—this man might end up showing up every Monday like clockwork.

"We've come a few times," I finally said.

"I'm new to the area, so I'm still discovering all the hot spots."

I wasn't sure I'd call this a hot spot, but I wasn't in the mood to argue. I had bigger fish to fry, so to speak. Mainly, I just wanted to get rid of him.

"Where'd you move here from?" Jamie asked, still eyeing the man with her sharp, perceptive gaze.

"Louisville."

My heart stuttered. Louisville? Chase had worked as a cop in Louisville up until six months ago. Could this man be connected with Chase through his time there? Even more, was this man somehow connected with the threat on Chase's life?

Suddenly, I was more than a little uncomfortable. The

man might seem goofy and unassuming, but was he? This could all be an act. He could be a part of this whole fiasco.

"Why'd you move here, Benjamin?" Jamie asked, emphasizing his name just a little too much.

"I took a new job."

"Doing what?" she continued, ever the inquisitor.

"It's all kind of hush-hush right now. Not that it would really matter if I told you, because what are the chances you would spill the beans? But, still, I took an oath, so I shall remain silent until I'm given freedom not to be silent." He raised two fingers in the air in some kind of Martian-looking, Mork-and-Mindy-like pledge.

Secret? Oath? Hush-hush? This was getting worse and worse by the moment.

"So you're telling me you have a job you're not allowed to talk about?" Jamie stared at him, her lips pursed and her eyebrows raised. "What are you? CIA or something?"

He laughed, slightly awkwardly. "I'd tell you, but—"

"You'd have to kill me," Jamie finished with a scowl.

I pushed my plate away, my appetite totally and completely gone. Stress was my best weight-loss method. Unfortunately, I'd had a lot of stress in my life lately, and I didn't need to lose any more weight.

Before we could offer, Benjamin helped himself to a piece of pizza.

"Be our guest," Jamie muttered.

"Don't mind if I do." He took a bite and murmured under his breath, "Oh, this is good."

I grabbed my purse, feeling ill at ease. I couldn't just sit here and pretend everything was okay. Not when I realized everything that was at stake. Not when the lives of people I loved could be on the line.

"You know, I hate to cut this short, but I really feel like I should get home," I announced.

"Are you feeling okay, Holly-Wolly-Doodle-All-Day Paladin?" Jamie asked.

I shook my head, scowling at my friend for using the nickname. I'd made the mistake of sharing with her once about how a boy in my seventh grade class had taken to calling me that. Now she liked to use it at the worst possible times. "Not really."

Benjamin slid out of the booth to allow me an exit, somehow wiping the sauce on his fingers all over the edge of the table and on his sleeves. I watched carefully so I wouldn't stain my clothes.

"I totally understand." He frowned at the pizza sauce on his shirt. "The pizza's on me. Literally and figuratively." He let out a weak, self-conscious laugh.

Jamie gave me a look that clearly indicated she didn't want to be left alone with this guy. "Unfortunately, I've got to run as well. Hate to bail on you, Benjamin." She emphasized his name a little too much.

"Oh, I get it. Maybe I'll see you two again sometime."

"Maybe," I muttered.

Jamie and I waved before hurrying out the door together, not bothering to look back.

"What was that about?" Jamie whispered when we were outside in the balmy spring night.

"I'm not sure." My words sounded wooden and forced. "It was weird."

"You look pale. Anything you need to talk about?" Jamie asked. Her gaze, as always, was eagle-eye keen and perceptive. She didn't miss anything.

Oh boy. Did I ever want to talk to her. But I couldn't, not

when so much was at stake. Benjamin's providential appearance had confirmed that.

"I'll be fine," I told her.

At least, I hoped I'd be fine. I *prayed* that I would be fine.

She stared at me another second before nodding. "Okay, but my killer instincts are telling me something's up."

"Killer instincts?" Did she know? I nearly gaped in surprise and horror.

"It's an expression."

"Of course." I laughed airily, realizing that I needed to get a grip.

That was easier said than done, though.

CHAPTER 6

As I lay in bed last night, the perfect idea hit me. Like, brilliant perfect. Like, if I wasn't such a good girl, maybe I'd be pretty good at being cunningly brilliant. Maybe—just maybe—I could match wits with Mr. Evil.

I'd spent the morning composing a letter, perfect down to the last word, and then had a courier run it over to Chase at the police station.

The only problem was that I'd forged the letter and signed a name other than my own at the bottom. No one should get hurt though, and that was how I'd justified my actions. I tried not to make a habit of doing deceitful things like this, though I wouldn't be able to prove it by my actions as of late.

As I sat at my desk staring at the various snapshots and trinkets that highlighted my life, I nibbled on my nails, hoping my plan would work. It was risky, but maybe I could outsmart the mysterious Shadow Man. Maybe.

I tried in vain to concentrate on my work. Instead, I pondered new paint colors for the otherwise drab, gray walls in our office. I wondered what would make this space stop smelling like days-old food even mere hours after being cleaned. I contemplated if it was a coincidence that so many people wore red, white, and blue to the office every day.

My focus was absolutely, positively shot.

At noon, my phone rang. I fully expected it to be Chase, calling to check in as he usually did. I had my entire spiel worked out as to what I would tell him when he mentioned the letter. I would encourage him to do just as it said. I thought I'd crossed every *t* and dotted every *i*, so he wouldn't be suspicious that it was a fake.

Instead of Chase's digits, it was a number I didn't recognize. With a touch of hesitation, I answered. People with numbers I didn't recognize called me all the time—that was nothing unusual in my line of work. But the Shadow Man remained on my mind, and I kept expecting him to pop up again.

"I'm trying to reach Holly Paladin," a male voice said.

It wasn't the deep tone of the man who'd threatened me, but the voice did sound vaguely familiar. "Speaking."

"I hope you don't mind me calling you at work."

I tried to sound perky and polite, even though the greeting was a strange one and lacking the professionalism I'd half expected. "Whom am I speaking with?"

"Oh, I'm sorry. Here I go again, making a fool of myself. This is Benjamin Radcliff."

"Benjamin?"

The man with no concept of social cues whom I'd run into not once but *twice* yesterday?

Unease sloshed in my gut. Benjamin had to be connected with this fiasco somehow. The man seemed so harmless, but maybe that made him perfect for this scheme. Right now, there were only a few people I could trust—namely, my family, Jamie, and Chase. Everyone else was a toss-up.

"I hope I'm not creeping you out by calling like this," he continued.

"Uh . . . *creeping out* is an interesting way to phrase it." I nibbled on my bottom lip as a sense of foreboding filled me. Was this it—the next step in someone's diabolical and senseless scheme? Would Benjamin ask me and test my "obedience"?

"I have a confession. It actually wasn't a *total* coincidence that I ran into you at the pizza place yesterday. It was only a half coincidence." His voice rose almost comically as he finished the sentence.

My throat tightened as I realized his implications. This conversation felt creepier by the moment. "You followed me?"

"Yes—I mean, no." He let out a nervous laugh. "I mean, I was in the area and I saw your Mustang in the restaurant's parking lot. How many people around here drive a car like that? I decided to take a chance and see if it was you. I guess that's pretty lame, huh?"

My cell phone buzzed in my purse, and I saw Chase's number. I desperately wanted to answer, but I had to play my cards right. If Benjamin was connected with this whole threat/fiasco, I couldn't tip him off that I was taking calls from Chase. I was walking a difficult line.

"What a coincidence." I pulled my gaze away from my cell and stared at a picture of Chase and me instead. There was nothing glorious about the picture on my desk. It had been taken after lunch at my mom's one day. The two of us were sitting on the couch, and Chase had his arm wrapped around me. We had dopey grins on our faces.

Well, I guess there was *something* glorious about the picture. It was the light that beamed from both of our eyes. The happiness there couldn't be faked or bought.

"That's what I said too! What a coincidence," Benjamin continued. "Anyway, I told myself that if I ever saw you again, I was going to ask you out. But I lost my courage last night. Especially when I realized I'd intruded on your girls' night like a bumbling idiot."

This was it. The man asking me out. This was the

moment when I was supposed to say yes or face dire consequences. I had to buy myself some time.

"How'd you get my number?" It was a valid question. And the only way I could think of to postpone him.

"Your friend said your name last night, so I googled you and saw you worked for Ralph Paladin."

"Googled me? Of course." My phone buzzed again. Chase was trying to reach me still. He wasn't usually that persistent unless he really needed to talk. This wasn't good.

My fingers itched to grab the phone and answer.

I hated feeling coerced. Hated it. But what else could I do?

"Anyway, what do you say? Do you have any plans for this Friday?"

"I'll have to check my schedule." Truth. Score. I hadn't exactly said no, so I was still abiding by the rules I'd never agreed to play by, right?

"Oh." His voice fell before instantly brightening again. "If not Friday, then how about Saturday?"

I searched my thoughts and came up with nothing, other than the Saturday night church service I'd be attending. Why couldn't I have other plans already? I couldn't say yes, nor could I say no.

Hello, rock and hard place. We're all becoming fast friends.

"I . . . don't know," I finally said. I just couldn't bring myself to say yes. I couldn't betray Chase.

"I know I'm probably coming on strong. It's my personality, if you haven't guessed that yet."

"I may have had an inkling." My phone buzzed again. Chase had sent me a text:

Call me ASAP.

What was going on? He wasn't usually so urgent, so he must have news of some sort.

"Are you dating someone? I mean, you're extremely attractive and kind, so I imagine you are. Girls like you don't come along very often."

I chewed on my lip for a moment as my thoughts battled it out. "It's complicated."

"Isn't it always?" He paused. "Look, think about it. I'll call you back, okay? I know this probably surprised you, and I also realize you're at work right now and can't talk."

I glanced around my cubicle. "That I am."

"So am I. Here comes my boss, for that matter." He lowered his voice. "I've got to run. *Ciao.*"

His boss? His secret boss with his secret company? There were so many strange things about the man that his phone call left me feeling even more perplexed than I did before.

How could a man who seemed so harmless be involved in this mess? And would the fact that I'd delayed answering him about the date still put Chase in danger?

Not if my plan worked out the way I hoped.

Maybe I was being too optimistic. I'd been guilty of it before.

But I really thought I could be onto something with this plan of mine.

***

An hour later, I'd tried calling Chase back several times, but he didn't answer. He must be busy doing his detective thing. As much as I'd like to think he was at my beck and call, he most definitely wasn't. He had important things to do outside of our relationship, things like saving people's lives.

"Did you see the news?" Henry the Tell asked, sticking his head over our shared partition.

I glanced up at him, not used to him being social. He was a numbers guy and thought chitchat was petty and a waste of time. The man had curly red hair that he kept cut short. It didn't matter what he wore, he always looked sloppy. I wasn't sure if it was his small shoulders, the beginning of a pooch at his stomach, or just poor fashion sense.

I snapped back to his question. "The news? No, what's going on?"

He crossed to my side of the gray divide, phone in hand and tinny speakers blaring. My eyes widened when I saw the news feed.

Riots had broken out in the downtown area. Police against those who didn't like or trust law enforcement. On the screen, I saw smoke and men in SWAT gear and people running, shouting, inciting violence.

My heart lurched into my throat. Chase. Was Chase there? Was that why he kept calling?

The picture was too small, and there were too many people for me to single anyone out. It looked like a madhouse, like something I'd see on a movie. A disaster flick, for that matter.

Please, Lord, be with Chase. Watch over everyone involved in this situation. Please.

"Whoever thought this would happen in our city, right?" Henry leaned back on my desk like the two of us talking was the most natural thing in the world.

"That's only a few blocks away," I realized with a shiver. Our offices were located downtown but not in an expensive area. In fact, we were close to the inner-city, low-income area of town where crime was rampant.

"We should be safe here. There's a police line. No one's going to get past it. I mean, look at those guys. They're geared up to fight terrorists."

Just as the words finished leaving his mouth, glass shattered on the other side of the building.

I rushed to my feet and saw the front windows of our office had been broken. The sound of a rowdy crowd roared from the street. Yells and screams and shouts mingled with panic. Too many voices collided together to make out any words.

"Get away from the windows!" I yelled. "This way!"

The rest of Ralph's staff—there were probably nine here now—darted to the back, where a door led to a hallway snaking between various businesses. Everyone tried to squeeze through the doorway at once, each desperate to get out of harm's way. I made sure everyone was out before following.

Swarms of people from other offices in the building crowded the area, and I felt myself being carried along with the flow. I couldn't stop moving if I wanted to. The tide was too strong.

In the middle of the craziness around me, a bullet rang out. Screams erupted, and any of the order that had once graced the mass exodus vanished. In their rush, people became careless. They pushed and shoved and forgot common courtesy.

Chase . . . he was in the middle of this. The thought was almost too hard to bear. I knew dating a detective came with a certain measure of danger, but right now fear and uncertainty threatened to overtake me.

How had the city I loved so much morphed into such chaos? Had no one been able to predict this was going to happen? Why hadn't we been evacuated? Or at least warned?

Questions swirled in my mind as I moved with the

relentless crowd.

Suddenly, someone grabbed my arm. I jerked to a halt, though the wave of people continued to jostle around me.

I turned and searched the crowd to see who'd grabbed me, but there were too many people pushing into me. Everyone blended together.

As I craned my neck, something sharp sliced into my lower back. A burst of pain followed.

I'd been stabbed, I realized as the pain came faster, harder.

Though my head swirled, I turned, desperate to identify the person who had done this to me.

Before I could, the crowds knocked me to the floor . . . and footsteps battered my already broken body.

CHAPTER 7

The doctors said I was lucky.

The knife blade hadn't hit any organs, nor had the wound been as deep as I'd feared.

I still wasn't sure how many people had stepped on me before two men in business suits pulled me to my feet and dragged me outside with the rest of the crowds. I must have passed out, only awaking after I arrived at the hospital, because I barely remembered anything.

After an initial evaluation, I'd had blood tests and a CT scan. I'd ended up with stitches and antibiotics and a lovely hospital gown that even one of my wide-strapped belts couldn't make look cute.

As I lay in the ER, the whole fiasco replayed in my head. The crowds. The man who'd grabbed my arm. The sting of the knife's blade. Everything seemed sharp and clear, yet at the same time like a blurry nightmare.

Now I had a bruised hip, an awkwardly placed future scar that I wouldn't even be able to brag about, and a fear that reached implosive levels.

All around me, something was in the air that I'd felt only a few times in my life. There was a zing of danger, of urgency, of something out of the ordinary taking place.

People were rushed past on gurneys. Paramedics and nurses exchanged instructions. Police officers paced with their radios crackling. I could barely see it all happening through the slit where the drape serving as a door didn't quite reach the wall.

"I can't believe this happened," Ralph muttered, running a hand through his hair and closing his eyes. He sat against the wall in a little fold-out chair that looked uncomfortable enough to be a torture device. His phone had been ringing nonstop since he'd arrived thirty minutes ago.

He'd come as soon as he'd found out what happened. He felt responsible for me, I supposed, as both a brother and a boss. Mom was trying to get here, but the streets were blocked off until the rioting crowds were contained. The hospital I'd been taken to was, unfortunately, not far from the chaos of downtown.

"Ralph, you should go," I told him when his phone rang yet again. "You have a bigger catastrophe than me to handle right now."

"I can't leave you." He shook his head, but it still hung low, like he didn't have the energy to hold it up straight. The good news was that he was comfortable around me. He'd never act this way while out in public or around reporters. But he let his true self—his attributes and his weaknesses—become known when he was around family. Everyone, in my opinion, needed a safe place, needed people to let their guard down around.

"I'll be fine," I told him, raising my IV-clad hand in an attempt to reassure him. However, a bruise had already formed there, showcasing just how battered I was. I quickly pulled my hand back down to my side and tucked it away. "Besides, the city needs your leadership."

He stared at me as if trying to gauge my words. He neither conceded that my idea was good nor leaned back to get comfortable for a long stay.

"If I need you, I'll call. I promise," I assured him. I was already bandaged, and my pain meds were on the way. "Besides, I suspect they'll be releasing me soon. They're going to need all the beds they can find here at the hospital, especially if people continue getting injured at this rate."

"How will you get home?" He looked up, weariness in his gaze.

"I'll figure out a way. I'm not helpless. I'll wait in the lobby for Chase to get me if I have to."

After several minutes of contemplation, he finally offered a firm nod and stood. "Okay. I think you're right. I need to try and help manage this situation. I'm really sorry this happened to you, Holly."

"There are bigger issues at hand than me right now. Go."

He kissed my forehead and stepped out of the little curtained-off area where I'd been propped up.

As soon as he was gone, I frowned. Though I'd just exalted the idea of having a safe place, I hadn't mastered letting down my guard around my family yet. I didn't like them worrying about me. They had enough on their minds as it was.

The worst news, even more than my injuries, was the fact that I hadn't heard from Chase yet. I'd tried to call, but he didn't answer. News reports said there'd been one fatality from the riots so far, but numerous others injured.

Police tried to hold the crowds back, but rioters had begun throwing bricks. They'd ravaged vehicles—breaking windshields, spray painting doors, and slashing tires. They'd looted stores and threatened further violence. It was ugly out there, and what happened today had shaken up the whole city, it seemed.

Tragedy had begun a cycle of more tragedy.

Around me I could still hear the doctors and nurses scurrying. Triage had been set up in the hallways. The scent of saline, rubbing alcohol, and maybe even urine filled the air. Everything reminded me of a scene from a disaster movie—only this was real.

Just then, the pink curtain moved, and I saw a shadow on the other side.

To my delight, Chase emerged. He wore his tactical gear: a black bulletproof vest, a utility belt loaded with who knows what, combat boots, and a whole load of appeal.

Tears rushed to my eyes when I spotted him. Praise God, he was okay. As far as I could tell, he'd gotten through everything without so much as a scratch.

"Holly," he muttered, his voice raspy and deep. He kissed my cheek before pulling the chair up beside my bed. He rested his hand on my arm, and something about his touch calmed me. "I'm so sorry this happened."

"It's crazy out there."

"You don't have to tell me."

All the images that had run through my mind came back at full force. I'd pictured him shot. I'd pictured him dragged into the crowds and used as an example to other police officers. I'd imagined myself without him. "I'm so glad you're okay."

My throat tightened with gratitude that he was sitting beside me now. People could never take moments like this for granted. Loved ones could be snatched away in the blink of an eye, and our lives could be forever changed. I'd experienced it before, and I knew I'd experience it again one day.

I squeezed Chase's hand, and something strange happened. I started crying. Not just tearing up but flat-out weeping, almost. I'd been so worried about him. I was so worried about us. Being injured in the riot and concerned about Chase's safety in the process had brought everything to the surface.

"What's wrong? Are you hurting?" He stood and leaned over me, obviously at a loss. I wasn't usually weepy, not unless stress was getting the best of me. That definitely described my life at the moment.

I sniffled and grabbed a tissue from the table beside my bed. "I just can't imagine life without you. There was a minute there when I had to. When I didn't hear from you and then I heard about the fatality . . ."

He didn't say anything. Instead, he pressed his cheek into my forehead. He must have surmised that I was sore and incapable of using my back muscles to pull myself toward him. He was right.

I gladly accepted his half embrace. My impromptu declaration of how much I cared for him wouldn't do much for my believability factor if I had to break up with him later. But my words had been honest. And sometimes you had only the present moment to speak the truth.

"I'm okay, Holly," he mumbled. "You're not going to get rid of me that easily."

His eyes crinkled on the sides as he studied me. His hand brushed my cheek, wiping a tear away. I could see the worry in his gaze, and the emotion made my heart pump wildly out of control.

If he only knew about the ultimatum I faced.

"Tell me about what happened to you," he prodded.

I filled him in from the time the glass broke all the way up to being trampled. He remained close as I spoke, his eyes riveted on mine.

Though I'd known him since we were in high school,

every time I saw him he took my breath away. I wanted to bury myself in him and never let go. Sometimes I just couldn't believe we were together, and I had to pinch myself.

He brushed my hair back from my face. "I tried to call earlier, but there was no answer. The riots took place in a location other than what our informants told us. The people organizing this act of so-called civil disobedience were a step ahead of us, and we didn't have much time to warn people."

I remembered his missed calls and nodded. I couldn't explain why I hadn't been able to pick up. The reminder made the weight on my chest feel even heavier.

"Did you give a statement to the police yet?"

I nodded. "I did. They took pictures of my wound and everything."

He frowned. "Do they think this was a part of the riot? That someone targeted you?"

I swallowed hard. "What else would it be a part of?"

His frown deepened. "You didn't see the person's face?"

I shook my head. "There were too many people around me. Everyone blended in with everyone. I have no idea how it happened or why."

He leaned back and let out a long, heavy sigh. "Senseless crimes really get to me. Why someone would do this to you . . ." As his voice trailed off, he shook his head. "I'll just never understand people, and I've seen it all. The more I see, the less sense it makes sometimes."

I understood. I felt his pain also. Some of the things I'd seen as a social worker kept me up all night, even weeks after I'd experienced them. I needed to stay focused right now, though. "What's going on out there currently?"

"The crowds have backed off, but I don't think we have

this under control yet. There's a lot of anger. The riots only seem to be feeding people's negative emotions."

"Are you in danger?"

He ran a hand through his hair and looked off into the distance. I'd wanted him to deny it, but I guessed that wouldn't happen. My denial didn't make the danger any less real.

"I'd venture to say every police officer in this town is in danger," Chase said. "In fact, I may have it a little easier because I drive an unmarked car and don't wear a uniform. If it makes you feel better, the city has called in the National Guard, and they're setting a curfew."

Maybe those two things would help. I had no idea, but maybe.

I squeezed Chase's hand again. "Do you need to get back to work?"

"I have a few more minutes. I won't be working on the front lines as much as I'll work behind the scenes to figure out who the ringleaders are in all of this. We heard grumblings that this might happen, so we planned to police the riots in Over-the-Rhine. Somehow these guys seemed to catch wind of it, and they moved their location at the last minute. That's why everything was so sudden today."

My thoughts turned from the riots to other ways Chase might be in danger. He hadn't brought up the letter I'd sent to him. But, of course, that seemed mundane after everything that had happened.

"So you won't be home as much?" I nibbled on my bottom lip as I waited for his response after blatantly fishing for information about that letter I'd sent.

He shook his head. "Probably not. It's just as well. I actually got a letter from the city today informing me that the drywall used by the previous owner of my house was from

China and it's contaminated. They recommend I evacuate immediately until contractors can fix this problem."

"Really? Chinese drywall?" I made sure I sounded surprised.

"Yeah, isn't that crazy?"

"I'd say. What are you going to do?"

"I'm not sure yet."

"I know!" I snapped my fingers. "You should go stay with Ralph for a while. I'm sure he wouldn't mind."

He tilted his head, as if he hadn't considered that idea. "You think?"

I nodded, probably a little too hard. "I can't imagine it would be a problem. But you definitely don't want to be around that drywall stuff. It can have nasty side effects. That's what they were saying on the news a few weeks ago, at least. Asthma, coughing, and who knows what other kinds of long-terms effects haven't even been diagnosed yet?"

"I was thinking another week or two probably wouldn't make a difference. I've been living in the house for six months already, and I haven't had any problems."

"You had a cold a couple of weeks ago . . . or so you thought. Maybe it was the drywall." I'd thought all of this through.

He shrugged, still appearing uncertain. "Maybe."

"I really think you should get out now. Better safe than sorry." I really hoped my plan worked. If Chase was out of his house, he'd be away from that bomb and then away from danger—at least, some of the danger.

He studied me for a moment, his blue eyes warm and intelligent. "You feel strongly about this, don't you?"

I nodded, trying to tamp down my excitement that my plan might actually work. "You've got to take care of your health. Sometimes you only have one chance to get it right."

"I guess that's true. Talk to Ralph for me and let me know what he says, okay?"

"Will do."

He sighed and looked at the curtain as another group of paramedics rushed past. Police radios beeped, and feet hurried quickly across the floor. "Holly, I don't want to leave you here."

"You've got stuff to do," I told him. "I totally understand. Go."

He kissed my hand, gratitude evident in his eyes. "If you need me, call. Okay?"

"I will. Don't worry about me. The doctors just want to make sure everything is stabilized. I'm good."

"I'll check in with you later, then. Stay out of trouble."

He'd only been gone for five minutes when I got a text from an unlisted number. I immediately knew it was the Shadow Man.

Sorry about your injury. I guess I just got a little carried away.

***

That night, Mom had picked me up and insisted for the rest of the evening that I take it easy. Then she and Alex had run off to meet with the wedding coordinator. As I lay in bed, I picked up my Bible and began reading Isaiah 43:2. The verse gave me another anchor of hope to hold on to.

"When you pass through the waters, I will be with you; and when you pass through the rivers, they will not sweep over you. When you walk through the fire, you will not be burned; the flames will not set you ablaze."

I prayed that those words would be true for my life, as I

felt wedged between this unending rock and hard place.

Today, however, I had a new perspective. In fact, I was nearly skipping. I actually would have been skipping except my body hurt too much to move like that.

No, I was overjoyed because Chase had temporarily moved in with Ralph. That meant the threat of Chase's house exploding while he was inside was off the table. And his every move was no longer being watched by hidden cameras. Meanwhile, I'd held up my end of the bargain, and I hadn't told Chase anything.

Maybe I really could outsmart the man who'd threatened me. I held my head higher at the thought. I wasn't usually big on one-upping people, but it felt surprisingly good.

Ralph's office downtown was closed today. Though the riots had ended, at least temporarily, the whole area was a mess, and people were being cautioned before heading that way.

Instead, Ralph's staff had set up a temporary office in a building owned by one of Ralph's staunch—and wealthy—supporters who happened to have some recently vacated real estate. I'd made it to work, even though I still felt like I'd been stabbed and kicked, which, come to think of it, I had.

When I glanced at the time and saw it was 1:30, I grabbed my purse and a sweater.

"In a hurry?" Henry asked.

"I have a task force meeting to get to."

"A task force, huh? Interesting."

I nodded, not sure why he was suddenly trying to be all nicey-nice with me. He hadn't given me the time of the day when I first started. He probably decided being my friend might be a good way for him to get ahead here in the office, since I was Ralph's sister and all.

"Hope you can solve the world's problems," he muttered.

I scowled. Now that sounded more like Henry. Honestly, I wished I could solve all of the world's problems too. I'd settle at this point for just solving my own problems, but that was probably wishing for too much.

Rather than respond, I hurried downstairs, hopped in Chase's car, and gave him a kiss on the cheek.

"What was that for?" He wasn't arguing. In fact, he looked rather pleased based on the warm glimmer in his eyes.

I shrugged. "Just because. I'm glad you're okay and that you're here."

"I'll take that explanation. You ready for this meeting?" he asked.

"I suppose. I'm interested in seeing what this is like, at least." I glanced at him as we took off down the road. "So, did you stay with Ralph last night?"

"The small amount of time I had to actually sleep, I was at Ralph's. I'm thankful that he's okay with me being his temporary roommate. In the meantime, I put in a call to the previous owner of my house."

My stomach clenched. "Really? Why?"

"Something just didn't ring true about that letter from the city. I mean, how did the city find out about the drywall before me? I'm going to need to find some contractors to do the remediation work and call my insurance company to see if they cover this. There are a lot of loose ends."

I hadn't thought about any of that. Dread filled me. Talks with the previous owner? Calls with the insurance company?

My brilliant plan might not have been so brilliant after all.

"Any updates on the car bomb?" I asked, trying to appear normal and not frazzled by Chase's last revelation.

"We think it happened in relation to the riots. Someone wanted to make a point."

I nodded, feeling rather numb. I knew better. I knew why someone had really set off that bomb. But the riots would be a perfect cover for the crime, and I'd bet anything that the perpetrator knew just that.

"There's one other thing I should tell you, Holly. I wanted you to hear it from me."

I instantly tensed. "Okay."

"There's a hit out on local cops. We don't think anything will come of it, but it's a possibility that some young, not-so-smart kids might take it seriously."

That news didn't exactly brighten my day or ease my worries.

The office building where the task force was meeting was only five minutes away, so we barely had time to talk before we pulled up.

Before I'd quit my job as a social worker, I'd been asked to join the Missing Persons Task Force that the mayor had put together. Various people in the community—from the police to social services to the DA's office—were meeting in the community services building once a month to dissect various cases.

As I walked from the car, a little kid who was probably eight years old ran up to me. Chase began talking to someone he knew by the front door as I turned toward the approaching boy.

"Someone told me to give you this." He stuck a piece of paper in my hands and then ran back toward the playground in the distance.

I looked back at Chase, but he was still absorbed in conversation. I quickly unfolded the square of paper. The words I read there made my blood go cold.

"You didn't think your little plan would work that easily, did you? I have other ways of killing your boyfriend. Back off or else."

CHAPTER 8

I shoved the paper into my pocket and glanced around me. That man was here somewhere. Was he watching me right now? Did he see me with Chase?

"Holly? Are you okay?"

I pulled my gaze up toward Chase and forced myself to nod. "Yeah, of course."

He squinted, evidently not believing me. "Who was that boy?"

"I may have met him through my social work," I said, my throat tight. It wasn't the truth, and I hated lies. *Hated* them. But I didn't know what to do. The lines suddenly seemed much more blurry than I would like.

"I see."

"Look, go on upstairs to the meeting," I told him. "I'll be right there. I want to ask that boy a question, okay?"

"As you wish," he said. "I'll see you in a few minutes."

Chase was a detective. He knew the cues when someone was lying. Certainly he knew me well enough to pinpoint when something wasn't quite right. At least he hadn't challenged me on it yet.

I took a step toward the park when Chase said, "Holly?"

I paused and turned toward him, certain he was going to call me out on my deceit. My blood pressure surged until I felt light-headed.

"Yes?" I kept my voice light, pretending everything was fine.

"You sure you're okay?"

I nodded and attempted to offer a reassuring smile. "I'm fine. Thank you."

I released my breath as I turned away from him. I didn't have any more time to waste. The longer I stayed here, the more likely it was that the man threatening me would get away.

I quickened my steps across the parking lot until I reached the playground. It was separated from the business area with a simple wooden fence, and a neighborhood backed up to the other side of the space.

I searched for the boy among the children there, but I didn't see him. As I looked, I also kept an eye out for the man who was tormenting me.

I had no idea what he looked like. I only had the impression that he was tall and large. As my gaze surveyed everyone, no one appeared menacing. In fact, I saw mostly moms and preschoolers. There were a few older kids. Maybe they were homeschooled, because otherwise they should have been in class. There were two dads talking over by a water fountain.

Finally, I spotted the boy who'd given me the note. He was running with two younger boys through a mazelike portion of the play set. I waited at the end for him to emerge, knowing I'd have to choose my words and actions carefully. The last thing I wanted was to scare the boy or have his mom call the police on me. Especially when considering that I was supposed to be meeting with the Missing Persons Task Force at the moment. Wouldn't that be ironic?

Finally he emerged from a twirly tunnel slide. His eyes widened when he saw me standing there, and he stopped in his tracks.

"Excuse me!" I called, keeping my voice light and friendly. "Who gave you that note?"

He shrugged and looked around him. "I dunno."

"Please, it's very important. Is he still here?"

The boy looked around and shrugged again. "I don't see him."

"What did he look like? Can you tell me that?" I knew I was wading through sticky territory. Stranger danger was real, and I was a stranger.

The boy squinted against the sun. "He was wearing a coat and sunglasses. He was in a car."

"You went up to a stranger in a car? You shouldn't do that. Do you hear me?"

His eyes dulled before brightening. "He paid me five dollars, though."

"Excuse me, ma'am. Can I help you?" A woman rushed over toward me. As she did, the boy scrambled away.

"Is he your son?" I nodded toward the young courier.

"Yes, he is." The young mom put her hands on her hips and looked ready to go all mama bear on me.

"A stranger just approached him and paid him money to give me a note."

Her nostrils flared. "I don't know what kind of game you're playing, but tell your secret admirer to find other ways to send you love notes."

I wanted to sigh, but I didn't. Her concerns were valid. Then again, so were mine.

"He wasn't a secret admirer," I explained. "He's a dangerous man who was using your son to advance his own agenda."

The woman didn't seem to care. She raised her nose

and turned around. "Stay away from my son. Next time, I'm calling the police."

I let out the sigh I'd been holding back. Communication was so difficult sometimes.

As I stepped away, I scanned the parking lot for anyone lingering in a car. Every vehicle looked empty. Which left me right back where I was before.

***

"So what do you think, Holly?"

I snapped my head toward my sister, Alex, and saw her expectant look. I'd been absorbed with my own life and had mentally checked out. We were sampling cakes at a local bakery that had been featured on a national TV show. Since then, this "cake artist's" work was now sought after and expensive. We'd come to see what all the hype was about.

I set my empty plate and fork on the table and swallowed. Everything tasted like sawdust lately.

"It's great," I finally said.

Alex narrowed her eyes and leaned toward me, lowering her voice. "I think it's terrible. A chocolate-and-bacon-flavored wedding cake?"

I blinked several times, certain I hadn't heard her correctly. "What?"

I looked at the placard in front of the cake and saw the description. Sure enough, it was a chocolate-and-bacon-flavored cake.

"It's the latest trend," the baker said. He scowled, obviously the uptight type who considered food an art. Even his name, Jean Claude, which he pronounced with what sounded like a fake French accent, sounded snooty.

I was all for creativity, but his disposition and nose-raised attitude zapped any fun from the room.

"I'm not into trends," Alex muttered. "I'm more traditional and classic."

"Then let's move to the mango-and-chili . . ."

Mango-and-chili-flavored wedding cakes were more traditional? What planet was this man from? Despite my doubts, we followed him down the line.

Alex's original baker had unexpectedly gone out of business, and now she was scrambling to find a replacement. Her wedding was coming up soon—as in, next Friday soon—and being behind was so unlike Alex.

My sister was everything I wasn't. In fact, I called her Alex the Great because there was nothing she'd ever failed at. Now my perfect sister was marrying her perfect match: a surgeon. Together, they'd begin to live their perfect life together.

Honestly, my mom, brother, and sister were all very similar. They were overachievers who continued to reach higher and higher. I was like my dad. We liked things simple. We found contentment in doing what we'd felt called to do, whether that meant looking successful in the world's eyes or not. I knew I wanted to be the person I was created to be, but being around the rest of my family somehow made me feel not good enough.

"So why do you look so distracted?" Alex asked, licking icing off a fork as we sampled the mango-and-chili cake.

The mango icing was delicious—if I was at an exotic resort for a weekend getaway.

I shrugged. "Just life, I suppose."

How I would love to have her opinion about how I should proceed. An assistant district attorney and smarter than a whip, she'd probably have some great ideas on how to handle this insane mess.

"Things are getting crazy at work," she said before I could formulate my thoughts or contemplate spilling everything. She moved on to the next sample: blue cheese and apple. "I think I'm getting married at the absolute worst possible time."

"What's going on?" Alex had my attention now, much more so than the cake.

She stuck a bite in her mouth and practically gagged. Jean Claude did *not* appreciate her reaction. "It's the trial for Arnold Pegman. Remember him?"

I shook my head, mentally reviewing any recent news stories I'd heard. I didn't even bother to sample the blue-cheese-and-apple concoction, and instead set my plate back onto the table. "I can't say I do."

"He killed his girlfriend."

"That sounds vaguely familiar."

"His trial got moved up to next week. Can you believe it? Right before the wedding."

She moved on to the next cake. I read the label: sweet potato and marshmallow. Really? Where were the good old white cakes with buttercream icing? Or, for a step up, maybe he could even have almond cake with fondant?

I shoved a forkful in my mouth and forced myself to swallow. "I take it you're on the prosecution?"

"Exactly. I'm not lead, but I've been very involved. Get this: William and I have to delay our honeymoon."

My jaw dropped. She might as well have said she was wearing a black dress on her wedding day. "No. They can't do that, can they?"

"They can and they did. The media is going to be all over this trial. Everything we say and do will be scrutinized by commentators wanting to make a name for themselves and people who think they're more important than they actually are."

"Why is this so hot?"

"Basically, all the people involved look like they're from Hollywood. Very camera-friendly faces, and the media love that. I'd like to say there's no bias toward pretty people, but there is. Other than that, the whole trial is based on circumstantial evidence. The defense knows it, and so do we."

"That stinks." I actually did feel sorry for Alex. Her career controlled her life at the moment. Then again, her job was arguably the first priority in her life, so maybe this was just par for the course.

"Holly, if there's one thing I've learned in life, it's that it isn't fair. Never forget that."

If only I could.

***

Somehow, Alex ended up hating all the cakes and convinced me to make her wedding cake. Tasting her choices, I couldn't say no. All the other bakers around who were available were either overpriced or no good.

I did like to bake, but I'd never done a wedding cake before. Alex insisted she wanted something simple, so I'd try to give her one that matched her expectations. She hadn't really left any room to say no.

But as I sat on my couch that night, I couldn't help but feel overwhelmed. Really overwhelmed.

I didn't want to break up with Chase.

I didn't want to go out with Benjamin.

I didn't want Chase to be injured in the middle of these

riots.

And I didn't want to make this stupid cake.

I took a sip of my raspberry tea and leaned back. Not even Peggy Lee singing in the background about it being a good day to be alive could soothe my nerves. I mean, I wasn't talking about a bad day or a bad week, even. I was talking about things that had the ability to change my entire future.

My phone buzzed. I saw I had a new email—from the task force meeting I'd stumbled through earlier today.

This was my first time serving on a task force, and I hadn't been sure exactly what to expect. We were tackling one case at a time, and today we'd been introduced to one involving a missing woman named Deborah Picket.

Six months ago, Deborah Picket didn't show up for work at the interior design firm she co-owned. Her husband, who worked for the government, called the police at noon when he realized his wife wasn't answering her phone. He claimed he slept on the couch the night before and didn't go into their bedroom that morning in order to let her sleep.

Her car and clothes were still at the house. None of the money in her bank accounts had been touched. And no one had heard a word from her since then. Coworkers said she never complained about her marriage and that she seemed happy. The woman had seemingly disappeared into thin air.

Although Deborah's husband, Tom, was suspected of her murder, her body had never been found nor any evidence to charge him. The only hunch the police had was based on the fact that Tom Picket was having an affair. He'd joked in an email about killing his wife so he could be with his girlfriend. He'd taken shooting lessons six months earlier, and he upped Deborah's life insurance policy that year. However, no charges were pressed by the DA's office.

Four months after Deborah disappeared, Tom killed himself without leaving any notes or confessions. Deborah's body still hadn't been located, and her family desperately wanted answers. I hoped this interagency task force would be able to help.

Each of us had left the meeting tasked with reviewing the case files. With the fresh sets of eyes on the case and the inclusion of people of different professions, maybe we could find a new lead. Nothing I dredged up would necessarily be used in court. We were simply looking for answers.

I finished my tea and put the cup in the sink. I had to get some rest. Maybe with a little sleep, things would look brighter. Then I could get a handle on how to deal with the hand life had given me at the moment.

I climbed the steps to my bedroom and stepped inside, visions of relaxation in my head.

Instead, my light didn't pop on when I flipped the switch. Instantly, my stomach clenched.

"I wanted to pay you another visit, just in case my earlier note didn't sink in," a familiar yet unwelcome voice said.

"It sank in just fine," I said, steadying myself with the doorframe. I wanted to run, to flee, but I couldn't.

"You haven't followed my instructions. There will be consequences."

"What kind of consequences?" I hardly wanted to ask the question. I didn't want to know. I just wanted this dilemma to magically disappear from my life. All the wishing in the world wouldn't make that happen, though.

"I can't tell you that. It would spoil all the fun. But there will continue to be consequences until you do as I asked."

"As you *asked*? I didn't exactly hear anything that left me wiggle room." My words had a bitter edge to them.

"You think you're clever, getting Chase to move out of his house. But you will not outsmart me, Holly Paladin. Let me make that clear. You're a means to an end—an irreplaceable means."

Well, there was that. At least I knew someone else was being targeted, and I was just being used. This was all about . . . Chase? He was the most logical choice.

"Can you just tell me what you want?" My voice cracked. "There's got to be another way to do this. Your methods leave a lot to be desired."

"You're not in a place to be defiant, Ms. Paladin." Anger simmered in his voice now, and I realized I'd pushed too much.

"Holly, I'm home!" The door opened downstairs. Mom. Mom was here.

I braced myself. Would one of those "consequences" the man had mentioned have something to do with my mom?

I prayed that wasn't the case.

CHAPTER 9

"Go downstairs and greet your mom like nothing has happened," the Shadow Man instructed. "Speak of this to anyone, and I'll accelerate this process. I expect results, Ms. Paladin. And soon."

With one last glance at the shadowy figure, I rushed downstairs. I wanted to get away from the creep, and I wanted to demand more answers. Leaving was the wisest choice, though.

Before I reached the bottom of the stairs, I slowed and attempted to compose myself. That was about as easy as calming a tornado. My insides felt like a disastrous mess.

"Hello, Mother," I said, walking gracefully to the bottom step.

"Holly! You're still up." Mom pulled off her coat and slipped it into the closet. "Was it all the sugary cakes that Alex made you try? I wanted to go, but I had the board meeting for the children's hospital. Our big fund-raiser is coming up two weeks after Alex's wedding. Life never slows down, does it?"

"Cake tasting was fine. I suppose Alex already told you she didn't like any of the samples?"

Mom paused in the foyer. "She mentioned that. She knows what she wants. I guess that's why she's as successful as she is today."

I rubbed my neck and quickly glanced behind me. Was

the man upstairs gone yet? I had to keep Mom down here long enough for him to leave. First of all, I wanted to keep her safe. Secondly, I didn't want to have to lie to her about what was going on.

"I was just about to go to bed when I heard you come in," I started, smoothing my skirt. "I wanted to say hi."

"You're looking a little pale, Holly. You're not coming down with something, are you?" Mom frowned and put her hand to my forehead.

I shook my head. "No, I think I'm just tired. It's been a long day, full of meetings and appointments."

Not to mention dealing with possible killers, death threats to my loved ones, and a strange man lurking in my house. I kept this last part silent, of course.

"So you're making Alex's cake?" As she breezed toward the kitchen, I caught a whiff of her rose-scented perfume.

I frowned. "Somehow Alex convinced me to say yes."

Mom raised her eyebrows and put the kettle on for her nightly tea. "Really? Now that's something I wasn't expecting to hear."

"Me either."

"But it's going to be such a beautiful event." Mom sighed, a far-off look in her eyes as she leaned against the granite countertop. "I wish your father were here to see it."

The weight on my chest grew heavier. Life would never feel completely whole again without my father here. "Me too."

She let out another long sigh before raising her chin. "We have no choice but to keep going, right? Life goes on. We just have to keep the memories of the ones we love alive in our hearts."

My hand covered hers, and I squeezed. "Dad would be really proud of you, Mom. You've really proven what a strong woman you are." Sometimes I forgot that my mom was still human beneath her well-manicured exterior. She seemed so put together, but everyone needed encouragement sometimes. I tried to listen to the quiet voice nudging me to follow His leading.

Mom patted my cheek just as the kettle whistled. She grabbed it and poured some water into a dainty teacup. The scent of spearmint rose with the steam.

"Thank you, Holly," she said. "I know he'd think the same thing about you. The ability to continue on in the face of grief and adversity says a lot about a person. There's a time to mourn and a time to continue on. It can be one of the hardest realizations to accept."

I fought a sad smile. It was strange. Sometimes I'd give anything to turn back time and have some extra moments with my father, to feel like a whole family again. But if I went back in time, it would mean giving up Chase. That was one of the ironies of life, I supposed. It was impossible to have it all at once. Some moments and people and relationships only came with time.

"Well, I'm heading to bed, Holly. I'll see you in the morning." She kissed my cheek, then hurried upstairs with her tea in hand.

"I'm coming behind you," I called.

I quickened my steps, hoping the Shadow Man wasn't upstairs still. She reached her bedroom just as I cleared the stairs.

"The window's open again? I need to have this checked out." Mom harrumphed as she gently placed her porcelain cup on her dresser, strode toward the wall, shoved the glass down, and clicked the locks in place. "Well, would you look at that?"

"Look at what?" I stepped into her room, my eyes

darting around in one last desperate attempt to make sure the man wasn't here.

"The lock is broken. No wonder it keeps popping open."

Interesting. Had the man arranged that so he could easily come and go? But how had he gotten in the first time?

"I can probably fix that in the morning. I just need to run to the store first." Dad had been a locksmith, and he'd made sure to teach me the basics. Though I was all girl, I'd still been content to pal around with him on the job rather than go to fancy galas with my mom.

"Thank you, Holly. We'll be fine for tonight. I mean, what's someone going to do? Scale the side of our house and break in?" She let out a laugh.

If Mom only knew, she wouldn't be laughing.

If she only knew.

***

Although things were relatively calm in the downtown area the next day, Ralph said we still needed to meet in our temporary offices to be on the safe side. I had mixed feelings. Part of me wanted to show the city that we wouldn't back down or be bullied. The other part of me craved safety and didn't think I could handle the stress of another riot breaking out while I was nearby.

I finished writing replies to three constituents. One wanted Ralph to endorse a bill that had been proposed. Another thought the crime in the city was growing out of control. And yet another needed a recommendation for the college of his choice.

With those letters printed and proofread, I stuck them in a folder so Ralph could approve them. When I finished that, I picked up my file on Tom Picket and reviewed the information there. Tom had been thirty-six and worked for the government, although his exact job title was undisclosed. He liked hiking and fishing and didn't have any children. Interestingly enough, Alex was the one who had told detectives there wasn't enough evidence to press charges against him.

It was funny the connections that could be found between my family members. Since we all worked with the public in one form or another, people we knew often overlapped.

I needed to look into Tom's background more, but first I had to stand. My body was still sore from being trampled and stabbed. Whenever I twisted my back the wrong way, my muscles quickly reminded me I'd been hurt and needed to take it easy. That meant that sitting too long in my office chair made me ache.

Which was what was happening now. I'd been at work for only three hours, and I already felt sore. I could take a pain pill, but I was afraid I wouldn't be lucid enough to function properly, and I didn't want to risk that.

As I stretched, my phone rang, and I saw that it was Jamie. Maybe chatting with my friend would help me perk up some. "Hey, girl," I told her.

"You weren't going to tell your bestie what happened?" Jamie said.

"Huh?"

"You were stabbed," she said bluntly.

"Oh, that," I muttered.

"Yeah, *that*. You know how I heard about this? I was covering the riots, and a witness said that Ralph Paladin's sister was injured. I guess she'd seen you being carried away in an ambulance."

"I'm sorry, Jamie."

She paused. "Are you okay?"

"I'm sore, but I'm hanging in."

"Get this, Holly. I know everyone thinks that car bomb was because of these riots, but I'm talking to sources who claim these protesters don't have the know-how to do stuff like this."

"What do you mean?"

"These people who are protesting aren't the engineer types. They're not guys who can make their own explosives, set them under an unmarked police sedan, and detonate it at a later time. I wonder if Chase is being targeted for some other reason."

Her words caused my stomach to drop. "It's an interesting theory."

"Just tell him to be careful, okay? And you be careful too. I mean, really? Getting stabbed? How does someone accidentally stab you?"

They didn't, I said silently. The Shadow Man had been there. If only I had seen his face. But he was among the crowd when everything happened, and stabbing me was his way of letting me know I was within his grasp.

We hung up, and I plopped back down in my chair. But not before Henry the Tell caught my eye and raised his chin. Great. He'd just heard all of that, hadn't he?

I stared blankly at my computer screen as thoughts swirled in my head. I just wished I could make sense of everything. It seemed an impossibility, though.

In crisis intervention training, I'd never encountered a scenario of "Break up with your boyfriend or I'll kill him." Who *did* stuff like this? Someone with a twisted mind, that was who.

I sighed and tried to focus by checking my email. I had to get over this brain fog. Every time I was supposed to be concentrating on something else, all I could think about was my own dilemma. Honestly, the best way to put my own pain in perspective was to concentrate on other people and how I could help them. Sometimes that was easier said than done.

As I scanned my email list, my eyes stopped at one in particular. It was labeled "Important," and the sender's name was "Jon Dough." Jon Dough? This had to be some kind of email scam.

Despite the internal alarms sounding in my head, I clicked on it, and a video popped on my computer. I sucked in a deep breath at what played out on my screen.

A Craftsman-style house, decorated with clean lines and classic architecture, filled my vision. The decorations were minimal, the colors monotone, and the whole place immaculately clean.

Ralph's house.

The feed switched from room to room. No one was home, but I saw Chase's things in one of the bedrooms. His coat hung on the back of the closet door. The football-emblazoned shaving bag I gave him for our one-month anniversary sat on the dresser.

I closed my eyes. Somehow that man had set up cameras in Ralph's house also. What else had he done? Another bomb?

As if to answer my question, the shot panned to the basement. The camera zoomed in on something in the rafters.

Something with wires and a blinking red light, all attached to a black box in the center.

A bomb.

This nightmare wasn't going to end, was it?

***

When Chase called an hour later, my nerves were paper-thin. Hearing his voice only deepened my uneasiness. Something was wrong.

"Holly, you need to get to your mom's house."

I instantly tensed in my office chair, expecting the worst. "Why? What happened?"

"Someone broke into the house."

My insides squeezed with apprehension and worry, feelings I knew all too well lately. "Oh my goodness. Is Mom hurt?"

"She's fine, just scared. The intruder tied her up and put her in a closet."

"How did you find her? Who called the police? Did you catch the person responsible?" The questions rushed out.

"This is the strange part: apparently the intruder called 911 before he left."

I closed my eyes. This was the consequence I was facing, wasn't it? The Shadow Man was sending a clear message. A little too clear.

This was my fault. I should have fixed the latch on that window. I hadn't had the time last night, so instead I'd wedged a dowel rod between the windowsill and the double-hung glass.

I should have hurried to the store right then, but I'd figured he wouldn't strike again so soon. My optimism might get the people I loved killed, and I couldn't let that happen.

"I'll be right there." I jumped up, ignoring the twinge in my back, and searched for my purse. "Have you told Ralph yet?"

"Not yet."

"I'll fill him in."

I hurried through the office and burst through my brother's door. He was meeting with three men I'd never seen before, but I didn't care.

"Holly?" Ralph stood.

"Someone just broke into Mom's house!" My voice sounded breathless.

"What?" His voice rose with surprise.

"Chase called. I'm on my way there now."

"I'll go with you." He took a step my way, ready to abandon his meeting.

"I can handle it," I told him, raising my hand before he ran me over. "You stay here. I'll keep you updated."

"Are you sure?"

I nodded. "Yeah, I'm positive."

With that, I hurried to my car. I held my breath as I cranked the engine. I'd done that ever since Chase's car exploded. The only thing that comforted me was the fact that I thought this man needed me alive. Killing me off at this point wasn't part of his plan, or he would have probably done it already.

Oh, Lord. What am I going to do?

My hands trembled against the steering wheel the entire drive home. As soon as I pulled up, I bypassed everyone—the police officers and paramedics and even a few nosy neighbors—and went straight to find Mom.

She sat on the couch in our formal living room, a cup of water in her hand. She slowly took a sip as a police officer lingered close. Despite her ordeal, she looked beautiful, with not a blonde hair out of place and her business suit still pressed and neat. If my superpower was kindness, hers was looking put together and composed.

I pulled her into a hug. "Are you okay?"

She nodded, appearing coolly frazzled as she rubbed her wrists. "I'm fine. Isn't it just the craziest thing? Nothing was stolen from our house, even. It doesn't make a lick of sense, does it?"

That factoid confirmed my suspicions even more that the whole purpose of this crime was to send me a message. *There will be consequences.* I remembered the man's threat.

"What happened?" My throat tightened as I asked the question.

She let out a breath. "I came home from showing a house. I planned to be here only long enough to grab something to eat. I was in the kitchen when I heard someone behind me. Before I could even turn around, a man put his hand over my mouth. He tied me up and stuck me in the closet."

"Did you see him?"

She took another sip of water. That's when I noticed her hand trembling. She *was* shaken. "No, he had a mask on. I couldn't tell anything about him, except that he was taller than me and he was as strong as the devil."

"Did he say anything?"

"He said, 'There are always consequences.' I mean, what in the world does that mean? It doesn't even make sense."

I knew exactly what it meant, unfortunately. I tried to subdue my thoughts from leaking into my expression and being a dead giveaway. "Well, I'm glad you're okay."

"I am too. I had a few moments in the closet when I had no idea what was going to happen. Was he going to set the house on fire? Come back for me? Destroy something your dad made?"

No, he was just making a point and sending your daughter a message—one she received loud and clear.

"I don't know, Mom. It all sounds crazy."

She turned toward an approaching officer just as Chase

appeared in the background. I hurried over to him, reminding myself that he was working and I shouldn't give him a hug. And if I didn't break up with him soon, someone could be seriously hurt next time.

"When I heard there was a break-in at your address, my mind went to worst-case scenarios," he told me quietly as he led me out of earshot of anyone else.

"I can imagine. What do you think went on here?"

"I'm stumped. Nothing was stolen. Nothing even looked rumpled, which would have happened if someone was looking for valuables. Maybe your mom got home just as the intruder came in. Maybe she interrupted him before he could start, so he cut the job short and left."

"Maybe," I conceded. "But why not just sneak out before he was discovered? Why tie Mom up and call the police?"

"I have suspicions that there's something else going on here. Is there anything I should know?" He stared at me, studying my face a moment.

That familiar lump formed in my throat. Did Chase have any clue what had happened? He couldn't. There was no way. "I . . . I don't think . . . I don't think so."

He narrowed his eyes for a moment. Great. My unyielding honesty was all too apparent. How was I going to pull off breaking up with him? Because that was what was going to have to happen, wasn't it? I didn't see any way I would get out of this. Not with the lives of people I loved on the line.

"What's wrong, Holly?" He nudged my chin back up.

"Nothing . . . I mean, I'm just shaken up over all of this. As you can imagine."

"There's nothing else?"

Why did he have to be so good at reading me? I'd loved

that about him up until a few days ago. "What else could there be?"

He finally nodded. "Okay, then. I'm going to get back to work here. I doubt the intruder left any clues, but we need to cover every base."

"Before I forget, do you have any idea how he got in?"

"The window in your mom's room was open. We think that's how."

My stomach sank.

Holly Anna Paladin had failed . . . again.

I had to do something before someone I loved died.

CHAPTER 10

That evening I sat alone at a table in one of my favorite diners, the Cosmic Café. A new owner had recently taken over and decided to play into its name. All around me the walls were painted a deep blue. Images of the stars were emblazoned on the dark ceiling, and plastic comets and planets hung above the tables. Even the music followed the restaurant's theme—usually from *Stars Wars* or some other melody that reminded people of space travel and sci-fi.

Chase and I never came here for the decorations or music, though. We came for the killer hummus and pita chips, as well as for the view. The massive windows on one wall afforded a photo-worthy view of the sparkling lights of the city. Despite the great location, only locals seemed to know the place existed, so it was never overly crowded.

We came here often enough that the waitress automatically brought us red pepper hummus with cucumbers for me and pita bread for Chase. She also brought some kalamata olives. The low lights and the smell of garlic and grilled meat always cheered me up.

But not today.

Right now, I felt beside myself. My fingers kept twisting together. My stomach was in knots. And I wanted to cry—ugly cry, at that.

I knew what I had to do. The puppet master who was

controlling my life at the moment had made it very clear just how serious he was about his "request." If I didn't break up with Chase, I feared just how many people would be hurt.

I could try to deny this all I wanted. I could try to reverse roles and pull the strings myself. But, every time I did, it only seemed to accelerate the situation. I didn't see any way out of this, and I'd examined the circumstances until I was exhausted.

I don't want to do this, Lord.

"Hey, beautiful!"

As I looked up, Chase planted a kiss on my cheek. His sweetness only made this harder and my heart heavier.

"Hey, Chase." I managed a half smile.

He squinted again, obviously picking up my vibe that something was wrong. Before he could say anything, a news story running in the background caught my ear.

"The trial for Arnold Pegman begins next week. Some have called this the biggest trial the area has seen in the past decade . . ."

"Alex is on the prosecution, isn't she?" Chase asked.

I nodded. "She has to delay her honeymoon because of it. Can you believe it?"

"That's unfortunate."

The waitress appeared. Barb was in her fifties and seemed to love working here. She was always upbeat and never complained, and one might think she had a financial stake in the restaurant because of her enthusiasm over the food. "What can I get you two lovebirds tonight? We have a once-in-a-blue-moon salmon kabob."

She always used extraterrestrial types of sayings. *You'll love this to the stars and back. The dish is out of this world. One bite will take you to a galaxy far, far away.* Usually, I found it endearing and cute. Not tonight, though.

The last thing I needed was to sit through an entire meal. I had to get this over with. "Just tea for me, please."

Chase's eyes cut toward me again, questions lingering in their depths. "I'll take a coffee."

The lump in my throat and the rock in my stomach seemed to increase in size.

"I'm telling you: you two are missing out," Barb said. Then she winked. "But I'll let you both get your heads out of the clouds long enough to come to your senses."

As soon as she left, Chase leaned toward me. "What's going on?"

His voice sounded serious. He knew something was up. I obviously wasn't acting like myself. I was trying to pull away, to calculate some way to make this both easier and believable.

I drew in a deep, albeit shaky, breath. "I don't know how to say this."

He squinted and reached across the table, resting his hand on my forearm. The motion usually grounded me, but right now it sent my nerves skyrocketing into space.

I'd been around Barb too long.

"Just say it," Chase urged, his voice low and husky. It always got to me when he sounded like that. "You don't have to watch your words with me, Holly. You know that."

The knot traveled from my throat and down my esophagus, all the way to my stomach. "I'm not sure this is working, Chase."

"You're not sure what's working?" He looked earnestly confused. As he should be. We'd both been on cloud nine since we started dating.

"Us."

He twisted his head as if he hadn't heard correctly.

"Us?"

I nodded solemnly. "It's me. I'm not sure I'm ready for a relationship."

He blanched, and I could see the wheels turning in his head. "Holly, are you just getting cold feet or something? I mean, I thought we were moving pretty slowly, but we can slow down even more if you'd like."

His consideration made this even harder. I desperately wanted to explain the situation to him, to ease any hurt he might be experiencing. But I couldn't. "I just . . . I just think this is a bad time."

He shook his head, as if still in shock. "Holly, you're not making a lot of sense."

"I just think we need to break up," I blurted. Despite my best efforts, tears rushed to my eyes. I tried to pull them back, but it didn't work. Moisture poured down my cheeks.

"Are you serious, Holly?" His voice sounded husky, confused, and uncertain.

I looked away from the pain in his eyes, feeling too weak to carry this through. I somehow managed to force a nod. For such a simple little action, it crushed my heart. "I am."

"I thought we had something good. Something really good."

"We do—we did, I mean. I don't know, Chase." *Offer an olive branch*, a voice inside said. Something to give him hope, to signal that this wasn't right. Maybe that was my only option for getting through this. "Maybe I just need some time."

He scooted back in his chair and raked a hand through his hair. "I don't know what to say. This is out of nowhere. I thought more of you, Holly. I thought you were different."

His words sucked the air out of my lungs. His shock was turning into anger, and I couldn't blame him. I'd blindsided him.

"I am different," I finally muttered.

He shook his head. "Then why are you pulling this stunt?"

Of course he'd seen through me. He knew something wasn't right. What had I expected?

I had no more words. I had no more strength, for that matter. If I sat here any longer, I was going to confide everything to him.

I stood quickly, and silverware clattered on the table. "I need to go."

"Holly—"

"I'm sorry."

Before he could stop me, I hurried to my car.

As more tears threatened to escape, I pulled out my phone and composed a message to the Shadow Man.

I broke up with Chase. I hope you're happy now.

Almost immediately, I got a response.

I'm never happy, Holly.

Something about his reply made my soul feel even colder than I did before.

***

"You look terrible," Ralph told me the next morning.

I leaned back in my office chair. I wanted to sigh or pout, but I didn't. Instead, I remained professional and stiff. If I gave in to my emotions right now, I'd be a blubbering mess for the rest of the day, and I couldn't afford that. There was too much on the line, and I had too many things to do both at work and for Alex's wedding.

Neither of those things took top priority with me right

now, but I was trying to stay focused so I wouldn't lose my mind. "Good morning to you too."

He crossed around from the partition and leaned against my desk. A paternal-like worry formed in the wrinkle between his eyebrows. "No, really. You look terrible. Are you okay?"

I shrugged, shuffling through some papers like I had a mission. In truth, none of the words registered with me. I felt numb. "Chase and I broke up."

"What?" His voice sounded choked. "Why in the world did you break up? Did he break up with you?"

"No, I broke up with him." I needed to get this revelation over with because extending it wouldn't make anything better. But saying the words aloud made a lump form in my throat. I wanted to wake up and discover this was all a nightmare. I wasn't that lucky.

"Holly, I have to say that surprises me. I'd never seen you so happy. What happened?" Gone was Ralph the politician, and in his place was Ralph my overprotective brother.

"It's complicated." How many times could I say that? But it was the easiest way to express what was going on without sharing too many details.

"Most relationships are. Looking at you now, I'd say you made the wrong decision. At least, that's how you're feeling. Am I correct?" He sounded like a guidance counselor—that was usually my role. I didn't like having the tables turned on me like this.

I shrugged again, desperate to keep my emotions under control. I flipped through some papers, trying not to break down. "It doesn't matter. What's done is done."

He stared at me another moment, looking like he wanted to demand details, but he knew better. Ralph was usually good at respecting people's boundaries, and I appreciated that about him. Especially since my mother could often be just the opposite.

"Well, if you need to talk, I'm here, okay?"

I nodded, trying not to show my gratitude. "Thanks, Ralph."

Just as he walked away, my phone rang. With lackluster enthusiasm, I answered. "Holly Paladin."

"Holly, this is Benjamin."

Bile rose in my throat. This was it. This was the second part of the plan rearing its ugly head. "Hi, Benjamin."

"I wondered if you'd thought about that date yet? You've been on my mind all week."

My jaw locked for a moment. He was acting so innocent in all of this when he was anything but. I was tired of skirting around the truth. "Let's just stop playing games. Yes, I'll go out with you. Are you happy now?"

"Uh . . . yeah, I'm happy," he muttered. "Wow. I wasn't quite expecting that reaction, but I'll take it. How about tonight?"

I stared at the picture of Chase and me on my desk, and my anger grew. "Is that what it has to be? I'm obviously not the one calling the shots here."

"Okay . . . um, well then. How about if we have dinner?"

"Name the place, and I'll meet you there. I mean, I realize you have my address. I'm not naïve. But we should still meet. No pickups."

"How'd you know I had your address?"

"Don't play dumb." Did he think I was totally stupid?

"Okay, well, I did google you, and your address did pop up. I mean, this is dating in the twenty-first century, I suppose. Doesn't everyone google everyone? But . . . anyway. Okay, how about 7:00 p.m. at Darcy's. Would that work?"

"Fine."

"Okay." He still sounded so confused and uncertain. What an actor. "I'll see you then."

I hung up and scowled at my computer as if it had personally wronged me.

"Man problems?" Henry stuck his head over the partition, not bothering to hide the curiosity in his eyes.

I scowled again, realizing my behavior wasn't very becoming or desirable. My stress was trumping my social graces at the moment. "Maybe."

"I'm sorry to hear that. I hope you get it all worked out."

"Thanks," I told him.

But deep in my gut—I, Holly Anna Paladin, the Forever Optimist—I knew things weren't going to work out, no matter how much I hoped for them to.

***

I didn't bother to go home and freshen up before my big date with Benjamin. No, I couldn't care less how I looked. I stayed late at work, trying to get caught up on everything I'd fallen behind on this week in my state of perpetual distraction.

Chase had texted me several times and left two voice mails. Each time I read one of his messages, tears popped into my eyes. If only I could get him to understand why I was doing this, then maybe my heart wouldn't feel so broken and raw.

At 6:45, I'd headed out to my car and driven to Darcy's. I'd been there once before. It was a family-owned Italian restaurant that tried to be higher class than it actually was. It boasted generic, canned music; cheap, white tablecloths; and tea lights that gave off an odd odor I couldn't place.

Of course Benjamin was already there. He stood and waved a little too enthusiastically when he spotted me.

I didn't even bother to smile. I simply nodded to him and sat in the booth across from him, dropping my purse beside me.

"You look lovely," he said. He wore a pale-blue shirt and a lemonade-colored tie. His hair was styled and his cheeks clean shaven.

For just a moment, something tried to surface in my mind. Had I seen him before that day in the parking garage when he climbed in my Mustang? He suddenly seemed vaguely familiar. Despite the thought that nagged at the back of my mind, I couldn't place the elusive recollection.

"Thanks." My voice sounded as lackluster as I felt.

He put his menu aside and began reorganizing the condiments at the end of the table. "I hope you don't mind, but I went ahead and ordered for you."

"How did you know I don't have any food allergies?" I wasn't usually mean, but this situation was bringing out the worst in me.

"You have food allergies?"

"No, but I might." I sounded juvenile, I knew, but for once in my life I didn't care.

"Oh, well, I'll try and keep that in mind. But I heard their retro chicken parmesan was to die for."

I was tired of putting up with pretenses. This conversation didn't really matter, and I couldn't pretend it did. "Who are you really, Benjamin Radcliff?"

He looked stunned for a minute before shrugging. "Well, my name is Benjamin. Like I said before, I'm from Louisville, but I moved here to work for a company that I'm unable to talk about yet."

My irritation only grew. "I know all that. What I mean is, who are you really?"

His eyes brightened. "Who am I really?" he repeated. "Wow, that's so esoteric. I'm spontaneous and fun loving. I like long walks on the beach—"

I had to stop him. Like, now. Immediately. "I'm sorry. You'll have to excuse me a minute because I need to run to the restroom."

I hurried across the restaurant and disappeared into the ladies' bathroom, not because I had to go, but because I needed a moment to compose myself. The area had spa-like decorations with sea-foam-green walls and soothing sand-colored tiles everywhere else. The scent of bleach mingled with the normal bathroom odors, and the combination turned my stomach.

I leaned against the wall, not something I would normally recommend in public facilities, and rubbed my temples. This was great. Five minutes into my so-called date, and all I wanted to do was sock the man. What kind of game was he playing? None of this made any sense.

"Holly Anna Paladin, what exactly are you doing?" Accusation rang in the voice.

I pulled my eyes open and spotted Jamie. Wait . . . Jamie?

"What are you doing here?" I whispered, pondering just how my timing could be so very bad.

She put a hand on her hip and gave me the diva-like stare. "The question is: What are you doing here? With that Benjamin weirdo of all people? What about Chase? Holly, what is going on?"

I almost—almost—poured everything out right then and there. But I stopped myself and sighed. "It's complicated."

She didn't break her stare, nor did any compassion wash over her features. "Uncomplicate it for me."

"I can't. Relationships are tricky." She had no idea. Absolutely no idea.

Nor did she believe me. Her gaze made that clear. "There's no way you went from Chase to Benjamin. He's not your type."

I shrugged. The last thing I wanted to do was argue the point. The thought of it exhausted me, not only mentally but physically too. This whole thing was taking a toll on me.

"He's perfectly nice," I finally muttered.

"He may be. But you're in love with Chase."

"Feelings are fickle. You and I both know that." I had to change the subject before I had a breakdown. "Now, why are you here?"

"You're not getting out of this conversation that easily, Holly. I'm your best friend. We share everything. The fact that you and Chase are having problems and you didn't mention it to me first says a lot."

My heart softened a moment. Jamie was hurt and confused, and she was upset with me. I deserved her anger because all of this was a major fail in the friendship department. "Jamie, you know I trust you with everything. But Chase and I . . . I can't really explain it. Not now, at least."

"I'm not buying it, Holly."

I let out a sigh. Why couldn't she just let this go? She was only making my inner struggle more volatile. "I don't want to talk about it anymore."

Tears flooded Jamie's eyes before she raised her chin. "I see."

She started to walk away with nothing resolved between us. I wanted to change that, but I couldn't. Instead, I grabbed her arm.

"How'd you find me, Jamie?" The question seemed so inconsequential compared to the steps back our friendship had just taken, but I had to know.

The scowl on her face proved to me that she felt the irritation I'd expected from her. "Ralph called me and asked if I'd check on you. I drove up to the office just as you pulled away. I decided to head home but happened to see you pull into this place. I wasn't going to give you a hard time, but then I saw Benjamin and started to get suspicious."

"I don't know what to say, Jamie."

"You don't have to say anything else." She pushed past me and out the door, pausing long enough to add, "I thought more of you, Holly. And I thought our friendship meant more to you. I guess I was wrong."

I leaned against the wall again, feeling like my world was falling apart and I had no idea what to do about it.

CHAPTER 11

I had no choice except to go back out and face Benjamin. But I felt even more dead inside now than I did earlier. Each movement felt heavy, almost mechanical. I couldn't get a deep breath because of the weight I felt pressing against my chest. My head buzzed with so many thoughts and so much confusion that I felt off balance.

Benjamin didn't seem to notice.

When I returned, our food sat on the table, and Benjamin had already eaten half of his. Go figure.

"You okay? I almost went to check on you, but it seemed a little inappropriate." He let out a laugh as his vocal pitch climbed into the stratosphere. "Or I figured you may have skipped out in the middle of dinner."

"I'm fine. Thank you." I raised my fork, said a silent prayer, and then began picking at my food.

If he thought I was going to attempt to make conversation, he was wrong. I wanted no part of this. I had no idea what purpose this was supposed to serve. If I was going to be forced into it, I wasn't going to make it easy on anyone.

Apparently, it didn't matter. Benjamin began talking. And he kept talking. And talking.

And he didn't talk about anything of substance. Not really. He mentioned restaurants he'd discovered since moving here. What he missed about Louisville. How he'd grown up in

Tennessee.

I moved pieces of pasta and chicken around my plate, and every once in a while glanced at him.

The man was so oblivious and unassuming. Maybe he was just a pawn in this whole scheme. Maybe he didn't even know the full extent of what was going on.

"So how's your food?" he finally asked.

I looked down at my plate. I obviously hadn't eaten anything, but Mr. Clueless didn't seem to notice. "It was fine," I muttered.

"Yeah, I thought it was super good. I'm really glad we were able to get together tonight, Holly. I guess sometimes persistence pays off, right?"

I nodded slowly but said nothing.

"So do you want to do it again sometime?"

I wanted to say no, but I hadn't exactly been given orders on what to say regarding a second date, had I? I didn't think so. "I have a pretty busy weekend coming up."

"Maybe next weekend?" The man was like a puppy dog. He'd easily take away my superlative of being optimistic. So. Easily. "I'll call you."

I stood as he dropped some cash on the table. I couldn't wait to get out of here. The problem was that I didn't have Chase to run to. We'd always talked at night, and he helped everything make a little more sense in my world. Now I felt so alone and burdened.

"I'll walk you to your car."

"Actually, I'm going to run to the little girls' room again." I nodded behind me.

"Little girls' room?"

I shook my head. "The restroom. My grandmother used to call it that, and it's stuck with me ever since."

"I see."

"I have one more question for you, Benjamin."

He paused. "Okay."

"That first day when we met by my Mustang," I started.

"I remember it well."

"I'd just come from an explosion downtown. I'd been helping casualties. I was covered in soot and blood, but you didn't say anything. Why?"

He shrugged. "That would have been rude."

He could *not* be serious. "Didn't it concern you?"

He shook his head. "Not really. I just figured you'd had one of those days."

"One of those days?" I repeated like a parrot. I just couldn't buy this. Of course, I had rightly concluded that he was clueless, so maybe this was all within the realm of possibility.

"Well, have a good evening, Holly. I'll talk to you later."

I watched him walk away, really hoping I'd never have to see the man again. I had a feeling that wouldn't be the case, though.

***

Someone was sitting on my porch as I pulled up to my house. Chase. Immediately, my spirit sank with dread. I wanted to talk to him so badly. I wanted to make things right between us.

But I couldn't.

This day was getting worse and worse. I wasn't sure I was strong enough to convince him our breakup was sincere. I couldn't bear the heartache in his gaze.

I gingerly made my way toward him, my muscles tensing more and more with each step. He was so handsome. But he was more than eye candy. He was also kind.

Life had broken him in the past, and those experiences had rebuilt him with depth and character. He loved justice, strove to be his best, and was open about his struggles. He wasn't perfect, but I couldn't help but think he was perfect for me.

"Hey there." My voice cracked as I tried to hold back my emotions. I stopped in front of him, the cool nighttime air around us making my feelings even more crisp.

When Chase looked at me, I saw the pain in his eyes. That sent me reeling again. How could I hurt someone I loved so much?

It was the lesser of two evils, I reminded myself. I was breaking his heart but saving his life. How many times would I have to remind myself of that?

"I was hoping we could talk." His voice sounded raspy.

I immediately wanted to sit beside him and rub his back. I wanted to listen to how his day went and maybe even fix him something warm to drink. That was me: the nurturer. I didn't mind all those gender-specific stereotypes that a lot of women rebelled against. I wouldn't push my ideals on anyone else, but I knew what I wanted for my life.

"Okay." I sat down beside him, pulling my jacket closer and ignoring my instinct to reach out. "What's going on?"

"I've been thinking all day, Holly." He shook his head slowly and uncertainly. "Can't we work things out together?"

An ache that had started at the back of my heart emerged full force and nearly had me flinching with pain. I wanted to say, "Yes! Yes, we can. Of course we can."

"I'm sorry, Chase. But right now . . . it's difficult." My voice cracked.

"You went back to the doctor, didn't you?"

"What?" I quipped in surprise.

"That's the only thing I've been able to figure out. You went to the doctor, heard some bad news, and now you're trying to protect me or something."

I put my hand on his knee and squeezed. He thought I was sick again. The poor guy. He worried about me too much.

As soon as I realized I'd touched him, I jerked away, afraid Mr. All-Knowing had seen me. "I'm okay, Chase."

His gaze captured mine, and I couldn't look away. "Then, what is it? If you want me to leave you alone, I will. But I hate having these unanswered questions. I didn't sleep last night. I felt like the one good thing in my life slipped away. You."

"Oh, Chase. Of course I don't want you to leave me alone—" I stopped myself, realizing I was a total idiot who should receive the Worst Liar of the Year Award. I tried to neutralize my expression. "Give me a little while, Chase. Please. Then we can talk. You just have to trust me. This is a really bad time."

"I can help you, then."

I wanted more than anything to throw my arms around him and erase the hurt I knew he was experiencing.

"This is one thing that only I can do," I whispered, wishing reality wasn't reality.

"Are you in trouble, Holly?" The concern in his voice nearly made me give in to the urge to spill everything. If we stuck together, maybe we could figure this mess out. Together. But who else would get hurt in the process?

The bomb flashed in my head. The image of my mom being shoved in a closet. Pictures of life being recorded at my brother's house.

I stood, feeling like giving in to all my weakness, but I desperately resisted the urge. "I need to go."

"Holly—"

"I'm sorry, Chase. Really sorry," I mumbled. I hurried inside my house and shut the door, ready to be alone and process the dastardly day I'd had. Ready to scold myself for my inability to figure this out before I had to hurt people I loved. Wishing I could bury my head in the sand and pretend none of this had happened.

I could, however, do none of those things.

Before I could travel to my room, Mom appeared. Her hands were on her hips, and she had a look of vast disapproval on her face: lips together, eyebrows pointed inward, and stiff shoulders. "Are you out of your mind?"

"What was that?" I knew exactly what she was talking about. Kind of.

"You broke up with Chase?" She asked the question like someone might ask, "You forfeited a million-dollar lottery win for a life of poverty?"

"How'd you know?" I leaned against the door, unable to move. I kept picturing Chase sitting outside. Maybe it wasn't too late. Maybe I could run back to him and clear up this whole mess. The temptation was so strong, so real.

"Ralph told me."

Ralph had a bigger mouth than I thought he did. I was going to have to talk to him about that.

But first I had to finish this conversation. "It's complicated, Mom."

"But Holly, you and Chase—"

I couldn't let her go any further. I couldn't bear to hear what she had to say. She was going to convince me we were perfect together, and I knew she was right.

"Chase and I are over, Mom." The words made blood rush to my cheeks.

"But you can't break up with him."

"Why not?"

"Because you love him." Her voice actually cracked with emotion.

I opened my mouth to speak but stopped midway and ended up gaping at her. I couldn't bring myself to deny it.

"You're just going to have to trust me, Mom. I'm a big girl, and I have to make my own choices."

"I just hate to see you throw your whole life away. You finally gave up your dead-end job, and you're working for Ralph—"

I breezed past her. This was becoming a bad habit with me lately. I didn't promote walking away from confrontations, but I felt cornered, and I didn't like it. "I thought we'd been through this, Mom. Being a social worker wasn't a dead-end job. It was very fulfilling. But I want to help Ralph, and I thought it would be a good opportunity to have a broader reach."

Here I was going again. Defending myself and my actions and my choices. This seemed to be a cycle with Mom and me. One minute she said she trusted me and accepted my decisions. The next minute she was telling me why I was wrong and why she knew better.

Times like this made me wonder if I *should* move out. Maybe we were having trouble letting go of that parent-child relationship because of the fact that I was the youngest and still living at home.

I mentally sighed. Nothing was ever easy. No matter how we tried to sculpt it otherwise, life was messy. Just when we perfected one area, another fell apart.

"Holly, I just don't know what you're thinking sometimes." She followed me as I started toward the stairs. "I only want what's best for you."

"Then let me figure it out. That's what's best for me."

Mom's lips parted for a moment. Then she shut her mouth completely. I knew she was disappointed in me for speaking to her like that. Maybe in the morning I'd apologize, even though I'd spoken the truth.

"Good night," I called over my shoulder.

She didn't say anything.

Make that three for three. I'd just ruined my three most important relationships in twenty-four hours.

This had to be a new record. And I had the Shadow Man to blame for all of it.

CHAPTER 12

When I got back to my room, I'd half expected to see the man there. I really needed to give him a name because calling him the Shadow Man was getting old. The Man in Black had a certain ring to it, as did Mr. All-Knowing. But thinking about this now was just a way of avoiding thinking about what a disaster today had been.

I leaned back on my bed, turned on my phone, and watched the video on my email again. I paused it on the bomb beneath Ralph's house.

How did someone just come and go in people's homes like that? How did this person know so much about bombs? How did he know about my relationships? About Chase's relationships? And how did he watch me all the time without me noticing?

I rubbed my temples. There was so much here to process. I had so many questions and so few leads to go on. But I knew for certain that if I was going to regain my boyfriend, my best friend, and my relationship with my mom, I had to get to the bottom of this.

Maybe this person was connected with one of Chase's old cases. That seemed the most likely. The guy could have been following Chase, seen he was dating me, and then decided he'd get some kind of satisfaction if I broke up with Chase.

But there was still more to this man's plan, I was sure of

it. Otherwise, why would I have to go on a date with someone else?

My head pounded harder.

If I was right about this being connected with one of Chase's old cases, then where did I even start to figure out which one? I had no earthly idea.

Benjamin said he was from Louisville, so maybe this was connected to one of Chase's cases from his time there. Out of curiosity, I googled Chase's name. Nearly sixty articles appeared with his name attached. I clicked on the one at the top of my screen.

Apparently one of Chase's most notable cases had been when he put away a man who'd killed two of his coworkers and covered it up. But that man was in prison for life. It made no sense for a closed case to be brought to light again like that, especially not when the suspect was behind bars.

I supposed another case was a possibility also. In some ways, however, I simply felt this was a wild goose chase. I was grasping at straws and taking my best guesses.

There had to be something else I could do here, some other way to figure out a solution. Right now, the only thing I knew for sure was that Benjamin was somehow involved. But how could I use that to my advantage?

As soon as the question entered my mind, an idea smacked me in the face. It might be a long shot, but it also might work. My strategy seemed like a better plan than tracking down random criminals who might be upset with Chase.

Spontaneously, I texted Benjamin and asked if we could meet for lunch tomorrow.

Yes, meet for lunch.

No, I wasn't losing my mind. What I was doing was taking action. Initiating. Putting the ball back into my court.

One way or another, I was going to get some answers.

***

I forced a smile when I saw Benjamin the next day. I'd just stepped inside Jalapeño on a Bun, a Mexican restaurant and deli that was nothing special, other than the unusual pairing of cuisine. The food was ordinary, the decorations boringly minimal, and the service lackluster. Normally, I'd avoid this place, but I needed somewhere ho-hum to meet Benjamin, and Jalapeño's fit the bill.

I'd picked a location that was purposefully close to the Chinese restaurant where Chase and I had met for lunch earlier this week. That Chinese restaurant was where I'd first run into Benjamin, which led me to believe that the man worked somewhere close. I hoped my theory was correct. I also hoped that, even though it was Saturday, Benjamin really was working 24/7 at this new start-up or whatever kind of secret company it was that employed him. There were lots of "ifs" here, and I desperately hoped this gamble paid off.

As mariachi music played overhead and the scent of cumin filled the air, I mulled over my plan, praying it worked. The more I thought about it, the more I concluded that Benjamin's association with this scheme was more of the clueless variety than the evil mastermind. With that fact solidified in my head, I waved to Benjamin and started toward the laminate booth where he was seated.

He was dressed in business attire again today—this time in a pink shirt and navy-blue tie. His hair was still wet, like he'd just gotten out of the shower. His eyes still looked bright and hopeful.

"You look perky today." He rose five seconds too late to

be proper. I was already down and my purse was settled in the corner near the wall.

"I'm feeling a bit better," I told him.

A plump waitress wearing a white blouse stained with what I could only assume was salsa placed a tuna salad sandwich in front of me.

"I hope you don't mind . . ." Benjamin started, pointing at my food. A tuna salad sandwich was also placed in front of him.

"But you ordered for me?" I finished.

He nodded. Maybe he'd grown up with a mom who'd taught him this was the polite thing to do on a date. I, for one, liked to choose my own food. But none of that was important right now. This was all a means to an end, and I just had to get through this lunch date for my plan to work.

I picked up a tortilla chip—it was baked, not fried. If I ate chips, I liked them to be crispy and greasy, which was probably the reason I didn't eat chips that often. Despite that, I popped one in my mouth, preparing myself to listen to Benjamin talk about himself again.

"So your brother is a state legislator?" he started.

Great. He was asking me to talk about myself. I had a feeling he probably knew more than he was letting on to. "That's right. Ralph Paladin. I'm working for him."

"And your sister is one of the district attorneys, right?"

I hadn't shared that information, had I? I was pretty sure I hadn't. He must have seen my confusion.

"That was listed in an article I read about Ralph. Not trying to freak you out." He let out a weak laugh.

Too late!

"I see."

"Your family is very connected in the area, it sounds

like."

"We're all just trying to make a difference in our own way, I suppose."

"What do you do for your brother?" He ignored his food and laced his fingers together, reminding me a bit of a psychiatrist.

"I'm the constituent services aide. Basically, I'm the one who answers correspondence and keeps an ear on district and local issues. I garner support for causes and offer research on legislation."

"Whoa." He shook his head, his eyes widened. "You must be pretty smart. Smart and pretty? Lethal combination."

I shrugged, never one for flattery. "I was a social worker. Titles don't really have much appeal for me. We only have a short time here on earth, and I really want to do the most good possible."

Something flickered in his gaze. Surprise? Admiration? I wasn't sure. "Sounds noble."

"That is yet to be seen." Some days I felt like it was the right decision, and other days I missed working on the front lines in the community.

I popped another baked chip in my mouth, stared at the overstuffed sandwich, and frowned. Before I could overthink it, I grabbed a fork and cut off a piece. The sandwich was way too messy to eat with my fingers.

"I always kind of wished I'd gone into a job more in the helping profession." Benjamin took a sip of his iced tea before twirling the ice around the glass, probably trying to disperse the sweetener he'd added.

"What do you do?" I ventured to ask. He finally had my attention. I needed to find out more about him, even if that meant pretending to be interested.

He laughed faintly, but the sound trailed almost uncomfortably toward the end. "I wish I could talk about it."

I leaned closer, hoping there was no leftover tuna salad on my lips. "I'm intrigued now. I mean, how can your job be such a secret?"

His lips twisted in a frown, and he picked up his tea again. "It's thorny."

"I understand thorny." I decided to take a page from Jamie and lowered my voice all conspiracy-like. "Can't you just give me a hint?"

He opened his mouth but immediately shut it, acting like he wanted to say more, that he'd thought about it, even, but changed his mind. "I wish I could. But I can't. Not yet."

"CIA?" No, I didn't really think that. And I wasn't usually this pushy. But with my life falling apart around me, I decided aggression might be a good thing. I didn't have time to waste here!

He laughed, his shoulders relaxing slightly. "No, it's not the CIA. Not nearly that exciting."

I leaned back and studied him a moment, narrowing my eyes with thought. "But exciting enough that you left Louisville and moved here. That's significant."

"Well, it was an opportunity I couldn't pass up." He pretended to twist his lips shut. "But that's all I can say. I'll have to remain a man of mystery."

I bit back a frown, realizing he wasn't going to tell me anything. I was going to have to find out on my own. Instead of pushing more, I took another bite of my tuna salad sandwich.

"So, it was the strangest thing yesterday. I was talking to some old classmates of mine and . . ."

I tuned him out as he continued to talk. And talk. And talk.

Finally, I looked at my watch. Ordinarily, I'd hate being rude. But when my arm was twisted and the man in front of me was somehow involved, I shoved my social manners aside. As Mom always said, there was a time and a place for everything. That included social graces.

"Unfortunately, I have to get back to work," I told him, wiping my mouth and pushing away the remainder—which was almost all—of my sandwich. "I'm working some Saturdays until I get settled on the job."

"Me too, now that you mention it." He glanced at his expensive-looking watch.

Just like he did yesterday, he rose and opened his wallet.

As he did, I tried to catch a glance of his driver's license as one of the bifolds flopped my way. Sure enough, the man's name really was Benjamin Radcliff. I also saw an address: 471 Warble Wing Street.

I stored that information away because a girl never knew when it might come in handy.

Benjamin paused at the front door and stared at me. I took a step back, afraid he might pucker up. No, thank you. Being coerced into going on a date was one thing; being forced to trade kisses? It wasn't happening.

"Seeing how things are going so swimmingly, we should do this again sometime." Benjamin stared at me, watching my every reaction.

I tensed at the suggestion. I hoped to put an end to this. Soon. Like, before we ever had to meet again. Or before he ever considered kissing me.

"Call me," I said instead. Avoidance. Noncommittal. Nonconfrontational.

I wasn't sure if I was being a lady or being spineless. I

just knew that I had to play this safe.

"Good-bye, then." He nodded.

I pointed behind me. "I'm going to freshen up for a moment. Have a good day, though."

As soon as he walked away, I quickly snapped into action. I slipped a fedora on. Cheesy? Yes. But I didn't care. I also slid on sunglasses, pulled my hair back in a ponytail, and shrugged into my coat.

I couldn't be conspicuous, right?

Ignoring a strange stare from a woman seated by the door, I slipped out just in time to see Benjamin disappear around the corner. I had to follow him, and I prayed I would find some answers.

CHAPTER 13

I quickened my pace so I wouldn't lose sight of Benjamin. My gut told me he worked within walking distance, and I hoped I was correct. If the man climbed into a car, I'd have no hope of catching him.

Thankfully, he paused at the corner, waited for the crosswalk light to change colors, and then headed across the street. This could be trickier than I thought, especially if I didn't want to be splattered against the asphalt in a tragic game of Frogger.

This dress was way too cute to get messed up like that.

The light turned yellow, so I started a light jog. So much for not being conspicuous. The light turned red just as I stepped onto the street. I ran across anyway.

The driver of a silver sedan laid on his horn when I blocked his path for three seconds. I glanced up, hoping Benjamin hadn't heard. When I saw him start to look back toward me, I pulled down my hat.

Stupid move, Holly.

Then again, I'd never been trained for these things. I was acting on a wing and a prayer here.

I continued to follow Benjamin for three more blocks. Finally, he ducked inside an office building. On the bottom floor, I passed a copy center, a deli, a small newspaper and magazine stand, and a coffee shop.

Benjamin paused by an elevator. As he lingered for a minute, I quickly ducked behind the newspaper stand. I grabbed today's edition and held it in front of my face. Every once in a while, I peeked around the edges and saw he was still standing there. A couple of people waiting with him exchanged chitchat.

The guy seemed so normal, in a dopey, clueless kind of way. I still couldn't understand his nefarious motivations. As the elevator dinged, he climbed on. I put the paper down and slowly made my way toward the doors. When I saw they were shut, I stepped forward and stared at the numbers up top.

This building *had* to have twenty floors. Of course. Four stories would have been way too easy.

The first stop was on the third floor, I noted. The elevator then stopped on floors eight, twelve, fifteen, and eighteen.

I was going to have my work cut out for me, especially if I wanted to search the floors without being noticed. That meant I was going to take the stairs. I had too many bad mental images of the elevator door opening and me stepping out into the lobby area of his so-called secret company and running into him.

I started my journey, wishing I'd worn different shoes. Why had I donned heels today of all days? I must have lost my mind.

And if I'd thought that after the first floor, I definitely thought it when I reached the third floor.

I pulled myself together, despite my urge to dramatically drag air into my lungs and walk with a slump, and I pushed the door to the third floor open. It was just a plain hallway.

I slowly walked down the corridor, keeping my sunglasses on to conceal my face, just in case.

The floor appeared dead. There was an accounting office, an orthodontist, and a credit union.

No go here.

I started toward the eighth floor, pacing myself this time. Certainly the man was already in his office, so there was no need to hurry.

I tried that floor and the additional four ones where I'd seen the elevator stop. One was a marketing agency that took up the entire floor, another was a law firm, one was a magazine, and the others were random businesses.

I'd done all of this for nothing, unless I considered walking eighteen floors my daily exercise. My jellylike leg muscles clearly did.

I still had no answers.

And I was taking the elevator down.

I climbed in on the eighteenth floor, crossed my arms, and leaned against the back wall. I'd be lying if I didn't admit I was frustrated. This had been my best chance to find some answers, and I'd blown it. Now where did I go from here?

The elevator filled up on various floors until all I could see were shoulders in front of me.

As the elevator stopped yet again—I mean, seriously, where were all these people going?—I spotted a familiar figure stepping inside.

Benjamin.

I quickly looked up. This was the sixth floor. But . . .

It didn't matter right now. All that mattered was hiding before he spotted me.

I ducked to the side, hoping to remain concealed by the tall man in front of me.

Thank goodness so many people had decided not to remain at their desks at the moment.

Benjamin's gaze traveled back to where I was, but then he quickly conformed to the unspoken law of official elevator standing formation. He faced the doors, his back toward me. There were at least three people separating us. As long as the space didn't empty too quickly, I should be okay.

And what was up with the sixth floor? I'd watched: the elevator hadn't stopped there.

The mystery around the man deepened. And where was he going now? He'd just arrived back.

The elevator stopped again two floors down. A couple of people got off.

I suddenly felt like I was perspiring—after all, women didn't sweat—and my muscles tightened.

I prayed that Benjamin didn't look back. That he didn't initiate conversation. That he didn't recognize me.

Why was my timing so terrible? I mean, of all the elevators he could have gotten on at just this time?

I was a terrible undercover investigator.

And to make matters worse, my phone rang at that moment. And I hadn't turned the ringer off. Which meant that everyone in the elevator glanced toward me as Sinatra began belting a tune from the depths of my Dolce and Gabbana—a present from my sister.

Awesome.

I slipped my hand into my purse and hit mute.

My heart was beating out of control as I anticipated getting caught. There were bigger implications at hand, more than me having to make up an excuse as to why I was there. The man who was threatening me might not take too kindly to me inserting myself into this situation. He'd already proven that there would be consequences, and I really didn't want to make this any harder than it had to be.

Finally, the elevator stopped on the first floor. Everyone flooded out. I pulled down my hat and took a step forward. But Benjamin had paused in the lobby and glanced back.

No!

Thankfully, just at that moment, a man approached him with an outstretched hand.

"It's Mark Reynolds. Thanks for meeting with me," the other man said.

Benjamin smiled. "Yeah, man. This is great. I'm so glad you found us okay. How about if we grab a cup of coffee and chat?"

My heart slowed, but only for a moment. I could perhaps buy myself more time. Benjamin would probably be here for at least twenty minutes. That might give me just enough time to slip back upstairs.

It was risky. I knew it was.

But I was also desperate.

As another elevator dinged and its doors opened, I slipped inside and hit the "6." I felt a bit like a dog chasing its tail at the moment.

My heart quickened again as I waited to get to the sixth floor. There was so much that could go wrong. All the possible scenarios kept floating through my head. My imaginings seemed innocent at first, but turned from innocent little thoughts to gripping nags that beat me over the head until I was submissive to all the fears they produced.

Okay, that was a little dramatic. But my brain was playing with me.

I licked my lips as the elevator door opened. Holding my head high, I stepped out. Thankfully, this floor had been broken into several different office spaces. Maybe, just maybe, one of the placards on the doorways would give me a clue as to what was going on.

I kept my chin up as two women walked my way. *Look like you're supposed to be here*, I told myself. I offered them a quick smile, my gaze skimming the office titles. Chiropractor. Counseling. Technology consultants.

None of those things seemed too secretive. At the end of the hallway I stopped by an office with an unmarked door. This space could simply be part of one of the other offices that had bought more than one location. Or it could be a company that had just moved in.

I paused when I heard voices coming from the other side of the door.

I glanced behind me and saw no one.

After a moment of hesitation, I leaned closer to the door. I could barely make out the voices. Finally, I pressed my ear against the wood.

"I think we've really got something good here," a male said. "We're going to blow this out of the water, and no one will be expecting a thing. Especially not the folks over at NSA. This is going to be the talk of the town. Mark my words."

NSA? Were these people terrorists? I'd just been joking about it when I mentioned the CIA to Benjamin earlier, but now I was getting a little nervous.

Blow it out of the water?

No one expecting it?

Talk of the town?

I swallowed hard. This was worse than I'd thought.

CHAPTER 14

As the voices got closer to the door, I quickly turned and headed back down the hallway. I stepped inside the women's restroom and waited, my heart pounding in my ears.

As the voices carried down the hallway, I cracked the door. A moment later, two men walked past. One was short and blond, and the other had red hair and a chunkier build.

Neither looked familiar. Nor did they look evil. Or like terrorists. I mean, I knew terrorists were becoming homegrown and all, but something didn't reconcile in my head.

The more answers I found, the more confused I became. I'd expected guys who looked scary. Maybe with tattoos or painful-looking scars or dark gazes. Those guys almost looked like kids.

Finally, when the hallway was clear, I stepped out. I headed toward the stairs this time, realizing going down would be easier than heading up. Before starting my journey, I slipped off my shoes.

As I was walking down, I remembered that phone call in the elevator. I pulled my phone from my purse and checked my missed calls.

My heart caught when I saw the name there.

Chase Dexter.

No.

Seeing his name again reminded me of everything I'd

lost. Even though I was fighting to be able to reveal everything and restore my relationships, when I stopped long enough to let my thoughts wander, an undeniable sadness washed over me. What if this . . . this—this glitch, for a lack of a better word—ruined everything between us? What if Chase gave up on me, if he didn't understand that there were forces at work outside my control?

I checked my voice mail, but he hadn't left a message. I hoped he didn't hate me. Like, I really hoped that, more than I realized I had the capacity to hope. So much that I ached deep inside my soul.

At ground level, I slipped my shoes back on before cracking the door open. When I didn't see Benjamin, I stepped out. As I hurried toward the exit, I spotted him still having coffee with the man I'd seen earlier. Papers were spread out on the tabletop, and the two carried on an animated discussion.

For a secret company, that meeting sure didn't look very secretive. I wished I could inch closer, but I'd be pushing too hard if I did. However, part of the conversation did drift toward me.

"I'm telling you that this could be a game changer," the man said. "But you've got to get focused. I know losing that other contract tore you up inside, but fixating on it won't do any good. We've got to focus on the present and get people excited about your ideas."

I froze, wanting to hear more. But Benjamin gathered his papers at that moment and stood. I had to go before I got caught.

The good news was that I had Benjamin's address and the name of the man he was meeting with.

So I had something to go on.

It was better than nothing. I would take what I could

get.

***

By the time I headed toward the youth center that afternoon, I was exhausted. Not so much physically as I was mentally and emotionally.

Before I'd left, I'd done an Internet search for "Mark Reynolds" and "Cincinnati." I eliminated several people and finally located a social media profile for the man I'd seen. But as I read information about him, I only felt more confused than ever.

The man appeared to own a company that helped entrepreneurs find investors. But how did that tie in with what I already knew? Could Mark Reynolds be trying to find people to fund terrorist activities?

This only seemed more and more confusing.

On a whim, I set up a fake email account on an online server and emailed Mark under an assumed identity. I told him I was looking for financial help with a new cookie company. With a touch of hesitation, I hit SEND.

I also searched for Benjamin Radcliff, but the only result I got was a man who was an Internet whiz. His picture did not match the Benjamin I knew. So that left me at zero again.

As I drove, I glanced in my rearview mirror. A black sedan had been behind me for the past few minutes. Was it a coincidence? Maybe. But now I was on guard and looking over my shoulder, trying to anticipate the Shadow Man's next move.

I pulled to a stop in front of an old storefront in the Price Hill area of Cincinnati. As I did, the black sedan sped past. The windows were dark and tinted, so I couldn't make out the driver inside.

Random Acts of Deceit

I stepped out and glanced up and down the sidewalk, which was besieged with graffiti and litter. The area had been grand at one time, but through the years had become tattered because of economic downfalls and crime and a changing urban environment. Today, it wasn't known as one of the most desirable areas to live in the city, but it had always felt like home to me.

Mom was working hard to try and restore the area to its former glory days. She saw potential in all the old buildings people had once taken delight in. She hoped people might want to flock to the area again and see the same beauty she did.

But if that happened, then those who lived here would just end up being shuffled. Another area would be encompassed by the crime prevalent here now. This culture would migrate to a new location, but it would still exist. I didn't know what the solution was either, and I'd thought about it often.

I pulled myself together and tried to forget about that black sedan as I stepped inside the youth center. The space had a social area near the front door with a few couches and chairs, as well as foosball and a Ping-Pong table. Beyond that was a kitchen with two brown shutters that could be closed across a serving window. Down the back hallway, there was the director's office, a bathroom, and a storage closet. Behind the building was a half parking lot, half basketball court. That's usually where all the guys hung out.

As soon as I walked in, the familiar scent of the place hit me. It smelled old, probably because it was. This place, according to word of mouth, had housed several different restaurants before being converted into a doctor's office. That had closed about twenty years ago, and the place had been abandoned until Abraham took it over five years ago.

I worked with a lot of the inner-city youth here. At first, I'd just tried to come alongside the teens, but through time the girls had requested that I cook and bake with them.

When I started, they liked to watch the boys or paint their nails. But somehow that had morphed into cooking and other domestic tasks. I was more than happy to share any skills I had with them. Plus, cooking somehow opened the door to all types of conversations about boys and home life and school problems.

Talking with them in the normal course of our relationship development seemed like the best kind of counseling. These girls would never sit down with someone to discuss their problems. But baking seemed to open doors that social services never would.

"Ms. Holly, you don't look too good," one of the girls, Yolanda, said.

She was a favorite of mine, but I supposed each of the girls was in her own way. Yolanda was sixteen and sprightly. She liked to wear clothes that were too tight and too low, she indulged in sprinkles and sparkles at every opportunity, and she loved being the center of attention.

I touched my cheek in surprise. "I don't?"

Yolanda leaned closer, scrutinizing my face. "Your eyes and forehead look all wrinkly."

My hand traveled to my forehead. "Wrinkly?"

"Is there anything you want to talk about?"

Ha! Wouldn't that be turning the tables? But I knew I had to develop a mutual respect with them, and that meant I couldn't always appear like I had it all together. No one could relate to someone who was perfect.

"I've had a hard couple of days, but I'm hopeful that everything will work out," I finally said, trying not to sound too resigned. Instead, I measured some flour and added it to the rest of the cookie mixture.

"Uh-oh. There's not trouble in paradise for you and that fine piece of meat you call your boyfriend, is there? Because I know about ten girls here who would go after a man like that in a heartbeat."

"Well, that man is way too old to date any of you." Chase was only twenty-eight, but these girls were teenagers. The idea was inappropriate, to say the least. I added some more chocolate chips to the cookies we were working on. "Besides, I didn't think you liked cops."

"We like *him*." Yolanda grinned.

Chase had come in with me several times, whenever he was able to leave work at a reasonable time. That didn't happen very often, but I thought his presence here had gone a long way in developing trust between the police and local youth.

"Could you check the oven and see if it's finished heating?" I cleared my throat, venturing into what I knew would be an uncomfortable subject. I decided to go there anyway because I honestly wanted to hear her perspective. "What do you think about all those riots that have been happening?"

She leaned closer and lowered her voice. "Between you and me, there's talk of more riots to come. And the oven is ready, by the way."

I paused. "There are talks of more riots. Really? I thought all that tension was dying down."

She snorted and tried to snitch some cookie dough. "No. This is the calm before the storm."

"The riots aren't going to solve anything." I began dipping dough balls onto the cookie sheet.

"How are we going to get our message across to the police? There's no other way they'll listen. People have had to take extreme measures."

I paused a moment, determined to drive home my point. "Look, I'm not saying there are no dirty cops out there. I'm not saying they don't make mistakes and that there's not injustice. But more violence isn't going to help."

She raised her finger in the air and shook her head. "You're talking to the wrong person. I don't have anything to do with this. I'm just telling you what I heard."

Just then the door opened and another one of our regulars, Tasha, walked in. She headed straight toward me, a manila envelope in hand and a confused expression on her face. "Someone told me to give this to you."

My throat went dry as I took the package. Mysterious packages were never good, at least not in my experience. "Really? Who was it? Is he still out there?"

Tasha shrugged and also snagged some raw cookie dough. Normally, I'd swat her hand, but I was distracted.

"Beats me," she said. "This guy caught me on the corner. Then he hopped in a car and pulled away."

"Tasha, think carefully. What did he look like?" Before I even opened the package, I had to ask her. People's memories were fickle, and every minute could make a difference.

"It's dark outside. I don't really know. He was a white guy. He wore a baseball cap and sunglasses and a coat."

Sounded like my earlier disguise.

Certainly she'd seen *something* that could help. I just had to guide her in remembering. "Was he tall?"

"Not tall, not short. Average, I guess. Hard to tell, really."

"Young?" I stuck the first pan of cookies in the oven.

"Not old, not young." Tasha paused. "What's going on? He didn't seem all that weird. He just asked me to give this to you because he was in a hurry."

Tension squeezed my stomach. So much for getting information out of her. That left me with the package.

My hands trembled as I opened the envelope. Pictures slipped out. Pictures of Chase. Pictures of Mom. Of Alex. Of Ralph.

I gasped. There was no message, but I knew exactly what the man was communicating: everyone I loved was in danger unless I engaged in the dangerous game he'd pulled me into.

CHAPTER 15

I was shaken when I pulled into my driveway. I was supposed to go to church tonight, but I didn't.

Shame on me, I know.

But Chase and I usually went together, and that just made things seem more complicated.

I'd go to church tomorrow morning, but I wouldn't go to Jamie's church as normal. Yes, I usually went to church twice on the weekends, but it wasn't because I was super spiritual or holier than thou.

I always said I went to my home church because it fed my mind. I'd grown up in the large congregation, which met in a multimillion-dollar building and boasted endless programs. The pastor could preach from the Bible and offer exegesis like no one I'd ever heard before. I came home persuaded in the faith and with a stimulated mind.

But Jamie's church fed my soul. The congregation was spiritual and spontaneous and made me feel satisfied in an entirely different spiritual way. The church itself met in a storefront in a poor area of town, and it probably had thirty members. But I loved it there.

Tonight, however, I'd stayed at the youth center longer than usual, and then I'd come home. I had to work on Alex's cake. At least, I had to formulate a plan to make it, whether I wanted to or not. Throwing something together at the last minute was not an option. If I did things, I liked to do them well.

I also had her bachelorette party coming up. I had to confirm everyone who was coming, check again on the catering at the restaurant, and plan a few games. The last thing I wanted was for the event to be a typical bachelorette party. Not if I was planning it. There would be no strippers, getting drunk, or acting foolish.

None of those things were really weighing me down, though. What felt so heavy was not being able to talk to Chase. I hadn't quite realized how much my relationship with him had come to mean until it ended.

Before I got out of the car, I glanced at my phone. The screen glowed gently against the otherwise dark interior of my Mustang. The silence around me brought with it a certain sense of melancholy. The truth always seemed to make itself known in the quiet moments. Sometimes, the truth was terrifying; other times, sad. Occasionally, it brought intense hope. Whichever option, the truth was always life changing.

I saw that I'd missed another call from Chase and three calls from Jamie. Talking to the people who really knew me, who knew how to read me, just wasn't an option right now.

I felt so alone in all of this, and I just couldn't stand it.

With a sigh, I slipped my phone into my purse and stepped outside. I unlocked the front door, expecting an empty house. Instead, voices broke my earlier solitude. I glanced at my watch. It was almost ten o'clock. This was unusual.

I peered around the corner and saw my mom and sister talking in the kitchen. They sat at the table with papers in front of them, and words like *schedule*, *flowers*, and *reception* kept popping up.

They paused when they saw me.

"Holly, you're home," Mom said. "You had another long

day."

I forced a tight smile, not really wanting to launch into all of this. "I've just been trying to catch up on some projects."

"Well, I'm glad you're awake, because I need to talk to you," Alex said. She walked toward me, a list in hand.

I knew Yolanda had told me I looked tired, but Alex looked especially worn out. Was it the wedding planning? On top of the big case she was working on? I wasn't sure, but my perfect sister hardly ever looked tired or overwhelmed. She was one of the most put-together people I knew. She took after Mom.

I sank down into a kitchen chair as she launched into a last-minute checklist for the wedding. I listened and nodded and offered whatever affirmation I could. She and Mom had been obsessed with this wedding for the past six months, but it had taken on a new urgency over the past few weeks. Every night it seemed there were meetings with the wedding coordinator or florist or reception hall.

"Everything okay?" I asked Alex at a break in our conversation. "You look really tired."

She glanced across the room to where Mom had exited so she could change for bed. Once Mom disappeared, Alex leaned closer.

"It's more than the wedding," Alex whispered. "This case is turning into a media circus. Everything we do is being scrutinized. It's crazy, and it almost makes me feel like I shouldn't be getting married right now."

"You can't put your life on hold because of this trial."

"Before this case, I would have believed that. But I just feel drained. The thing is, there's already so much going on in the city with the riots. William has been working a lot at the hospital, trying to stitch up people who've been injured. I feel like I'm losing my mind."

"Your wedding should be special," I told her. "I hope everything doesn't wear you down so much that you don't get to enjoy what's billed as the best day of your life."

She snorted, her blonde bangs flying in the air. "I've given up on that fairy tale a long time ago."

I blinked, certain I hadn't heard her correctly. "What do you mean?"

"I'm not an idealist like you," she said. "Marriage is a logical next step for my life, Holly. It makes sense for William and me. We're established in our careers. We're well suited for each other temperament-wise, and I think we'll get along well in our life journey."

I frowned, something not settling right with me. "But your heart is involved also, right?"

"That's the problem with marriage today, Holly. Too many people base it on feelings. That's why we have a 50 percent divorce rate in this country."

"I agree it shouldn't be all feelings. There should be respect and commitment and character involved. But love needs to be part of the equation too, right?"

"Everyone makes their own choices. William and I think this is the best for us." She grabbed a shortbread cookie from a plate at the center of the table and took a crumbly bite.

I leaned back, curious now. "Have you ever actually felt infatuated with someone, Alex?"

She chuckled, short and quick. "Yeah, I suppose I did once, and that was the biggest mistake of my life. You remember Brandon Gordon, don't you?"

I searched my memories for a minute, and I had a vague image of a man with a shaved head, a full beard, and an earthy vibe. The man I remembered was a hipster before hipsters were cool. He always dressed like he was getting ready to go hiking, wearing cargo pants and tight T-shirts and munching on granola. "Maybe."

"You would have only been twelve when I dated him. We met my senior year of college, and I was ready to give up everything for him. I'm so glad I didn't. That would have been my biggest mistake ever." Her words left no room for doubt.

"Why? Tell me what happened." My sister and I didn't chat like we were equals very often. It felt good to have a heart-to-heart about boys. It made Alex seem more human and less like an overly educated Stepford wife.

"He was an engineering major, and he got accepted for his dream internship at a big company in . . . Dubai."

"Dubai?" Why hadn't I heard this story before?

Alex nodded and took a long sip of coffee. She downed coffee like an athlete downed water after a marathon. "He couldn't pass it up. It was with a private defense contractor, and it was basically his dream job. He asked me to come with him, but I would have had to drop out of law school."

"So you chose your career over love?" I tried to sound nonjudgmental, but as soon as the words left my lips, I realized I'd failed.

Her lips puckered out in a frown. "It sounds so dramatic when you say it that way. I couldn't throw away my life to support his dreams. I have more purpose on this earth than just getting married and having babies."

I was certain she had no idea how harsh her words sounded. I understood her point, but her commentary made me cringe. "I see."

"Besides, there was more to it than that. I mean, Dad thought I could do better. Mom told me I needed to finish my education. Ralph thought he was weird. Even you. You used to kick him."

"I would never do that."

She laughed. "Oh yes you would. And you did. You always made it look like an accident, and you seemed so innocent that people believed you. I knew better."

I tried not to smile at the mental picture that formed. "Moving on . . . did you ever talk to Brandon after that?"

She shook her head. "I didn't for a long time. Then he called me a few years ago. He'd started his own company and was doing some work with the Department of Defense as a private contractor. It sounded like he'd done really well for himself."

"Did he want to get back together? Be honest," I prodded.

"I think he'd be too proud to suggest that. I've always wondered what happened to him since then. Sometimes I wish I had fought harder to make things work between us. You know, maybe trying things long distance for a while. But that's all water under the bridge now."

"And you met William."

"And I met William." Her gaze locked on mine, like she was selling her closing argument in a court case. "He's a good man, Holly."

"He is. He's very nice . . ."

She frowned again. "*Nice* isn't a bad word, Sis."

"I never said it was. I'm probably one of the nicest people around, so I'm not throwing it out as an insult. In fact, I think kindness needs to be valued and utilized more in our society today."

Alex lowered her gaze. "Besides, not everyone can have a perfect relationship like you and Chase."

I frowned. She hadn't heard? How was that possible?

Then I knew. Mom hadn't told her because she was doing everything in her power to make Alex's big day perfect. It was all I'd heard for the last several weeks. *Don't upset Alex. Don't let anything spoil your sister's fairy-tale moment. Alex deserves a stress-free day.*

"What?" Alex asked, studying my face with a touch of suspicion.

I swallowed hard and contemplated my options.

Could I really lie about one more thing?

CHAPTER 16

I might as well tell Alex, I decided. There was no way I could keep this from her for so long. I didn't need her finding out at the rehearsal dinner when Chase wasn't there. "Chase and I broke up."

"What?" Her voice screeched unusually high for my poised sister.

I nodded, that familiar weight returning to my shoulders and to my heart. "It's true."

"Why?"

"It's complicated." How many times was I going to use that excuse? Every time I opened my mouth, that's what came out. I was even getting tired of hearing it.

"Did he break up with you?" Her voice sounded hushed, as if her realization had to be the truth. As if Chase would naturally be the one to reject me.

I shook my head, ignoring the silent jab. "No, I broke things off."

Her lips parted. "Have you lost your mind? You and Chase are great together. I've never seen you so happy. Not even when you were with that Rob guy."

I frowned. Rob was the man I thought I was supposed to marry. We'd courted, vowed to save our first kiss until the wedding day, and seemed to have been cut from the same cloth. But when Dad became ill and I spent most of my time taking care of him, Rob had split.

"I guess we all learn from our mistakes. Maybe our exes aren't even mistakes, for that matter. Maybe they're people who help us learn along the way, you know? When our relationships don't work out, we realize what we really want in a partner."

"That's so optimistic of you." She said it like an insult. "I guess Brandon helped me realize that there are some people who are just too smart. His IQ was at the genius level, but that didn't mean he was wise in matters of the heart . . . or the mind. I mean, he gave me up for a job, right?"

"And Rob made me realize that just because a person goes to church doesn't mean he shares your worldview. It doesn't mean he's your match." I sighed. "And now that we've had that *tête-à-tête*, we should probably talk about your wedding."

Alex gave me her lawyer look, reminding me that nothing easily got past her. "Now, you want to change the subject. Interesting diversion. For the record, I still think Chase is the total package. I know he has issues from his past, but don't we all? I don't want to see you throw that relationship away."

I shrugged, unsure what else to say. "Our breakup is still fresh, you know. I'm trying to process everything. It's going to take some time."

"Well, when you want to talk, I'm here."

"Thanks, Alex." But I had no intention of burdening my sister with more problems before her wedding.

***

I was standing in line at my favorite coffeehouse the next

morning after church when someone grabbed my arm. My head snapped toward the person, and I saw Jamie standing there.

"Jamie?" I'd never run into her here before. Like, never. "What are you doing?"

"We need to talk." Her eyes were narrowed, and her lips pursed in that sassy manner she was known for. "Since you didn't return my calls last night, I decided to come here instead."

"How'd you know I was here?"

"You're more predictable than you think, Holly. You come here almost every Sunday after church. And Mama Val isn't happy that she didn't see you this morning."

I frowned as I grabbed my coffee. I wanted to get out of this conversation. I really did. But Jamie didn't take no for an answer, which made her an excellent reporter but an exhausting friend.

"I should get home to help Alex with the wedding planning." I knew my attempt wouldn't work, but I had to at least try.

"Sit down for a minute." Jamie grabbed my elbow and led me to a table.

The next thing I knew, we were sitting across from each other. The cappuccino machine squealed in the background, people chatted amongst themselves, and acoustic music crooned overhead. The normally soothing scent of coffee and cinnamon was void on me today.

I glanced around. The table where we sat was away from the door and partially concealed by the coffee counter. No one seemed to be watching me, and no one looked vaguely familiar. Maybe I should calm down.

"So I was covering a story yesterday," Jamie started, "a shooting in Clifton."

Of all the things she was talking to me about, this was it? I took a sip of my coffee and nodded. Maybe this conversation would be easier than I thought. "Okay . . . ?"

"I ran into Chase."

Realization washed over me. No, this talk would be just as difficult as I thought. "I see."

She narrowed her eyes. "He told me you broke up with him. I couldn't believe it, though. I had to hear it from your own lips first. I thought you were just going through a rough patch."

I swallowed hard as she waited for confirmation. Tears tried to prick my eyes, but I held them back. "It's true. I called things off."

Every time I said the words aloud, it drove home the reality of our breakup. Basically, it had broken my heart.

Her hand went to her hip, which jutted out, and she did her head tilt. "Holly Anna Paladin, what's going on? First, I run into you with that weird Benjamin guy. Then I hear you and Chase went into Splitsville? Something is majorly wrong in the universe, and I have to figure out what. It's my mission in life at the moment."

"That's a little dramatic, wouldn't you say?" I rubbed the side of my coffee cup uneasily.

Her smile disappeared. "Holly, Chase looked torn up. I mean, seriously."

My heart thudded in my chest at the thought. Poor Chase. I didn't want to put him through this. I didn't want any of this.

"So, while he was at the crime scene, he just up and told you about us? That doesn't sound like Chase." Again, I was trying to use a diversion tactic in order to keep myself from losing it and spilling everything.

She gave me a "duh" expression. "Don't be silly. I

cornered him afterward, of course. You know guys don't talk about stuff like romance and breakups. He said he was confused and that he hadn't gotten any sleep. What is going on? I'm going to keep asking you that until I get an answer. You know I will."

"It's complicated, Jamie." This had become my standard answer. I mean, what else was I supposed to say? But even I was becoming sick of it.

"Uncomplicate it for me."

Would I ever love to. That's when I realized we were virtually hidden in our corner nook, and that the coffee shop was so noisy it would be nearly impossible to eavesdrop. I had a secret fear that I'd been bugged—maybe my coat or my purse—which had made me paranoid about discussing the situation. But if there was ever a time and a place, it was now.

"A man cornered me in my bedroom and told me I had to break up with Chase or he'd kill him," I blurted. "And that I had to date Benjamin."

Jamie stared at me, unblinking and stoic.

"Come again," she deadpanned.

"You heard me right. Then Chase's car exploded, and the man locked my mom in a closet and planted a bomb at Ralph's place."

"This sounds like a Lifetime movie." Jamie leaned back in what looked like shock. "It's so outlandish it doesn't seem real."

My shoulders slumped. "Believe me, I was dazed at first. But the man keeps making it obvious that he's dead serious. I didn't know what to do. But I know that I can't risk Chase's life."

"Why didn't you tell Chase?"

"The man planted cameras and a bomb at Chase's place. I thought I'd figured out a way around it by convincing

Chase to move in with Ralph, but then this all-knowing Shadow Man sent me a video feed that had been set up at Ralph's. That's how I found out about the bomb there. I don't know what to do or how to get out of this. I've tried to examine it from every possible angle, and I only feel trapped."

Her gaze locked with mine. "We can figure this out, Holly."

I glanced around again. No one looked our way or seemed to be paying a bit of attention to us. Still, I lowered my voice. "I never know when I'm being watched or when he's listening to my conversations, Jamie. Even talking to you here might be putting the people I love at risk."

She let out a long sigh and surveyed the room a moment. "You have no idea who's behind this?"

I shook my head. "No idea."

She suddenly sat up straighter and tapped her nails against the table. "I can help you."

I shook my head again. "What if helping gets you killed? I couldn't live with myself."

"This is what I want to do. It's not a Holly decision. It's Jamie's choice, so there's no not living with yourself. Let's just make that clear. Now, I want you to write down everything you know and send it to me."

I wanted to argue, but I knew I'd be wasting my breath. "I don't trust that anything on the computer won't be intercepted."

"That's why I want you to handwrite it."

"What?" Coffee jostled from my cup at my exclamation.

Jamie nodded. "I know it's old school, but old school is just what we need here. After you write it down, stuff it in the book that I let you borrow."

"Which book?"

"The one on coconut oil."

"Oh, that one." She had let me borrow that. I'd have to try and find it, I supposed.

"Give it back to me, and no one will be the wiser."

I chewed on the idea for a minute before nodding. Maybe she was onto something. It was better than any plans I had come up with so far. "I have to admit that your plan is simple but brilliant."

"Girl, you can always count on me. Never forget that, okay?"

I nodded, grateful for my friend. "I won't, Jamie. Thank you."

"Anytime."

"There's one other thing."

"What's that?"

"You have any plans today?" I asked her.

"Not really. Only to aggravate my brothers. You have something in mind?"

I smiled. "I do. But only if you're up for an adventure."

CHAPTER 17

We took Jamie's Ghettomobile—her name, not mine—toward the east side of town. Her vehicle was actually an old minivan her parents had given her last year when they'd upgraded. It wasn't much to look at, but it got her from Point A to Point B.

"Turn here," I told her.

As we traveled, my cell phone rang. It was Ralph. I tried to sound normal as I answered. "What's going on, Bro?"

That was my first mistake. I never called my brother Bro.

"Uh, not much. How about you, *Sis*?"

I had to smile. "Just hanging out with Jamie."

"Listen, I know it's Sunday and you're not officially working. But I wondered if you could swing by our new office for a minute."

"Really? You want me to come by the office on a Sunday?" I needed to talk with him about boundaries sometime.

"Yeah, really. It won't be long. I promise."

I glanced at Jamie, and she shrugged. "Fine. But just a few minutes."

"Great, I'll see you then."

I hung up, thankful the address where we were headed was in the same basic direction.

"What was that about?" Jamie asked.

"Not sure. But I need to swing by work for a minute."

"Your family wants you to be just like them."

"What do you mean?"

"They want you to be married to your work, to your causes."

"Is that a bad thing?"

"Part of the beauty about you is how much you focus on people, and on not having your life so scheduled that you don't have time for relationships and unexpected moments. Isn't that what you want? You talk about going back to simpler times."

I frowned. "That is what I want. Life seems to get in the way sometimes."

"I just want you to be careful."

I nodded. "I will be."

We pulled off the interstate and drove to the office building. I left Jamie in the van listening to music and singing along at the top of her lungs. Then I hurried inside and found Ralph.

"That was fast. Thanks for coming. Have a seat."

I sat across from him, anxious to get out of here. "So what's up?"

"I want to organize some peace talks."

"What do you mean?"

"Because of the riots. I want to try and get leaders from both sides together to talk through a plan of action. I think it could be a really good PR opportunity, not to mention good for the city."

"I don't know if that's something we're equipped to handle, Ralph. The idea is nice. I want to help find a solution here also. But . . ."

"I want you to make this first priority, Holly. I think this is important to our constituents. It could show the community how much this office cares about their well-being. That's why I want to move back into our downtown offices also. If we show fear, so will the rest of the businesses here. It just looks bad."

"Ralph . . ."

"I've thought a lot about it, Holly. This is my choice."

I subdued my sigh. "Did you talk to Chase and get his opinion on all of this?"

Ralph froze and stared at me. "Have you?"

I pressed my lips together, knowing this argument was over. His words felt like a verbal slap. Of course I hadn't talked to Chase, and Ralph knew that. He'd also made his opinion very clear about how he felt concerning our breakup.

"I'll get right on that, then, *Senator*." I said the word with a little too much emphasis. Before I could see his expression, which was bound to convey irritation, I turned and headed toward my desk. I needed to grab a few things for my impromptu assignment.

"Politics can be a hard life," someone said beside me.

I knew who it was. Henry. Why was he here? And why was he talking to me still?

The man hadn't given me the time of day up until last week, and I was fine with that. Our personalities didn't connect, and being civil with each other seemed good enough. Now all of the sudden he wanted to be chatty?

"Why would you say that?" I looked up and saw Henry's floating head peering over the partition.

"I overheard a little of your conversation with Ralph. I wasn't trying to, I promise. But his office is close to my desk. Your voices carried."

"That's just splendid." I stared at the blank piece of paper in front of me, a paper I would soon need to start jotting ideas for Ralph's so-called peace talks between the police and those who felt wronged by law enforcement. It sounded like a disaster in the making, a disaster I was going to have to insert myself in the middle of.

"Remember this, Holly. Politics always requires compromise. Always. Don't let anyone ever tell you differently."

Compromise? I knew, in some circumstances, finding middle ground was a good thing. But I didn't believe in compromising my convictions. And nothing that anyone ever told me would change my mind on that.

***

I was back in the van ten minutes later. Jamie didn't seem to mind the time to herself. She was still singing along to Lecrae and hardly seemed to notice my arrival.

"Everything good?" she finally asked, turning the radio down.

"Just work stuff. Riot stuff. Politics stuff. You know." I raised my phone again to view the map. "But enough of that. Let's keep going."

Fifteen minutes later, we turned into a neighborhood on the east side of Cincinnati. A few lefts and rights later, we stopped in front of a small house in a revitalized neighborhood. There were no cars out front, which seemed to indicate no one was home.

The house was plain with white wood siding and no ornamental features like shutters, eaves, or even a covered porch. The flower beds were bare, as well as the windows, which had no curtains.

It was Warble Wing Street. Benjamin's house.

"You sure someone lives here?" Jamie asked, staring at the house with doubt pooling in her eyes.

I shrugged. "He said he just moved here from Louisville."

"Louisville." Her voice rose in pitch. "Isn't that where Chase lived before he came here?"

I nodded, and Jamie gave me a knowing look. "I've considered that also."

Suddenly, Jamie cut the engine and opened the door. "Let's go."

Alarm rushed through me. "Let's go? Go where? We were just driving past."

"We're not going to get any answers just driving past. We need to investigate."

Dread pooled in my stomach. Jamie was right. Driving past wouldn't do any good. But the pressure I felt when I thought about what was at stake nearly paralyzed me. I mean, what if Benjamin came home? What if he caught us here? What would we say then?

"Consider it a random act of kindness," Jamie said as I scrambled to catch up with her. She was halfway across a green, weed-infested yard.

"How does that help?"

"When you think you're doing something to help someone out, you're okay with it. Remember those random acts of kindness you did that nearly got you killed a month or so ago? All you need is the right reasoning, and you'll find your motivation."

"I have the motivation. I just fear the consequences." *Lord, I can't handle any more loss in my life,* I prayed quietly.

The verse from Isaiah came back to mind. "When you pass through the waters, I will be with you; and when you pass through the rivers, they will not sweep over you. When you walk through the fire, you will not be burned; the flames will not set you ablaze."

"We'll be careful."

Before I could say anything else, Jamie marched into the backyard. I quickly followed. It was just as plain as the front, with no shed, swing set, or patio chair, even. There was an old deck leading to the back door, but the structure was green and warped and had nails popped up in various places. Jamie charged straight to the back door and peered inside.

"What do you see?" I asked, tiptoeing through the prickly grass to reach her. My heels sank into the moist ground, which made it hard to hurry.

She frowned and came back down on her feet. "Nothing. Absolutely nothing."

"You mean it's empty?"

"I mean it's bare. Sure, there's a fridge and an oven, even a kitchen table. But there's nothing that looks personal."

"Well, it is a kitchen. It's not the most personal room of the house." I peered in also and confirmed her initial assessment.

She wandered off the deck toward another window. "Fine. Give me a boost." She pointed to the window above her.

"Really?"

When Jamie didn't say anything, I laced my fingers together and bent down. She used my hands as a rung of sorts and stepped onto them. After grabbing the windowsill, she boosted herself up.

"Well, there is a couch and a chair and a rug. No pictures that I can see. I don't know, Holly."

"Just one more window," I said. I hurried to the other side of the house, where I assumed the bedrooms might be. I, however, didn't ask Jamie for her hand. I stood on a bucket instead.

I grabbed the window and pulled myself up. I gasped at what I saw inside.

"What is it?"

"It's like an electronic supply superstore. There's a table with all kinds of stuff on it. Wires and computery-looking things. Maybe this is where he makes his cameras and bombs."

"That's not good."

Suddenly, I froze as a new sound caught my attention. "Did you hear that, Jamie?"

"Hear what?"

I listened again but didn't hear anything. That didn't matter, though. "A car door slammed, Jamie. It was close."

"I didn't hear anything."

Just then, the door opened in the room as I stared inside. I dropped to the ground below, nearly spraining my ankle in the process.

"Someone just walked into the house," I whispered, pulling her down beside me. "I'm pretty sure it was Benjamin."

"We've got to get out of here," she whispered.

"Let's go."

CHAPTER 18

It was only after Jamie and I were safely back in her van with the doors locked that I released the breath I held. "That was close," I muttered.

Jamie nodded. "You're telling me."

"He's got to be the guy, Jamie. Maybe he's a one-man show. Maybe he threatens me in disguise and plants these cameras and bombs, and he's also the one who wants me to go out with him."

"Maybe. But we still don't know who he really is or why."

"I did an Internet search on him, but nothing came up. It seems like he's covered all his bases there and wiped out his true identity."

"So what now?"

I shrugged. "I have no ideas. Unless we go to the office."

"The office?"

"I followed Benjamin back to his work. You know, he said his job was a secret and all. I wanted more information."

She raised her hand to give me a fist bump. "Girl, you do have some moxie. What did you discover?"

I guess I had forgotten to mention all of this, hadn't I? "A possible terrorist plot."

"What?" my friend screeched.

I explained to her what had happened and what I'd

overheard.

She put her car in drive. "We've got to go there. Now."

"But . . ."

"No buts. Holly, you do realize that if there is a terrorist plot going on, there's a lot more at stake than you originally thought?"

"Of course." I mean, I guess I had realized that. But hearing her say it out loud put it in perspective. Everything seemed so sketchy, and nothing seemed definite. Put it all together and I couldn't think clearly. "It's Sunday. I doubt anyone is there."

"We'll just have to find any of the millennials there."

"Why would we do that?"

"Because if they're from our generation, they just might be working on Sunday, especially any of them who are trying to establish their career or get a business up and running. I don't like working on Sundays either, but sometimes it happens. When we do find someone, maybe we can ask questions."

It was a good thing I had Jamie as a friend. She knew how to take initiative unlike anyone else I knew, and she was lighting a fire under me as well. She was just what I needed.

"It's just all confusing, though. I mean, I saw the guys who left the office. Neither looked dangerous."

"They're the scariest kind of bad guys. They blend right in with society, and no one ever thinks twice about them. Holly, you have a civic duty to follow through with this."

She was making me wish I'd never mentioned anything to her about any of this. But I couldn't take my words back now. I directed her downtown, to the closest parking garage, and then to the sixth floor of the building. Knowing Benjamin was home, we took the elevator this time.

When I showed her the office door, I noted that there

was no sound coming from the other side. Just as I suspected, this had all been for nothing.

"What are you thinking, Retro Girl?"

I had to smile. That was a code name I'd used once when I'd broken into someone's home. Long story.

"I'm being paranoid, Girl Genius," I told her. She'd come up with her own code name. No surprise there.

Her hand went to her hip, one of her "I'm empowered" stances. "Well, I'm taking action."

Before I realized what she was doing, she pounded on the next door down, one that was labeled Thomas and Sons. I gawked in horror, but before I could object, someone pulled the door open and stared at Jamie with a somewhat dumbfounded expression on his face.

"You don't have to knock," he said. "We are a business."

Jamie smiled, not the least bit ruffled. "I have a question."

"Okay . . ." The man was pale with short blond hair, a rumpled shirt, and coffee breath. A miniature poodle wagged her tail at his feet.

"Someone I know went into the office next door. I can't figure out what kind of business goes on there, and I was hoping you'd help me."

His eyes narrowed, and his lips pressed together in a tight line. "You do realize I have a company to run. I have organic dog treats to distribute to the world."

"Just answer the question," Jamie insisted.

I squirmed, halfway wishing I was as aggressive as Jamie and halfway realizing I would never be Jamie, no matter how much wishing I employed.

"I don't know who's next door. I haven't met them yet." He leaned against the door now, looking ready to make a run for it if necessary.

"So you have no clue whatsoever?" Jamie continued.

"That's correct. No clue whatsoever. Now, if you'll excuse me . . ."

"This is very important," Jamie said. "Like 9/11 important."

That stopped the man in his tracks, and made me squeeze the skin between my eyes in horror. She'd brought up 9/11? We didn't have enough facts here. What was she thinking? That proclamation could cause major alarm.

"Should I call the FBI?"

"Not yet. But we need information."

The man crossed his arms, his gaze now pensive. "All I know is that whoever is running that company isn't friendly. We tried to introduce ourselves, but the guy in charge wouldn't let us in the door, and he said he couldn't talk about the business yet. It was strange, to say the least."

"Anything else?" Jamie continued.

"We've seen men and women coming and going pretty consistently," the man said.

"These men and women have anything in common?" Jamie said.

He shrugged. "They were black, white, Asian, Hispanic. I guess the only thing that struck me was that they were all attractive."

"Interesting," Jamie murmured. "Anything else you're not telling me?"

"Who are you anyway? Are you law enforcement?"

"I'd tell you, but I'd have to kill you."

He stared skeptically. "That's all. You'll have to direct any more questions to law enforcement. I might call them myself, for that matter."

"You'll be tipping these people off to the investigation and ruin six months' worth of work. I'd appreciate your cooperation. If you see anything else, let me know." Jamie started walking away.

"I don't even know your name."

"I'll be in touch," Jamie called over her shoulder.

And with that we slipped onto the elevator.

***

That night, I picked up the picture at my bedside, and a sad smile played on my lips. The photo was of Dad and me at my college graduation. I proudly wore my graduation gown—with gold ribbon for honors, of course—and he had his arm around my shoulders, a proud smile on his face.

I'd always been Daddy's little girl. He would hate to know I was struggling so much. And I missed his advice, his hugs, the love that could only come from a father.

Tuesday it would be two years since he passed from pancreatic cancer. Two years since my world changed. Two years since I had to find the strength to move on without him to guide me.

I marveled sometimes that my sister had chosen to get married the same week that we'd mourn the anniversary of Dad's death. But sentimental things like that didn't affect Alex. Or Mom. Or Ralph, apparently. No, I seemed to be the only one who cared.

That fact often left me feeling alone.

"Sometimes I feel like I'm only making a mess of things," I mumbled, staring at Dad's smiling face. How I'd give anything to see him again. To hear his advice. To have just one more hug.

I sighed and set the picture back down.

Instead of dwelling on my grief any longer, I grabbed my laptop and pulled up my fake email account. To my delight, I had a response from Mark Reynolds.

"I'd love to meet with you and get some more information about what kind of investors you're looking for. I'll need a business plan, a proposed amount that you need, and a projected growth chart. Are you available to meet tomorrow?"

My heart sped for a moment. My fingers trembled as I replied. "Yes, I can meet at six," I wrote. "Where's your office located?"

I hit SEND and then waited with bated breath. How long would it take for him to reply? I smiled when I got an immediate response.

"How about we meet at Bend or Break for coffee?" he wrote. "Do you know where that is?"

I was going to have to plan this carefully. But I could manage it.

I nodded, as if he could see me. "Yes, I do. Sounds good. I'll see you tomorrow."

Maybe I'd find some answers after all.

CHAPTER 19

The next morning, I put the finishing touches on the "peace talks" Ralph wanted me to organize. Things had come together rather quickly, and the meeting would take place in the afternoon. In the meantime, I was taking an early lunch. It was the worst possible day to do so because I had so many other things going on. But I had to take charge of my life, and this was one way of doing so.

Jamie and I met at Benjamin's office building. I pulled my hair back in a braid and put a gray scarf over my head and oversized sunglasses. I thought it was an Audrey Hepburn look, but I still got some strange looks. Some people just couldn't appreciate the classic fifties look.

"You ready for this?" Jamie asked as we stepped into the lobby.

I nodded. "Ready as I'll ever be."

"Benjamin headed down to Kentucky today, so the timing is just right."

"You followed him?"

"I didn't exactly follow him. I just camped outside his house this morning to see where he was going."

"Perfect."

"Let's go, then."

She'd called me last night, and we'd come up with a plan. It could be dangerous, but Jamie was never one to back away from challenges. I'd be right there to bail her out if needed. Hopefully, it wouldn't be needed.

We stepped into the elevator and traveled to the sixth floor. As calmly and coolly as possible, we started down the hallway. At the unmarked office door, I raised my hand to knock. Before I could, Jamie grabbed the handle and twisted it. She plastered on a smile as the door opened, and she stepped inside.

My heart fluttered in my chest as I followed behind her. Two men were sitting at desks in the room, and they both immediately froze and looked up at us.

They were the two men I'd seen leave on Friday. The unassuming-looking ones.

I quickly observed the space. The office was oddly arranged with one nice desk by the door and several other messy desks in the background. Boxes were everywhere, as were piles of papers. There were several computers, overflowing trash cans, and a whiteboard with a list of names across it and arrows connecting various people.

Names of terrorists, maybe?

Before Jamie could launch into her speech—she'd concocted some story about looking for a dentist office—one of the men stood.

"You must be our 12:30. You're early. And you brought a friend with you?" The redhead eyeballed me before nodding approvingly. "Perhaps we'll give you some bonus points. She should work."

Bonus points? What kind of twisted game were these men playing? Or was it human trafficking? This kept getting worse.

"Come, sit down." He cleared off his desk with a sweep of his arm and pointed to two chairs.

Jamie and I glanced at each other before moving the boxes of envelopes from the chairs and sitting.

"Again, thanks for coming. I assume you've heard what we're planning?" he started, sitting across from us.

The blond stood in the background. Both looked all-American, which was a perfect cover for homegrown terrorists. No one would suspect them.

Jamie and I nodded. But I wondered what we were getting ourselves into here. Maybe we were in over our heads.

"Oh, you know what?" The man leaned back and shook his head. "I'm so rude. My name is Albert Kay, but you can call me Al K. Just don't add the 'duh' on the end or I sound like an extremist. Get it? Al K. Duh?" He laughed at his own joke. When we didn't follow suit, the sound faded. "Anyway, this is one of my partners, Lewis, but you can call him Toaster. Benjamin wasn't able to come in today."

"I'm Helena," Jamie said.

I fluttered my fingers. "I'm Anna. You can just call me Anna." I couldn't resist throwing in the last part, as I tried to match their outlandish introductions.

"Great," he said, unfazed. "Welcome to Segreto."

Segreto? Was that the name of some people who hated America? My tension ratcheted up several levels. I couldn't decide if it was a fitting name for a terrorist group or not.

"Now that we've got that over with, you do understand our confidentiality agreement, right? We don't want NSA getting wind of this. It would destroy everything we've worked so hard for."

"Of course," I said, anxiety rippling through me.

"We'd hate to ruin anything," Jamie added.

"Our launch will be on Friday. Our website will go live, and we'll be off and running. That's not much time to get everything organized, but I think we're on track. We have all the right people in place. To say this will make headlines is an understatement. People will know who we are, and our message will be out in an explosive kind of way."

Launch? Launch as in a bomb? It certainly would make headlines. Explosive ones at that.

"You seem so . . . unlikely for this type of thing," I told him.

He thought about it a moment before shrugging. "Perhaps. But that's the beauty of it, right? No one suspects us. Besides, we're just the recruiters here. We've done research so we can have a good feel for what's going on. But a lot of people in this country are going to disapprove. We're prepared for that."

Recruiters? They were recruiting for a terrorist organization, and we were going to be pawns in their plans to destroy America. What if the FBI burst in right now? How would we explain this?

My jitters intensified.

"You've certainly done a good job keeping this on the down low." Jamie nodded. "What can we do to help?"

Duh glanced at Toaster.

"How about we start with pictures?" Toaster said.

A tremble rushed through me. A photo would mean the FBI would have proof I was here. I didn't want that. In fact, if Chase knew what I was doing right now, I'd never hear the end of it. I was in over my head. This whole thing was getting stranger by the minute.

"We need to freshen up first," I said, grabbing Jamie's arm. "Is there a bathroom here?"

"Just down the hallway. How about you run there and be back in five? Sound good? Toaster over here is our go-to guy for photos and profiles. Remember, as of Friday your picture will be everywhere—all over the news—so you'll want to look your best. We'll get set up."

I nodded and forced myself not to rush out the door. It would look too suspicious. But as soon as I was in the hallway, I wasn't sure I wanted to ever go back in that office.

"What are we getting ourselves into?" I whispered.

"Girl, I have no idea." Jamie took my arm as we hurried down the hallway. "But those men are strange. Benjamin probably fits right in."

"What should we do?"

"We should go back and confront them." Jamie nodded with a newfound determination.

"What will that prove? It may just get us killed."

We ducked into the bathroom. I stood at the mirror a minute, staring at my pale reflection. I really needed to get more sleep and eliminate stress, or I was going to wrinkle prematurely.

"At least we'll get some answers. Right now, we're getting nowhere. Not really. Not with Mr. Al K. Duh and Mr. Toaster. What geeks. And I usually dig geeks."

"It sounds like they're planning some kind of . . . of . . . event here on United States soil. I mean, they did mention the NSA again. I wasn't hearing things before."

"Nothing's making sense." Jamie adjusted a springy curl. "That's why I think we should just ask questions. Gather info. Then report what we know."

"What if asking questions gets us killed?"

"By those two? I have a hard time picturing it."

I splashed some water on my face, hating how my anxiety kept creeping upward to dangerously high levels. "Someone is threatening to kill Chase. If these guys are associated with that whole fiasco, they could be more dangerous than they appear. The fact that they're unassuming makes them even more dangerous."

"Let's go back. I'll see if I can buy time before the pictures, and we'll ask more questions. We've got this, okay? We just have to play it cool."

I nodded nervously. "One more thing first." I pulled out my phone and typed in "Segreto." A moment later, I had the answer I needed. "There's nothing listed by the company title, but the word means *secrets* in Italian."

"Secrets? How mysterious. Should we think they're Italian terrorists?"

I threw my hands in the air. "At this point, I don't know what to think. I didn't even think Italians were terrorists."

Jamie froze. "Racial profiling?"

My cheeks heated, and I feared I'd overstepped some kind of racial/cultural boundaries.

Then Jamie burst into laughter. "Just kidding."

I let out my breath. "Not funny."

"I thought it was." The two of us locked gazes. "We go back for just a little while longer. If it gets uncomfortable, I'll feign having a stomachache and we'll leave. No one really ever questions that excuse."

"Good to know."

"We've got this, okay?" She put her hand on my forearm to bring me down to reality.

I nodded. That was easy for her to say. The lives of her loved ones weren't on the line. At the same time, I was so thankful she was with me. Doing this was way more natural for her than it was for me.

With a deep breath, I stepped into the hallway, and we went back into the office. Toaster held a professional-grade camera in his hands. I pictured my mug shot splashed across newspapers, along with "Ties to Terrorism" and "Homegrown Terror" as headlines. It wasn't a pleasant image.

"Just a few snapshots," he said.

"I think I'm getting cold feet," Jamie said.

Al K. Duh paused. "What do you mean?"

"I just don't fully know what I'm getting myself into."

He stepped closer. "I know this can seem overwhelming, but I thought we already prescreened you for scruples? It's one of our biggest prerequisites. I mean, we want all types of people here. The innocent, classic beauties." He looked at me and then turned to Jamie. "Women of color are also a big hit. Then we have the vixens and the party girls and naughty teachers."

Now I was really more confused than ever. What in the world did different types of women have to do with dominating the world? Before I could stop myself, "What?" slipped out.

"Didn't Benjamin go over all of this with you?" Toaster said, lowering his camera and frowning.

"Maybe we didn't understand as well as we'd thought," Jamie said.

"We're going up against Nelson's Secret Affairs," Al said. "We can't let them know that their biggest competition yet is about to blow them out of the water."

"Nelson's Secret Affairs?" I parroted, trying to make sense of this conversation.

I'd heard of them before . . . but where? Why? Why exactly did the name leave a bad feeling in my gut?

Now that I thought about it, I realized I'd heard about them on the news. They were a dating website for married couples who didn't want to remain faithful to their spouses.

My mouth gaped open a moment. These people were

starting a website that would be in competition with . . . NSA. Not *the* NSA. The *other* NSA.

It was all starting to make sense.

"You're a dating website?" Jamie said, her hand going to her hip.

"Yeah, what did you think we were?" Al snorted.

"Terrorists?"

CHAPTER 20

Jamie and I stared straight ahead in the elevator after we left the office, unable to even look at each other. Were there really words after that experience? Yet there were things we needed to say.

"That just beats all. You know what I'm saying?" Jamie's voice sounded deflated.

I nodded numbly. "Do I ever."

"They're launching a website to help married people cheat on their spouses." Jamie shook her head. "Some people."

Al K. and Toaster had claimed they didn't support extramarital affairs, but they couldn't control what other people did. I could read their bottom line: money. Since they'd moved into their office, they'd been paying people to sign up for the website to increase their credibility on opening day.

They seemed to think if Nelson's Secret Affairs heard about what they were doing, they'd feel threatened and somehow try to shut them down. *Dateline*, the TV show, was doing an "explosive" story on their company launch on Friday. Everything made sense.

I was still in a daze over the information.

"What are you thinking, Hol?" Jamie asked as we stepped out of the elevator.

I shook my head, trying to snap out of my stupor. "I really don't know what to think. I guess, aside from the craziness of all of this, I can't figure out what this has to do with Chase. Or why the death threats? I mean, that just doesn't make any sense."

"I concur. This all doesn't fit together, does it? Deaths threats over a dating website would be extreme. Even a site like this one."

"I feel like I'm back at square one. I mean, what can all of this have to do with me?"

"Don't give up, Hol. We'll figure something out."

I frowned as we stepped onto the sidewalk. "Until then, I think I need to go take a shower. Just being in that office makes me feel dirty. And I've got the peace talks coming up."

"Peace talks?" Jamie asked.

I nodded. "Yeah, that's what Ralph's calling it. It's between the family of Ricky Stephenson, community leaders, and the police."

She let out a halfway-amused grunt.

"What?"

"I wouldn't want to be in that room."

"Why not?"

"Anytime the subject of race comes up, it's just uncomfortable. It doesn't matter what's said—someone's going to hear it the wrong way. On both sides, not just one. Good for you guys for having the gumption to initiate this, but I wouldn't want to be there. There are too many opportunities to screw up. You know what I mean?"

We reached the corner and stopped. Jamie and I would split ways as we each headed back to work.

"All too well," I told Jamie. "Ralph, however, thinks this will be a great opportunity."

"Good luck with that," Jamie called. "I'm sure I'll hear how it goes."

***

I was rushing around, trying to make sure everything was in place. The press was going to be here for the talk, and I wanted to do my part to make this a success. The family of the slain man was already here and huddled together on one side of the table. Ralph was talking with them and making general chitchat. The mayor had also come, as well as a civil rights advocate, a city council member, a young man named Booker Jones who had acted as one of the ringleaders of the riots, and the police chief.

I wanted more than anything to rehash what had just happened with Segreto, but I couldn't afford to lose my focus.

Finally, it was time to start. Cameras had been set up in the background, and reporters waited, probably hoping for something to go wrong because that was more newsworthy. Thea, Ralph's public relations coordinator, went to the lectern and welcomed everyone. Then a local news anchor stepped up as moderator.

The first ten minutes went smoothly. Everyone remained civil. The discussion was calm, and everyone aired their feelings, both good and bad, about the situation.

Halfway through, I looked toward the back of the room and saw a familiar figure step inside.

My heart immediately sped with pleasure before dropping with dread.

Chase had come. I was delighted to see him, but also reminded of the difficult circumstances I'd been thrust into.

What I wanted to do was to fall into his arms and tell him everything.

Then I remembered the threats, the pictures I'd

received, and the bomb in Chase's car.

The situation this evil man had put me in made me want to do something really . . . really mean. I wasn't good at being mean or thinking of ways to inflict pain on others. But this man made me want to explore the darker side of my personality.

"No one here understands what we're going through!" The boy's mom jumped to her feet. Her gaze zeroed in on Ralph. "And you. You claim to be a Christian. Where are those Christian principles of love right now?"

Ralph's eyes widened. He hadn't been expecting that one. Just as the surprise flashed in his gaze, a steady calm replaced it. "I'm trying to practice love by finding solutions."

"You only want to look good in the eyes of your constituents. Where were you right after this happened? Why weren't you on the news condemning my boy's death? I was against these riots and protests when they first started, but now I've realized they're the only way to truly get any attention."

My gut twisted. It was just as I feared. This was a mistake. Everyone in the room seemed to tense right along with me.

"I want you to know that your voice is heard," Ralph continued. "Everyone in this city matters."

God loved everyone; therefore I needed to also. It had become an unofficial mantra of mine. God especially loved the brokenhearted, the widows, and the orphans—those our society ignored. I wanted to be one who lived my life in such a way that these people could see Jesus through me.

And if God loved everyone, that had to include even the bad guys. Even the Shadow Man. Even the vile men starting Segreto. Even people who hurt other people.

Loving them didn't mean that they didn't deserve justice. It didn't mean that I had to be a doormat. But it did mean that life was precious and souls were capable of redemption.

Matters like these riots were so complicated. Violence bred more violence, and the end result could be even deadlier than the incident that incited all this. There were no easy solutions.

I held on to my pad of paper from my position against the wall and braced myself for whatever might happen next.

"I want you to feel free to express your opinions." Ralph's words seemed to calm everyone, and some of the buzz left the air.

Ralph was a great mediator. He really was a great guy in general, and I knew he would take it to heart that someone called out his Christian beliefs in the middle of this mess. Politics were messy and complex, and certainly he knew that going into this. But sometimes expecting things and experiencing those things were entirely different.

With a sigh of relief, I glanced around. My gaze fell on Chase, and my heart lurched. What was he thinking? Did he hate me? I had to resist the impulse to keep looking at him.

Finally, an hour later, the so-called peace talks came to an end. Was anything accomplished? No, not really. But at least people had been able to air their viewpoints in a somewhat healthy manner.

I lingered behind as people began to trickle out.

"Can we talk a minute?" Chase stepped toward me, looking just as uncertain as I felt.

"Of course."

We stepped outside, away from anyone who might be listening. As I anticipated the conversation, my throat tightened. I'd been ready to marry this man. It seemed so unfair to be in this situation now. But I'd learned that life was terribly unfair, no matter how much some people might want to deny it.

"I know I should probably leave you alone." Chase shoved his hands into his pockets. A gut-wrenching somberness seemed to encase him. But there was another emotion there also. Almost a hardness. Had bitterness set in?

The last thing I wanted was for him to leave me alone, but I couldn't tell him that. "Don't be silly."

"You know, I kept thinking I messed up and somehow blew it with you," he said as we began a slow stroll down the busy sidewalk.

Now, I really wanted to go closer. I wanted to put my hand on his chest and tell him it wasn't him. I wanted to throw my arms around him and bask in his strength and protective embrace. I wanted the Shadow Man to disappear and this whole fiasco to have never happened.

"You . . . you didn't," I told him.

Our gazes connected, and I prayed he could see the truth and agony in my eyes. It was probably too much to ask. As much as I wanted to believe we had some kind of unexplainable connection where we could speak without words, who could predict something like this? Besides, he was viewing this situation through the lens of his hurt. Nothing was ever clear when that filter was used.

Chase paused on the corner, and his gaze changed from hurt to almost angry as he looked down at me. "Then I heard you went on a date with someone else already. Is that true?"

I gasped, his question hitting me like a blow. "How in the world did you hear that?"

Emotion glimmered in his eyes. Hurt. Anger. Confusion. "That's not important. Is it true?"

I licked my lips. The worst thing someone could ask me to do was hurt someone I loved. That's what made all of this more difficult. How was I ever going to get through to him?

"Chase—"

He looked away, closing his eyes in the middle of the jostling crowds wandering by. "That means yes. Wow. I thought I knew you better than that, Holly. All of this was really about the fact that you met someone else. I was a fool." His head swung back and forth, his shoulders hunched: it was classic body language for grief. I'd caused his grief, and I hated myself for that.

"It's not like that, Chase." I put my hand on his arm, but he shrugged it off.

"Then what's it like?" His words hung in the air.

My heart lurched into my throat. This was going worse than I could ever have imagined.

"Please don't tell me it's complicated," he said.

I closed my eyes, feeling like my world was falling apart around me. I had no idea what to do about it or how to fix this. *Lord, what can I do?*

"Chase—"

He straightened, his demeanor changing from open to completely closed. "Don't bother giving me your excuses, Holly. Sometimes you think you know someone, but you don't." He turned and walked away.

A sob caught in my throat. I'd just lost the love of my life.

Would he ever forgive me for my deception?

CHAPTER 21

With a heavy heart, I left work later that day and went to meet Mark Reynolds. I showed up at the coffeehouse ten minutes early and found a corner booth with a bird's-eye view of the front door. Then I waited.

My heart almost felt numb. I didn't want to hope. I didn't want to get excited. Yet I felt like I couldn't hurt any more than I already did. All the things I'd worked so hard to accomplish in my life—primarily my relationships—were being destroyed one by one.

A waitress brought me a latte, and I slowly sipped it. I didn't even have any ruse worked up as to how I could get information from the man. I had no cover, no delicately crafted story, no brilliant plan. I definitely didn't have a business plan, proposed budget, or any projections.

No, I was going to wing it. In fact, maybe I'd just come right out and ask the man what he was working on with Benjamin Radcliff.

As I sat there, I remembered the hurt in Chase's eyes, and my heart ached. How had he found out that I'd gone out with Benjamin? That's what didn't make sense. I'd wanted to shield him from any unnecessary pain.

Things rarely worked out the way I wanted them to, though.

I glanced at my phone. It was a quarter past six. Mark

Reynolds was late.

Had he seen through my invitation to meet? Again, how would that have happened?

Just then, my phone rang. I knew it wasn't Mark because he didn't have my number.

No, it was Benjamin.

I scowled but decided to answer. I needed to get a few things off my chest, and I was in a no-holds-barred mood.

"Why are you doing this?" I demanded.

"Uh . . . hello to you too," Benjamin said.

"I'm tired of being polite. I'm tired of playing this game."

"I really hate the dating game also."

"Dating game?" Was this guy really this clueless? He was certainly a good actor. "I'm talking about the game you're playing with my life."

"I'm not a game player, Holly. If you can't tell, I'm foot-in-my-mouth real."

I sighed. He wasn't going to admit anything, was he?

"You put cameras in my house, didn't you?"

"That would be creepy." He said the words almost comically.

"Stop playing. I know about Segreto. I know about the equipment in your house. And I just give up. I can't do this anymore."

"You know about Segreto?"

"I do. Unfortunately." I saved my lecture.

"Then you should know that I'm one of the founders. I'm the technical guy on the team."

I squinted. "What?"

"It's true. I'm in charge of the web design and the database management. I also sweep the houses where couples meet to make sure everything's on the up-and-up. Privacy is very important to our clients."

My jaw dropped. "You're not serious."

"Of course I am. I've been doing some marketing also, but Al and Toaster are really in charge of recruiting and running the books. I hope you'll keep this all quiet."

"So me meeting you had nothing to do with Segreto?"

"No. Why would it? You're not married, are you?"

I sighed. Could the timing when Benjamin and I met be just a coincidence? An awful, awful coincidence that had led me on a wild goose chase?

I sighed. It appeared it was.

And it appeared Mark Reynolds was probably just trying to get the start-up company some capital in order to help the business take off.

***

When I walked inside my mom's house, I discovered Alex's best friend from college had arrived.

Heather.

Heather was the daughter of a prominent judge. Her mother had been in some not-very-well-known films. Though Heather had gone to Harvard, today she enjoyed a life of luxury as a trust-fund baby. She loved to name-drop about the various celebrities she either knew or had met, and those people always ranged from movie stars to political figures.

I couldn't believe it sometimes that she and Alex were such good friends. They seemed like polar opposites, but Alex said they balanced each other out well. Maybe there was a side to Alex that I didn't know existed.

Heather was certainly pretty enough, though I didn't

know how much of it was real and how much of her beauty she'd paid for. I supposed the good news was that, if she'd had work done, her surgeon had been skilled enough that everyone could only guess.

She had streaked blonde hair and a tiny, fit body. She put my gentle peppiness to shame with her loud, extroverted peppiness. Despite our differences, she always called me her little sister.

I'd never called her my second big sister in return, but she didn't seem to notice.

"Holly Anna!" she squealed, coming straight at me with outstretched arms. She pulled me into a hug that conveyed we were long-lost relatives. "It's so good to see you."

"You too, Heather."

"You look great." She stepped back, and I feared she might squeeze my cheek with "older relative" admiration.

"I didn't realize you were coming early." I spotted my mom and sister in the background, sipping on warm drinks at the table and sending me amused glances.

"Of course! I had to help with my best friend's wedding." She waved her hand in the air, her cell phone wrapped in her fingers. When she'd visited last year, her nose had always been pointed toward the device.

"Are you staying here?" *Please say no.*

"No, I'm staying with Alex. I'd been meaning to ask you. Do you need help with the bachelorette party?"

No way was I letting Heather help me. No, she'd have us playing beer pong and flirting with shirtless men boasting dollar bills stuck into their belts. "I think I've got everything covered."

She glanced at my sister and then turned back toward me, her voice almost condescending as she spoke. "Are you sure? I've got a lot of experience with this kind of event, experience beyond church social kind of stuff, you know."

Anger began to grow inside of me. "I'll be fine."

She looked at me another moment, uncertainty evident in her overblown expression of consideration. "If you're sure."

"I am. Anyway." I stepped away from her. "I've got to go. But it's great to see you."

Before anyone could stop me, I headed upstairs. I needed to email Mark Reynolds. He'd stood me up. Even though I was fairly certain he wasn't a part of this, I wanted to confirm that.

I did a light check in my room—it worked, so I should be okay without any shadowy figures hiding. Then I grabbed my computer and pulled open my in-box.

There were no emails from Mark.

Strange.

I sent him another email, asking where he was.

Immediately, I got a response, just as before.

"Sorry. Something came up. Maybe another time."

I narrowed my eyes. Normally businessmen would offer a makeup time. They'd at least sound more apologetic in today's consumer-driven society.

Still fuming from everything that had happened today, I typed back. "How about tomorrow?"

I hit SEND and then waited. I expected a response to pop into my in-box again, just as it had in the past.

Instead, nothing happened. There was no reply.

I leaned back against my pillows, trying to figure out my next plan of action.

But I had no good ideas. All my plans thus far had only made things worse. My whole family was suffering because of me.

I grabbed my extra pillow and hugged it.

All my hope was beginning to fade faster than the sunset.

CHAPTER 22

The next day, I realized that those peace talks had only increased my workload by about 300 percent. I had people from the area emailing and calling me with their concerns, with their solutions, and with their opinions. I could hardly keep up. If Ralph had wanted to spark discussion, he'd definitely succeeded.

"Can we talk a minute, Holly?" my brother asked midway through the morning.

"Of course."

I went into Ralph's office and shut the door. As soon as I saw him, I noticed the circles under his eyes. Something about him just seemed heavier, and it wasn't his weight. It was something unseen, something invisible.

"What's going on?" I sat in the seat across from him.

He squeezed the skin between his eyes. "It's getting to me, Holly."

"What's getting to you?"

"I've been attacked on so many fronts since I took office, but it's only getting worse."

"But you knew that was going to happen. You can withstand the storm of people's opinions. You just have to stay firm."

"I just got off the phone with Roy Childers."

"From church?" Roy taught Sunday school for the

college-age class.

"Yes, that one. He just scolded me for an hour."

I felt a wrinkle form between my eyebrows. "About what?"

"Everything, but especially for using my religious beliefs both in politics and to guide me in my decisions. I mean, I got an earful. I guess I expected criticism from some people for the stance I've taken on things. I didn't expect it from the church."

I leaned against the chair and let that soak in. "Wow. I'm so sorry, Ralph. But you have a lot of supporters. Never forget that. You answer to someone whose influence goes beyond these earthly realms."

"Thanks, Holly." He raised his shoulders. "I knew I could count on a pick-me-up talk from you. Don't mention this to Mom or Alex, okay?"

"Really? They'd want to know and support you."

He frowned. "Alex is already stressed out enough. I just want her to enjoy her big day without worrying about me, and Mom has enough on her mind."

I nodded, appreciative of his compassion. "I understand. I'll keep my lips sealed. I promise."

I went back to my desk and decided to do my daily scan of local headlines. I'd liked to stay on top of the local news even before I had this job, but now it was doubly important. I needed to feel the pulse of the community.

My eyes zeroed in on one particular headline, though. "Local Executive Found Murdered."

My eye scanned downward, and I gasped.

A picture of Mark Reynolds stared back at me.

He'd been . . . murdered?

No wonder he hadn't shown up last night. Did the Shadow Man realize I'd made contact with him? Was that why the man had died?

Familiar nausea began to gurgle in my gut.

"Hey, Holly," someone called.

I turned toward Henry as he popped his head over the partition again. This was a bad time. I wasn't in the mood for chitchat, especially not with the Tell.

"Yes, Henry?" My words lacked enthusiasm.

"I was wondering . . ."

"Yes?" I could hear the annoyance in my voice and tried to mentally silence it.

"I was wondering if you'd want to go out sometime?"

My breath caught. Everything came together in my mind in slow motion. "Come again?"

"Would you like to go to dinner sometime?"

This was it, wasn't it? *Henry* was the one who'd been supposed to ask me out. I'd been wrong all along about Benjamin. Benjamin *had* been telling the truth last night when he told me about his job as a web guy.

That familiar tightening of my stomach happened again, and I prayed I wouldn't barf right here and now.

"This is so sudden," I muttered.

He shrugged, like he didn't have a care in the world. "I heard you and your boyfriend broke up. There's no time like now to start playing the field again."

"I have a lot going on." My palms were suddenly sweaty. Mark Reynolds was dead. *Dead.* Henry still stared at me, waiting for an answer. "My sister's wedding is this weekend and all."

His eyes brightened. "Don't you need a plus one?"

"A plus one? At her wedding?" I blurted, trying to think fast. "We're going to have to talk about this somewhere else, Henry. The workplace seems like a terrible place to have this conversation."

"I'll take that as a yes, then. And of course we can talk later."

His head disappeared as he sat at his desk.

I suddenly knew I had to get out of this building. Now. Or I was going to lose my mind. And, at this point, I needed to hang on to every ounce of sanity possible, especially when considering my heart was already broken into a million pieces.

***

I escaped from the office and headed to the cemetery. I found my dad's grave and sat there, a bouquet of dandelions in my hands. Dad used to pick them for me when I was a little girl, and now I always left some at his graveside when I visited.

My head swam with thoughts as I sat there.

The Shadow Man had kicked this all up a notch, hadn't he? He'd resorted to murder.

Murder.

But I'd gotten an email from Mark last night.

That's when I realized that someone else had sent that email. The Shadow Man, maybe? Had he been monitoring my email all along? He'd probably known I'd see that news story today and get the message loud and clear about what happened when I defied him.

And now Henry was somehow involved.

"Dad, what am I going to do? I'm in another mess, but this time my participation has been involuntary."

Of course there was no answer.

"And I had to break up with Chase. What if he never forgives me? What if he never speaks to me again or if he doesn't believe my explanation? Sometimes moments like these can set in motion a whole series of negative consequences. The snowball effect."

That's what had happened with Rob. Everything had been going swimmingly until he found out my father was sick. I'd canceled a couple of dates so I could be with Dad, and the whole relationship had fallen apart shortly after.

Of course, it was like I'd told Alex. Maybe our past relationships helped us learn along the way. The people we dated helped us realize what we really wanted in a partner.

Dad had told me from a young age that I should never settle. He'd told me that I should only be with a man who treated me right. That didn't mean I had to date someone who always brought me flowers or gave me gifts—that didn't equate to love. But I should be with someone who made me feel like I could be my best.

Chase had been that person. Even with his problems, I'd believed in him. He'd believed in me. And I'd seen my happy ever after with him.

Tears filled my eyes again. I hated feeling so weepy lately, but sometimes life took sad turns, and it was better to deal with the emotions than ignore them. Ignoring them only led to more problems.

It had been two years today since Dad died. Two years. Life was strange because sometimes I felt like I'd moved on. Then I felt guilty for moving on because moving on essentially meant getting used to life without my father. I didn't want to ever get used to that. His life was more important than that. That's when the grief would set in again and create a vicious cycle.

"Everyone else acts like they're okay. Like life is normal," I whispered, staring at his headstone. "I know the rest of the family grieves you in their own way, but I feel like such an outcast and like no one else understands how important you were to my life."

I just wanted to be a little girl again, at a time in my life when my biggest problem was not being able to eat all the chocolate I wanted or watch that PG-13 movie that all my friends raved about. I wanted to go back to a place in my life when I'd been able to sit in my dad's lap and he was somehow able to make everything better with just a hug.

"Hey, Holly," someone said softly behind me.

I gasped and turned, fully expecting to see the Shadow Man.

Instead Chase stood there. My heart sped a moment.

"Chase?" I said his name aloud, unsure if I was seeing things. The last time I'd spoken with Chase, I was pretty sure he hated me.

He sat down beside me on the grass and picked up one of the dandelions I'd brought. He absently twirled it between his fingers, a far-off look in his eyes. "I'm sorry to intrude."

I ran my hands under my eyes and wiped away the moisture there. I was sure I looked like a wreck, but for once in my life I didn't care. "You're not interrupting. How'd you even know I was here?"

"Jamie told me."

I squinted in confusion, trying to figure out how that had worked. "Jamie?"

Chase nodded solemnly. "She called me earlier and told me you were coming here. She told me to bring this." He pulled out a small device from his pocket, one that I didn't recognize. "And an open mind."

Leave it to Jamie to intrude. Unapologetically, at that. I wasn't sure if I wanted to hug her or never speak with her again.

I pointed to the device in his hand. It was a simple black

box with a switch. "What's that?"

"It's a frequency jammer that blocks anyone from listening in on what we say."

"I thought only spies used stuff like that."

"You'd be surprised." He shifted, still seeming melancholy but curious. "What's going on, Holly? Jamie insisted there was more to the story than I could possibly understand."

"So, if, hypothetically speaking, there was a bug on me, that thing would make sure no one was listening in?" I pointed to the device he held.

He nodded, worry wrinkling the corners of his eyes. "That's right. Now, do you want to tell me what's going on? I've tried to guess a million times, but I've had no luck. You're putting my detective skills to the test here."

Would this really work? I looked around. There were no other cars at the cemetery, nor was anyone else in sight. Maybe this was my one opportunity to come clean. Was I willing to take the risk?

CHAPTER 23

"Holly?"

I looked at Chase, and that ever-present hurt showed in his eyes. That's when I broke. I had to tell him the truth. I only hoped I wasn't making the biggest mistake of my life. I hoped my words didn't get him killed.

"A man said if I didn't break up with you and go out with someone else, that he'd kill you." My words collided with each other in a fast-paced string of emotion.

"What?" The skin around his eyes crinkled with confusion.

I nodded. "I thought I'd outsmarted him, but he has a bomb set up in your house. That's why I sent you the letter about the Chinese drywall."

"You sent that?"

I nodded with a frown.

He shook his head, but just for a second. "Okay, I'll address that later. Say the first part again."

I slowed down as I repeated the beginning. "But then he broke into my home, stuffed my mom in the closet, and set up another explosive device at Ralph's. I knew he was serious and that if I didn't listen, everyone I loved would be hurt. Not to mention the fact that he killed Mark Reynolds."

"Mark Reynolds?"

I poured out the whole story. From the man who'd

given me the ultimatum right up to Mark Reynolds.

Chase reached forward, and his hand covered the side of my face. I instinctively leaned into the action, relishing his touch. "Oh, Holly . . . you should have told me."

"And gotten you killed? I couldn't do that. I couldn't live with myself if something happened to you because of me."

He hooked a piece of hair behind my ear. "So who's this guy who asked you out?"

"His name is Benjamin Radcliff. At least, that's who I thought it was, but Jamie and I followed him. Well, I followed him—" I stopped myself, realizing I was being entirely too long-winded. "Long story short, it turned out he's opening an online dating service for people who are married. I think he may have been in the wrong place at the wrong time, because he wasn't the right guy."

"How do you know?"

"Because today Henry Tell asked me out."

"Henry Tell?"

I sighed. "He works for my brother."

"And now you think Henry is the person behind this?"

"I can't help but think there are two people. I mean, the Shadow Man—"

"The Shadow Man?"

"That's the name I gave to the man who broke into my house. He just seems to always be in the shadows and know what I'm doing at all times." I looked around. "Maybe even now."

He glanced around also. "There's no one here, Holly. It's just you and me."

His words gave me the confidence to keep going. "He said someone would ask me out and I had to say yes. That makes me think that he's working with a partner, or at least someone he's using as a pawn in this twisted little game."

"I say it's time to stop playing by his rules," Chase said.

"You think that's possible?"

He nodded. "I do. I'm going to do some research. This guy can't hack into the police computers, so he won't know that I'm looking into him. My search will be untraceable."

"Thank you. That would mean a lot." I paused, soaking in his strong features as the sunlight hit his face. I was so thankful he'd come here for me. "I have to wonder if you're the target here. I mean, could this be someone from one of your past cases?"

"It's a possibility. I can't think of anyone who'd go to these extreme measures to get back at me. Most of the really dangerous guys I've put in jail are still in jail. The rest of them don't seem this clever. They're more the types who would just outright shoot me rather than play a game like this."

"I would love to hear a profiler's version of what this could all mean. None of this feels typical, not even for a killer."

"I agree."

"But, Chase, I think it's best that I stay away from you until this is resolved. If I lost you . . ." My voice caught.

I put my hand on his chest and hoped he could see my affection for him in my gaze.

Based on the way his eyes widened, he did. "You're probably right. It would be for the best if we act like we've broken up. In the meantime, I'm going to send someone to your place. He'll appear to be an exterminator, but I'll have him look for any cameras or bugs."

"Won't you need to have that approved by the police department?"

He shook his head. "I won't go through them. I know someone who will do it for me. I won't have him remove the cameras. That would be too obvious. But at least we'll know if this man is telling the truth. Also, have your computer checked for malware, okay? Maybe have Ralph check everyone's computers."

"How can I update you?"

"We'll go through Jamie. How's that sound?"

I nodded, part of the weight that had been pressing on my shoulders disappearing. "That sounds like a great plan. I can't tell you how thankful I am that we talked. I'm . . . I'm so sorry for hurting you." Tears pricked my eyes again. "I'd give anything to plant a huge kiss on your lips right now. But since I can't do that, we'll have to take a rain check, okay?"

His gaze was so full of tenderness and concern that my heart welled with gratitude. I didn't take this man for granted, not for one minute. "Okay."

"One more question. How did you know about my pseudo date with Benjamin?"

"Someone sent me a picture."

Of course. The Shadow Man had thought everything through, hadn't he? He wanted to ensure that Chase and I didn't end up together.

As soon as I reached my car, I heard the phone ringing inside. I wanted to ignore it. But I couldn't, especially not when I saw Ralph's number. I asked Chase to wait one minute.

"I'm coming back to work. I just had to do something," I started.

"It's not that. Holly, I just got a call from the police. Apparently there was some kind of explosion at my house. I'm on my way there now."

***

I let Chase leave before me; then I followed five minutes later. By the time I pulled up to the scene, there were two fire trucks, an ambulance, and three police cars at my brother's. I parked on the street and hurried toward the crowd of onlookers.

I supposed the good news was that Ralph's house was still standing and, to my knowledge, no one had been hurt. Had the bomb gone off because the Shadow Man knew I'd been talking to Chase? Was this another warning?

I found Ralph and joined him on the other side of the police line. The worry that had lined his face earlier had only deepened.

"This had to have happened because of someone who opposes me," Ralph said low enough not to be overheard.

I blinked with surprise for a moment. Of course, that was a natural assumption, and I had to leave it at that. He had no clue about what was actually going on. "You really think one of your critics would take it this far?"

"I've gotten numerous threats, Holly. Someone wanted to prove that he or she was serious."

"This is crazy."

"You're telling me." He shook his head. "We live in a crazy world. Add politics into that, and you have an even more volatile mix to contend with."

I spotted Chase in the background. He exchanged a quick look with me and waved at my brother.

Ralph gave him a nod. "I really think you made a mistake when you broke up with him, Hol."

"I never took you as one who was that concerned with my love life," I told him, surprised by the subject change, especially in the face of what had happened to his house.

A frown puckered his face. "I just hate to see you throw something good away. But you have your reasons, right? You're a big girl."

"That I am. Besides, maybe you should worry about your own love life. When was the last time you went on a date?"

He laughed. "It's been a long time. Too long. It's even more complicated now with this new job." He glanced at me. "Speaking of which, did I hear you're bringing Henry with you to the wedding?"

Unease sloshed inside me. "Maybe."

Ralph raised his eyebrows. "Maybe? That's not what he said."

"He talked to you about it?"

"Henry seemed to be gloating. I've noticed him watching you over the past week or two, so I guess I shouldn't be surprised."

I barely had time to let that sink in when Chase approached us. "It's still too hot to go inside, but the investigator said that early indications point to the basement as the source of the explosion. I told him you don't have gas lines in your house. Is that correct?"

Ralph nodded. "I just have electric. I have no idea what may have caused this."

"Did you store propane or anything in the basement?"

"No way. All of that kind of stuff is in the shed out back. My dad taught me better than that."

Chase scribbled on his pad. "They'll keep investigating, of course. But until then, we're both going to have to find somewhere else to stay."

"I'll probably stay with my mom. She has enough rooms. You could probably stay there too." Ralph cut a quick glance at me, probably expecting to see disapproval.

"I'll figure something out," Chase said. "Until then, I'll

be in touch. And, Ralph? Watch your back. I'm not sure what's going on, but I don't like it."

CHAPTER 24

I needed a break from doing work on my computer, so I decided to open the file I'd received at the task force meeting. I skimmed the contents and refreshed myself on all the details on the missing persons case.

Almost everyone concluded that Tom had killed his wife, hidden her body somewhere, and then killed himself. But where was her body? And Tom was the one having the affair, so did he kill his wife just to get her out of the way? The thing that bothered me was that the police didn't press charges, so Tom should have been home free. Why would he take his own life when there were no impending consequences? Had he done so out of guilt?

The interview with his girlfriend didn't provide any answers. She claimed Tom would never kill his wife or take his own life.

However, there was one thing that I found suspicious. Hidden cameras had been found in their home.

One of them—either Tom or Deborah—had been spying on the other. Had Deborah suspected an affair and tried to find some proof?

I didn't know. I really needed to examine all of this more. But, before I could, someone leaned against my desk with palms planted flat against the stacks of papers beneath them. "Hey there."

"Jamie? What are you doing here?" She'd startled me, to say the least. I'd been in my own world, thinking about my own problems.

"I was in the neighborhood. You said your door was always open."

"And it is. Of course. What can I do for you?" I prayed she wouldn't try to talk too openly, especially considering that Henry was right next to me. I was more certain than ever that he was eavesdropping on everything I said. Wasn't that convenient? No wonder the Shadow Man had been able to keep tabs on everything I was doing. He had his own personal spy within arm's reach of me every day.

"I was wondering what you thought of my new lipstick?" She puckered her lips and turned toward the side for a better angle.

I stared at her a moment. That question was so unlike Jamie, who liked looking nice but not in an overly done, makeup-loving type of way. I went along with her line. "It's lovely."

"I made it myself using coconut oil."

"I shouldn't be surprised. You do love your coconut oil."

"It keeps me young and healthy. What can I say?" She paused, something unspoken shifting in her gaze. Her voice remained normal, however. "Besides that, I heard about Ralph's house. Is everything okay?"

"You're not coming to get the scoop for a newspaper article, are you? Under the guise of showing me your new lipstick?" I didn't really think that's what she was up to, but there was more to her visit here than this chitchat.

"I would never do that. I am truly worried."

"Well, no one was home when it happened, we have no idea at this point what exactly did happen, and things could have been much worse. Much."

"I'm glad you're okay. You know I can't rest if I think something happened to my bestie." She straightened. "All right. I've got to run. You take care of yourself."

"Thanks for stopping by, Jamie."

As she walked away, I looked down. There was a folded piece of paper where her hands had been.

I smiled. She'd just passed me a note, I realized.

My best friend was brilliant.

***

I waited until I could slip into the bathroom before reading the note. "I talked to Chase. He told me to convey to you that there are no past cases he dealt with that he can tie to all of this. He doesn't think this is about him. P.S.—This note will self-implode in five seconds. HAHAHA. But seriously. Destroy it."

If this fiasco wasn't linked to Chase, then who was it linked to? Me? Why would someone possibly want to threaten me this badly? That didn't make sense in the least.

I sighed, ripped up the note, and flushed it down the toilet. I was probably overreacting, but, seeing how Ralph's house had just been blown to smithereens, I couldn't take any chances.

I composed myself and stepped into the hallway, nearly colliding with Ralph. "You're back," I muttered.

"There was really nothing else I could do at the house. I'm waiting to hear from the inspectors. I can't even go inside right now. I figured I'd be better off keeping my mind occupied at work."

"You're probably right."

"There's talk of the protests starting again, Holly."

I jerked my head back. "What? Is that what Chase said?"

"I just got off the phone with the mayor. There are rumblings that someone's trying to organize something a few blocks from here. The police are trying to maintain a high presence there so things won't get out of control. But I'm keeping my eye on it in case we need to evacuate. I can't have anyone getting hurt again." He frowned at me.

Instinctively, I touched my wound. I was taking regular pain pills since it happened, and my discomfort was minimal. Still, I didn't want anyone else to go through what I had. "Sounds wise. Keep me updated, okay?"

He nodded, but his face looked taut. "Okay."

My cell phone rang just then, and I saw Mom's number. I answered quickly.

"Holly, did you really send an exterminator over?"

I smiled. Chase hadn't wasted any time, a fact that I appreciated. "That's right. I did."

"Why in the world did you do that? You know I have someone come out every quarter to spray."

I thought quickly. "But I saw a spider."

"A spider? One spider?"

"That's right. It was kind of big. It freaked me out, so I called another company. It happened so fast that I forgot to mention it to you."

"I'd say."

"Don't worry, Mom. I'm paying for this."

"Good to know. I hope that spider is worth eighty-nine of your hard-earned dollars, though."

Oh, it would be. Definitely.

***

There were disadvantages to my brother moving back home. For example, he knocked on my door at 3:30 a.m. I was less than ladylike as I stared at him with sleep in my eyes and my hair rumpled.

"The riots started again," he told me.

I ran a hand over my face. "Okay . . ."

"I want to schedule a press conference for this morning."

I blinked, trying to kick my brain into gear. "You want me to start on this now?"

"Actually, yes. I want to be ready first thing. The riots are even worse this time. A building was set on fire. Another officer was injured. It's getting really ugly."

"I thought you said the police were prepared for this."

He shook his head. "Rioters struck at a different part of town and totally threw everyone off guard. It's weird, but it's the same thing that happened last time. Everyone thought the riots were being organized in one place, and instead they happened closer to the business district."

It was strange how someone seemed to have the upper hand.

"What do you want to say at this press conference?" I asked.

"I want to ask the people of this city to consider the safety of others, to be careful, and to remind them that violence is never the answer, no matter what side of the law you're on."

"Is violence the answer if someone pulls a gun on you?"

Ralph shook his head. "What?"

"That's what the press is going to ask, Ralph. Is violence never the answer? Or is it always a last resort? The people rioting consider this a last resort, the only way their voice can be heard."

"Are you on their side?"

"No. I find all of this maddening. But I can understand desperation and fighting for what you believe in. The issue isn't as black-and-white as people make it out to be, and I agree you need to speak, but understand that there's nothing you can say that will make things better."

"I've been accused of being a racist." He ran his hand over his face.

"I know you're not, though. You know you're not. I know you're a man of principle. Stand strong."

He nodded. "Thanks for the pep talk."

"I'll start jotting some ideas. Then I'll send it over to Thea, and she can take over from there."

"Thanks."

I showered, dressed, and then sat down with my laptop to begin working on Ralph's project. When I opened my computer, the reminder popped up that tonight, in less than twenty-four hours, was Alex's bachelorette party. I'd nearly forgotten. Thank goodness I'd sent the invitations two weeks ago.

There was so much going on lately. Ralph was in the middle of these riots. Alex had her trial starting—today, as a matter of fact. Mom was planning the wedding. I was trying to juggle a psycho's threats with my work, love life, and friends.

It looked like no one in this family had time for a wedding. And that was just simply unacceptable.

CHAPTER 25

The day had started with a headache, which only increased as the hours went on. First of all, Ralph's office had again moved to its temporary location for the day because of the less-than-peaceful protests going on. The press conference was slated to begin anytime now, and, as an official conflict hater, I dreaded what a spectacle it might become. Add to that the fact that Alex's big trial started today of all days, and what did you have? You had a Paladin family circus on TV. Every time the news came on, someone in my family was mentioned.

In between all those phone calls and questions, there was my mom. She was trying to get everything ready for the wedding. William's family was in town, and she was showing them around, as well as confirming floral arrangements, photographers, caterers, etc.

Maybe I'd just go to the mountains for my own wedding one day. Or go to a small chapel where only my family and friends would attend. I just didn't want all this stress in my life.

All these worries really meant nothing, however, with the lives of those I loved on the line.

My life was the picture of chaos.

I stood in the wings as the press conference began. Just as Ralph took his first question, my cell phone rang. I saw Mom's number and stepped to the side.

"Everything okay?" I whispered.

"No, it's not. You'll never believe this."

I braced myself for another whammy. What would it be this time? Had she been injured? Had someone else's house exploded?

"It's your sister's dress. The woman altering it ruined it. She absolutely ruined it."

"What?" I tried not to sound irritated, but I kind of did. I mean . . . I supposed I would take that catastrophe to the kind that had been brewing in my mind.

"She gathered it in the waist too much and made it a size 2 instead of a size 6. And it's four inches too short. Four inches!"

I paced away from the stage area and lowered my voice. "Can't she fix it?"

"No! The material is gone. She cut it off. You can make clothes smaller but never bigger. Didn't I teach you that?"

This was no time to rehash my home economics lessons Mom had reviewed with me over and over as a preteen. No, I had to stay focused right now. "How did this happen? I mean, Alex went in and the seamstress took measurements, right?"

"She did, but she claims all the numbers got changed after she entered the information in the computer. Can you believe that? It seems like an unlikely story. What am I going to tell Alex?"

"Nothing yet. She can't handle it if you do. Let me think if there's another way to solve this."

"Your poor sister. Everything that could go wrong is going wrong with her wedding. First the baker, now her dress . . ."

"Even if the wedding goes wrong, it's the marriage that's important, right?" I sounded like my dad. And I didn't sound like a woman, for that matter. I mean, didn't every girl want her wedding to be a fairy tale?

"Holly, at least make sure she has a nice bachelorette party, okay? Promise me that."

"Of course, Mom." At that moment I wondered if I had truly put enough time and effort into making it special. I'd been so distracted lately.

Before I could think about it any more, I heard someone tell Ralph that it was easy to sit in his office and wax philosophical about life, but that he needed to get out on the streets and put his money where his mouth was.

Could this day get any worse? As I saw Henry approach, I knew it could.

***

Henry cornered me as Ralph's voice droned on in the background. The man, at one time, had not seemed imposing. But knowing what I did now, I felt uncomfortable around him, to say the least.

He flashed a smile that didn't reach his eyes. His hands were tucked into his black slacks, and an odd emotion lingered in his eyes. Malice? Boredom? Something else? I wasn't sure.

"I'm excited about the wedding this weekend," he started. "I figured I should probably accompany you to the rehearsal dinner also, but I don't know the details yet. What time should I pick you up?"

My lips parted at the man's guts and gusto. He had some nerve. "I don't believe I invited you to either of those things."

He stepped closer and crouched toward me, looking more serious than I'd ever seen him. "Come on, Holly. You know the deal. I'm going with you."

I narrowed my eyes and leaned toward him, even though the pervasive smell of onions on his breath made me want to barf. "How could you be a part of this?"

"That's not important."

"It's important to me." My voice sounded hard, harder than I thought it could sound. It made me feel tough for a moment.

"Look, let's get this over with, okay? Then we can both move on."

"You think you're going to move on here in Ralph's office after being a part of something like this?"

"If you know what's best for you, you'll keep your mouth shut." His lips moved, but his teeth remained clenched together.

I sucked in a quick breath. "Is that a threat?"

"It's the truth." He straightened as a couple of other staffers got closer, and his voice changed from threatening to friendly. The press conference had ended, and people began dispersing. "Now, what time was that rehearsal again?"

I had to unlock my jaw before answering him. "I'll meet you there."

"Where's there?"

"I'll tell you tomorrow."

"Oh, come on." He narrowed his eyes and hissed out a sigh.

I crossed my arms. "It's on a need-to-know basis. And we're not there yet."

"You don't know what you're playing with, Holly," he warned as soon as the other staffers were a safe distance away. "You're in over your head. So am I, for that matter."

"Who is this guy who's pulling the strings?" I asked.

His face hardened, and he looked around. "I can't tell

you."

"How are you connected?"

He stepped away, ready to brush me off. "I can't talk about it."

"Henry—"

He paused and jerked his head toward me. The dark gleam in his eyes shook me to the core. "Just drop it, Holly. If you know what's best for you, you'll just be compliant. Understand?"

I stared at him, stared at his eyes. That's when I identified one of the emotions there. How could I not have seen it earlier? It was fear. Henry was afraid of something or someone.

Before I could say anything else, he turned and stormed away.

***

I hardly recognized most of Alex's girlfriends. A few were from college. One was from high school; three more worked with her at the DA's office. Then there was me. I wasn't quite as well versed in partying as the rest of the group, apparently. Or, at least, my parties consisted of dainty cookies, tea, and great dresses.

Despite that fact, I'd arranged to eat dinner at a trendy restaurant on the Kentucky side of the Ohio River. We had a private room on the water. Alex wanted the whole thing to be fun but classy.

Of course, I hadn't gone the traditional bachelorette party route. But I had a tasty menu, some silly games, and some ideas for keepsakes that would help Alex remember this, not to mention the "Bride-to-Be" T-shirt and felt-covered headband with a cheesy-looking veil my sister had donned at Heather's request.

"What a fabulous room!" Heather said, turning in circles.

I carried out my duties as maid of honor and welcomed everyone. We played a few games, and then everyone went through the buffet line and sat down at a U-shaped table arrangement to eat.

I really wanted to think about everything else except this party. I wanted to think about the Shadow Man. I wanted to think about Chase and what it would be like to plan a wedding with him one day. I wanted to think about how to get out of the dilemma I faced.

But Alex deserved my attention, so I turned my concentration back to the conversation around me. Heather had already been through the fact that she knew Johnny Depp, that she had an inventor friend who'd developed a way to hack into cell phones and eavesdrop, and that she'd been invited to the White House for a special breakfast next month. When she wasn't talking, she was texting obsessively.

"I always thought this would be Brandon," Heather said at a break in the conversation. She slipped her phone back into her pocket.

Alex snorted before taking a bite of a mozzarella stick. "Really? He's so ten years ago, Heather."

"Oh, you two were in love. Admit it. You all but forgot about your friends because the two of you were attached at the hip."

"We had that crazy kind of infatuation. But I'm much better suited for William."

"We're just glad you're happy," another friend chirped. "What's the saying? You have to kiss a lot of frogs before you meet your prince?"

"Oh, come on now," Alex moaned. "Brandon wasn't exactly a frog."

"And you're not exactly marrying him now, right?" Heather winked. "Anyway, a bachelorette party is no place for talking about your ex." She picked up another shrimp and popped it in her mouth. "Now, I brought some stuff that should really help us to have some fun." She pulled out a bottle of vodka from her purse. Everyone around cheered.

Oh great. I wanted Alex to object, but she didn't.

This was going to be a long night, one out of my normally reserved comfort zone.

Despite my innocent little bachelorette plans, somehow the whole evening turned into drinking games and an episode of Professional Women Gone Wild. I just stood back and watched the whole disaster unfold before my eyes.

Two hours into everything, Heather walked toward me holding her stomach, her face pale.

"Have you had too much to drink, sweetie?" I asked, patting her back. I'd been the girl who'd held her friends' hair back after parties one too many times.

"I can hold my alcohol," she mumbled. "I don't think it's that."

"What else would it be? A stomach bug? Don't tell Alex—she'll freak out at the mere possibility of getting sick right now."

She opened her mouth to respond but instead hurled all over the floor . . . and my feet.

Nausea churned in my own gut at the sight and smell.

Heather moaned and snapped me back to reality.

"You should sit down," I told her, trying to tame my gag reflex.

I led her to a seat and then scrambled to find a trash can. Before I could, she threw up again.

This wasn't good.

I finally located a trash can. It was huge, lined with a thick black bag, and made to hold way more than vomit, but I pulled it over anyway. Then I grabbed some linen napkins and handed her one.

"I'll get you some water."

The party seemed to be slowly halting around me as people realized what was happening.

"Heather? You can't be sick," another one of Alex's college friends said. I thought her name was Sarah, but I wasn't 100 percent sure. I only knew that she came across as snooty.

Just as Sarah reached us, she grabbed the trash can and all the contents of her stomach flooded into the bag.

What in the world was going on?

Alex started toward us, but stopped in her tracks. "You guys are both sick. You've got to be kidding me."

Just then my phone buzzed. I looked down and saw that I'd gotten a text message.

Didn't anyone ever tell you not to eat shellfish?

CHAPTER 26

We didn't know for sure, but it appeared the shrimp was ground zero of the food poisoning implosion that had swept the bachelorette party. It was the only food Alex and I hadn't eaten, and we were the only two who weren't sick at the moment.

The reason Alex and I stayed away from the shrimp probably went back to one of my aunts, who'd once told us that shrimp were bottom feeders and that the ones raised in China were fed pig poop. That had pretty much ruined our chances of ever wanting to eat the food again. Or buy anything edible from China, for that matter.

Four people had been rushed to the ER, three went back to their hotel and insisted they could handle it themselves, and the health department was now investigating the restaurant. All in all, the bachelorette party had turned into a complete failure.

So much for ensuring that nothing went wrong on Alex's big day, other than that which was out of our control—like the trial and her postponed honeymoon.

As everyone else trickled away, I followed Alex outside to the deck overlooking the Ohio River. The sparkling lights from downtown Cincinnati glittered on the other side of the glossy black water. Boats slugged atop the glimmering river, and the air was just cool enough to frost our breath. Spring might have been officially declared, but it was still cold here in the City of

Seven Hills.

Alex leaned against the railing a moment. I mirrored her stance—a tip I'd picked up in Counseling 101—and gave her a moment to collect her thoughts. She had the amazing ability to remain composed, despite the chaos around her.

Then she buried her face in her hands. "It's like there are signs all around me that I shouldn't do this."

I patted her back, trying to follow her logic. "Do what? Have a breakdown? It's okay not to be strong all the time."

She gave me a sharp look. "I mean get married, Holly. There are signs that I shouldn't tie the knot."

My cheeks flushed with alarm. Alex was not sounding like Alex. She wasn't a doubter. She made a decision and stuck with it. That was how she'd always been. Confident. Sure of herself. Unwavering in her decisions.

"You're reading too much into this," I started. "It's just food poisoning. It could happen anytime to anyone. It just happened to occur with your bridal party and closest friends two days before your wedding."

My words sounded lame, even to my own ears. But at least I was trying, when what I really wanted to do was bury my head and pretend none of this had happened. I mean, the troubles just kept piling on. I barely had time to absorb one before a new problem was added to the heap.

"It's not just this party. There was the baker," she reminded me.

That's right! I promised to make her wedding cake. I'd nearly forgotten, which was a horrible thing because the wedding was quickly approaching. I was going to be up all night, wasn't I?

"I've got your cake covered. It will be fine."

Her frown didn't budge. In fact, it might have deepened

as she continued to stare out over the river. "There will be no honeymoon, thanks to this trial."

"At least you can take one later, maybe when it's warmer. Maybe it will actually be a blessing in disguise. Just think about the Bahamas in the summer."

"You mean during hurricane season?"

"Minor detail," I murmured.

"And then there's my dress."

I froze. She wasn't supposed to know about that. I hadn't accidentally said anything, had I? "Your dress?"

"Don't play dumb, Holly." Her shoulders slumped as she pulled her goofy veil off. "I know all about it. I called the bridal shop today, and the seamstress confessed everything. She said she'd told Mom and assumed I'd gotten the message. Basically, she didn't want to be the one to break the news to me. So, as of right now, I have nothing to wear on my wedding day."

"You'd look beautiful in anything. You could wear white flannel pants and a baggy shirt, and people would still be in awe. They'd think you were starting a new fashion trend or something. I mean, society is becoming more casual. Who wants fancy stuff anyway?"

She let out a laugh for the first time since we'd stepped outside, but the sound quickly faded. "There's also the fact that I'm afraid I'm going to lose my job with the DA."

"What? Why would you say that?" All this self-pity wasn't like my sister.

"I've been so distracted, Holly. I've been making dumb mistakes. I mean, the timing on this case was horrible. And so many things have gone wrong with the wedding. My mind is shot."

"I'm sure you're doing great."

She frowned. "You're such an encourager. I wish I saw

life from the same perspective as you."

I shrugged, wanting to embrace my optimistic side but still remain real and let people know their feelings were important and relatable. "I just try to look on the bright side. It always makes me feel better, even when things don't quite work out as I'd hoped."

She turned toward me, a new emotion in her eyes. Before I even heard her words, I braced myself. She was about to drop something on me.

"Do you like William, Holly?" Her eyes left no doubt that her question was earnest and sincere.

Whoa. Where was this coming from? I replayed our conversations, starting back a few days ago, and finally stopped on the one thing that could be the only possible explanation in my mind. "It's all this talk about your ex, isn't it? It is messing with your head."

Her face twisted with doubt. "Brandon? No. I'm totally over him."

"Then why?"

"It's just all the signs—"

I had to stop her before she went any further. "Come on, Alex. You don't really believe in signs, do you?"

She stared at the river a moment before shrugging and looking more melancholy than I'd ever seen her. "I don't know. Maybe I'm more superstitious than I've given myself credit for."

"If you and William can weather this week together after everything that's happened, then certainly you can weather the storms that come in the future."

"But what does it take to make a marriage work, Holly?"

She was asking me this? My sister never asked me for advice. She never had to because she knew everything already. I was both flattered and on the verge of second-guessing anything I might tell her.

"What do you think it takes to make a marriage work, Alex?" Classic counseling move. *Turn the question back on the person who's asking. Buy yourself some time. Let them come to their own conclusions because then they'll value the decision more.*

"I don't know." She threw her hand in the air. "If the guy makes you happy, if you think you're a good pair who are willing to compromise and look out for each other, if you have chemistry. All those things play into making a relationship work."

"How about if he makes you better?" I asked softly.

She glanced at me, wrinkles forming in the corners of her eyes. "What do you mean?"

"I mean, does William make you a better person? Does he challenge you? Does he make you grow?"

She let out a scoffing grunt. "That's so not what marriage is about, Holly. If it was, I'd marry my counselor or Preacher Dan. For that matter, I'd marry self-help guru Tony Robbins. That doesn't mean I'd be happy, though."

"Well, that's the advice Dad gave me." Yes, I'd pulled the dad card. I knew there was no better way to get her to listen, since coming to her own conclusions hadn't been as effective as I'd hoped. Now it was time to use our father's wisdom to guide her. Of course, it was always easier to apply this wisdom to other people's lives instead of my own. That was one of the ironies of life.

"Dad told you that? When?"

"When I almost married Rob. Don't get me wrong. I think there's more to it. I think you should be compatible and attracted to each other. But I think marriage has a much deeper meaning than we often give it credit for. It can make us stretch and grow."

"Dad told you that?" Her voice clearly indicated she didn't believe me.

"We had a long talk in the study one day. Ella was singing in the distance—"

"Who's Ella?"

"Fitzgerald, of course. Don't you know me at all?"

She rolled her eyes. "You and your music. I should have known. Continue."

"Anyway, Dad had a heart-to-heart with me about Rob."

"But Rob broke up with you. So you're saying that Dad gave you that advice, and before you could apply it, Rob called things off and left you heartbroken?"

When she put it that way, it didn't make a lot of sense. I had to regroup a moment. "And Rob breaking up with me was the best thing that could have ever happened. I know it sounds harsh, but Rob was just a guy who fit every requirement on my list. There was a connection we were missing, something that can't be spelled out on paper. And the fact that he bailed on me when Dad got sick just went to prove his character."

Her gaze locked on mine, and I could tell she was truly listening, truly searching. "But then you had Chase, and you let him go."

I frowned. "Have I mentioned that it was complicated?"

"Several times."

I shrugged. "I'm really hopeful that things between Chase and me will work out. There are just a couple of unresolved issues that need to be fixed first."

"You're pretty smart for a little sister, you know."

I punched her arm, because I was a nerd like that. "You're pretty smart yourself."

Before we had any awkward Hallmarkesque moments, I straightened. "Now, let's get you home. You need your sleep before the big weekend ahead."

CHAPTER 27

It was midnight. I'd been up for way too long, and I felt like I was losing my mind as I stared at the cakes in the oven.

I'd gotten Alex home and then briefly met up with Jamie, only long enough to give her a rundown on the bachelorette party and to pass her a note to give to Chase. I let him know about all the developments that had happened today. Until I knew if I was being bugged, I had to play it safe, and this was my best bet right now.

Then I'd come home and started baking. My first attempt at the cake had been a flop. The middle had sunk, and the cake was crumbly. Why had I ever agreed to this?

The timer dinged, and as I pulled new cakes from the oven, my cell phone beeped. Who in the world was texting me at this hour? With a sigh and a wipe of my flour-dusted hands, I grabbed my phone from the counter.

Meet me at Sixth and Vine Street. Bring five thousand dollars. Come alone.

The Shadow Man, I realized. After my initial alarm, I replied, "I don't have that kind of money."

Yes, you do. In the safe in the library.

What? How did that man know that?

Then I remembered the cameras. How long had they been set up? Just a couple of weeks ago, I'd added more cash into the hidden strongbox. Had the man seen that?

I liked to keep cash on hand. I knew it sounded crazy, but sometimes I liked to gift people with money. It was easier to do it with cash so I could stay anonymous. I usually kept around five thousand dollars in the safe. That money had helped people pay heating bills, buy groceries, and purchase new cars.

I'd been saving up to help one of Ralph's staffers, whose husband was battling cancer. I'd planned to give the family some money next week, after the wedding was over and I could think more clearly.

If I gave that money to the Shadow Man, the other family would miss out.

"What if I don't?" I whispered aloud as I texted him back.

There will be consequences.

My fear was turning into anger. I mumbled under my breath as I responded, "Why are you doing this?"

That's not for you to know.

I closed my eyes, another headache coming on. That, mixed with my exhaustion, was making me more emotional than usual. I texted him and asked him when he wanted to meet.

In 30 minutes.

Thirty minutes? Great. He wanted me to go downtown in the middle of the night with five thousand dollars. What exactly was he setting me up to do? It seemed like nothing but trouble would come from this.

As if to confirm it, a picture popped on my screen. It was of Alex sleeping in her bed. There was an alarm clock behind her. I read the numbers there: 12:05.

I gasped. That man was in my sister's room. He was going to hurt her if I didn't do as he said.

My companions, rock and hard place, joined me again. I texted him back:

Fine. I'll be there.

But I wouldn't like it.

***

I stood on the street corner, unease overtaking my entire body to the extent that I felt light-headed.

This was a bad idea on so many levels, I realized. Not just because I was downtown while riots were going on only a few blocks away.

It was in the middle of the night. I had a lot of cash. And no one knew where I was.

I was giving this bully, the Shadow Man, a lot of leverage.

Somewhere I'd heard it was a bad idea to negotiate with terrorists. I felt like that was exactly what I was doing right now. I was negotiating with someone who only wanted to ruin people.

As a chilly wind swept through the downtown streets, I pulled my overcoat closer around my neck. *I'm in a life-threatening situation, and all I have to protect me is this lousy coat.* I could design a new bumper sticker and capitalize on that saying.

The good news was that the riots were several blocks away. Every once in a while, I could hear a loud pop in the distance. But for the most part I felt insulated from that scene.

A couple of guys who looked like they were up to no

good walked by across the street. Their jeans sagged way below their waistlines, they had an urban swagger, and cigarettes dangled from their lips. As they let out some catcalls, I wanted to shrink and disappear. Instead I remained on the corner with a bag full of cash and a spirit filled with uncertainty.

A light fog hung around the street, reminding me of a spy movie. Only, in movies you knew things would turn out okay. Too bad that wasn't the case in real life. In my moments of doubt, I wondered if the bad guy was going to get away with all of this while I suffered.

I shivered and pulled my coat closer. I couldn't shake the feeling that someone was watching me. Yet whenever I looked around, I didn't see anyone—other than those rough-looking guys who'd just turned the corner. Everyone else was sleeping, like normal people did at this hour.

Speaking of hour, it was past 12:30. Where was this man? Was this all part of his plan somehow?

As I stood there, I had a startling realization: What if this wasn't about Chase? What if it wasn't about me either? What if I was just a means to an end?

Instead, what if this whole upheaval was about someone else?

Someone like . . . Alex.

In an instant, I felt more alert. I could be onto something. I mean, my sister was in the middle of an emotionally charged trial. Someone had been in her bedroom tonight. Maybe that food poisoning had been meant for Alex, not everyone else.

And every episode that was connected with me was somehow connected with her. When Mom had been left in the closet or Ralph's house exploded . . . those things had affected Alex as well as me.

But why? What purpose would all this serve? My thoughts raced a mile a minute.

Maybe if Alex was taken out of the trial because of all these personal challenges, then the prosecution would suffer. Maybe the bad guy wouldn't be put away. Maybe this was all a case of manipulation.

My theory wasn't much to go on, but it was something. It was the best lead I had right now.

Footsteps sounded behind me, and I twirled around. A man in an overcoat, wearing a fedora pulled down over his already shadowed gaze, approached me. I gripped the bag with the money, sorrowful about many things, but especially sorrowful at the moment about not being able to use this money as I'd wanted.

Kim and Steve could have used this.

Instead, I was letting someone else control my life. It seemed pathetic. And desperate. And so much against everything I believed in.

Just then, the man flicked his head up, and light from an overhead street lamp grazed his face. I sucked in a deep breath when I recognized him.

CHAPTER 28

It was . . . Henry?

His steps slowed when he spotted me, and a moment of uncertainty washed across his face.

What was he doing here? He frowned as he approached. When he stopped in front of me, he shifted awkwardly, remaining distant as if afraid to get too close.

"I need the money," he muttered.

Anger surged in me, heating my blood. "Have you been behind all this?"

"I don't know what you're talking about." He glanced down at my hands and licked his lips. "I just need the bag."

I shook my head. He needed to realize exactly what he was doing here. If he didn't know it already, I was going to inform him. "I was going to give this money to Kim, you know. They have so many bills. And instead, you're taking it from me? You're taking it from a family who's struggling with cancer. The disease isn't just affecting them healthwise, but this disease has made it so they're close to losing their house. You're spineless."

Henry sighed. "There are other, more important matters at stake here."

"More important than a man's life?" My voice was full of judgment, and I didn't care. I wanted him to feel the guilt he so rightly deserved.

Henry's eyes darkened with annoyance. "Just give me

the money, Holly."

I remembered the video of Alex sleeping in her bedroom and thrust the bag into his hand. I supposed there was more than one life at stake here. I'd give this to him now, but I'd do my fighting best to get it back. "I hope you can live with yourself."

Just as his hand connected with the handle, men encircled us.

"Police! Hands up!"

I sucked in a deep breath. What in the world was going on here? Who had called the police?

And what did this mean for Alex and the man watching her sleep?

***

I sat in an interrogation room, going over everything that had happened for the forty-seventh time. The detective talking to me had left ten minutes ago, and I'd been sitting alone ever since.

"Holly?"

I turned around and saw Chase standing in the doorway.

"Hey there." My greeting was Academy Award worthy. Not.

He handed me a cup of coffee. I unwrapped my arms from across my chest—I'd practically been hugging myself—and gratefully took the warm drink. I was desperately tired, to the point of feeling achy and cranky.

"Thank you." Again, our dialogue was riveting. I just couldn't quite set my mouth in motion and say anything graceful, thoughtful, or thought provoking.

"I heard what happened. How are you?" He squeezed my arm, the warmth in his gaze making me flush.

I shrugged, reality slamming into my mind again. "I don't know how I am anymore. I'm just tired and confused and wishing I'd been able to convince you to take that trip to Hawaii that I mentioned not long ago."

A smile curved half of his face. "Now, that conversation is starting to make more sense."

"I was hoping I'd have the chance to explain myself sooner rather than later."

Any amusement left his gaze as he lowered his voice. "You shouldn't have gone alone at night like that. Especially with the riots and everything that have been going on lately."

"I know. But that man was in my sister's bedroom. How could I not risk it?" My voice caught as my inner struggle continued.

"You were risking your own life by going out there tonight, Holly." Chase's voice was a mix of scolding and concerned, of affection and worry. I wanted to both storm away and give him a kiss.

Instead of doing either of those things, I chose to go a different direction. I really had to remain focused on figuring this out and stay away from my emotions. Stress and lack of sleep had clouded my thinking. "I wonder if this is about Alex, Chase. Has anyone gone to check on her?"

"An officer just stopped by. She's fine. Confused, but fine. Why do you think she's the target here?"

I explained my earlier thoughts to him, including the food poisoning last night, the camera in her bedroom, and her delayed honeymoon. I thought I'd sounded rather convincing. Chase must have agreed because, when I finished, he nodded slowly.

"You could be onto something. Although, I have to say that your entire family has reasons why someone would want to threaten them." He was silent a moment and stared off into the distance. "Maybe it is tied in with this Arnold Pegman trial. Let me do some digging."

"That would be great." I took a sip of coffee, trying to gather my thoughts. The brew was bitter and strong, but I swallowed anyway and attempted not to let my disgust show on my face. "What did Henry say? Can you tell me anything?"

Chase rubbed his chin. He looked tired. All of this was taking a toll on him also. "He claims he's being manipulated and someone made him meet you and collect the money."

Was that true? Or was Henry working with someone and in on this whole plan the entire time? Henry was a smart man. He could have definitely concocted a scheme like this, all the way down to the last detail. "What kind of leverage does he claim someone is holding over him?"

Chase shook his head. "He won't say. He said he was being threatened and that it's random and he's just as much of a victim as anyone else."

"Do you believe him?"

"I think he knows more than he's letting on. The detectives are still questioning him, though."

I began pacing, trying to sort my thoughts. "There's one other thing: How did the police know to show up tonight?"

"That's the strange part, Holly. An anonymous caller let us know that a shady deal was going down at 12:30 on Sixth and Vine. That's why the police questioned you as well. It wasn't clear exactly what was going on."

"The only person who knew we were meeting was the Shadow Man. What if he called in the tip?"

"Why would he do that?"

There was only one reason I could think of. "To frame Henry."

CHAPTER 29

I leaned back against my chair, trying to process that thought.

Someone had set Henry up, made him play this twisted game, and then called the police. The Shadow Man was obviously done with Henry and whatever part of the plan he'd needed him for.

Was that what the money was all about? Was it just a way of making Henry look bad?

"What are you thinking, Holly?" Chase asked.

"I feel like I'm so close to finding answers, yet I'm so far away. Someone has planned this down to the last detail."

"I think we're dealing with a very dangerous individual," Chase said. "This person is smart. He has a background that allows him to go in and out of houses, to plant bombs, and to manipulate people. His motive still isn't clear, but all of this almost seems like it's building up to something."

"Like the Arnold Pegman trial?"

"It's a good guess. I can't imagine what else it would be. You're right. Alex could be involved. Maybe this is all about witness intimidation and trial tampering."

A moment of silence fell as I absorbed those thoughts. If this was about someone associated with Arnold Pegman, then the whole pool of suspects would become larger. Who knew what kind of people were linked with him?

In fact, he'd been military at one time. Maybe that

would give him connections with people who knew about bombs and using manipulation and violence to get what they wanted. It wasn't that everyone in the military was like that. Not by any means. But the wrong person in the military could use the skills they learned to do horrible things. Didn't things like that happen every day? People went crazy?

I needed to process this. Chase was my best bet as far as finding answers. He was going to look into the trial. He had access to information about who was involved.

I looked up at Chase, who was waiting patiently for me to continue. "What about the exterminator? Did he find anything?"

"He found ten cameras. They're the size of a quarter, and they're very well hidden. Of course, he left them there. Taking them would be too revealing."

My stomach clenched again. "That's not comforting."

"It shouldn't be. I need you to know how dangerous this is."

"I do, Chase." I glanced around the interrogation room for a moment. "Do you think they're going to let me go or that I've implicated myself in all of this?"

His gaze flickered toward the door, and he sighed. "I'm fairly certain they'll let you go. I'm sure they already gave you a stern talking-to about what you did and the importance of allowing police to help in matters like these, right? Going at it alone is never a good idea."

"Of course." I wasn't going to argue. I'd known it wasn't a good idea when I went out. I'd known that if Chase found out, he wouldn't approve. None of this was a surprise.

He knelt down in front of me. "I thought I'd lost you once already. I can't let that happen again. Please tell me you won't ever do anything like this again. Please."

I nodded. "I'll do my best. But I'm just trying to make sure everyone I love is safe."

***

The police let me go thirty minutes later after I signed a statement confirming my side of the story. If all went well, I'd get my money back sometime next week. The good news was that at least I'd get the cash back and would eventually be able to give it to Kim.

Henry was being held, and he was probably facing charges. I was anxious for more details to be released from his perspective. What had he been thinking? Could he fill in any of these blanks?

Chase drove me back to my car, which was still parked downtown. Silence crackled between us during the ride. Finally, we pulled up beside my Mustang. He put his sedan into park and turned toward me.

At once, I forgot about my problems. I remembered the hit that was out on local police officers. I remembered those who'd already been injured at the riots. The gravity of the situation hit me at full force.

"Be careful out there." My words came out almost as a croak.

"I will," he said. He leaned toward me, and his lips brushed mine. The hazy look in his eyes made my stomach do somersaults.

He let out a deep breath and pressed his forehead into mine. "I've got to go."

I wanted to tell him I loved him, but the words wouldn't leave my lips. Those stupid rules of etiquette that had been so ingrained in me now prevented me from saying anything. The guidelines were supposed to help me, not hinder me.

"Good-bye, Chase," I said instead.

I climbed into my car and cranked the engine. Chase didn't move until I backed out and started down the street.

As I waited at a traffic light, my phone buzzed. Dread filled me. There was only one person I could imagine would be texting me at three in the morning.

My suspicions were correct: it was the Shadow Man.

Next time lives will be lost. You've been warned.

My heart squeezed. I just couldn't shake this guy, could I?

As I continued down the road, something began nagging at the back of my mind. I paused and squeezed my eyes shut for just a second. What was it? Something just begged for my attention.

As I reviewed everything it might be, my mind stopped at the Arnold Pegman trial. I thought about the theory that this was all connected with the prosecution, with someone associated with Arnold who wanted to fix the trial and ensure he wasn't convicted.

But I already knew all that. Some new piece of information wanted to make itself evident.

That's when it hit me. I'd gotten a letter from someone in the community. They'd begged Ralph to plead to the governor in favor of Arnold Pegman.

It wasn't unusual. People wrote to senators all the time, trying to get their endorsement or asking legislators to urge the governor on their behalf for a pardon or any number of other things. In this case, there was absolutely nothing we could do, even if we wanted to, because the man hadn't been convicted yet.

But what if that person, who knew I was related to Alex, had gotten angry when we hadn't responded to his request? What if he decided to take matters into his own hands?

I had to get into the office, despite the riots. And I had to find out that person's name.

If I had a name, I could put an end to this once and for all.

It was a gamble. I'd told Chase I wouldn't do anything like this, but the benefits outweighed the risks. I had to do something!

The parking lot closest to Ralph's office was also closest to the riots. This was going to be tricky, but I hoped I could manage it.

I was definitely wading through waters and fire, and I prayed desperately that God would be with me despite my stupidity.

My hand shook as I locked my car and stepped into the great unknown. My heels clacked on the sidewalk. I could hear the chaos of the riots. Smoke hung in the air, and violence seemed to sizzle in the atmosphere. I could see the police line. I could see cops forming a human barricade. Was Chase there?

Please be with him, I prayed silently.

I skirted away from that area and headed toward Ralph's office. The plan had come to me quickly, but I had a good idea of how to get where I needed to be while avoiding the protests.

I glanced at the building I'd just passed. If I could get inside, I could cut through the hallways there, go through a couple of alleys, and get into Ralph's office through a back entrance.

If I wanted to end this madness, I had to find that name. It wasn't on my computer. It had been a handwritten letter, and it was in my desk.

That's when I remembered my promise to Chase. I'd told him I wouldn't do something like this. I'd promised him.

What was I supposed to do, though? I had to get to the office somehow. I took a step back when a hand covered my mouth.

At once, my life flashed before my eyes.

CHAPTER 30

I froze, waiting to see what the man behind me would do next. Would he pull a knife? Drag me into a car? Shoot me?

Then I realized I had to take action instead of feeling immobilized. At once, I swung my leg back and kicked, thrashing with all my might. I had to fight until I got away.

As I jammed my elbow back, the man's grip loosened just enough for me to slip away from him. Fighting back had worked!

I twirled around, raised my hands like I might throw a right hook, and spotted . . . Chase?

"I could have been a killer," he growled, his jaw clenched.

My mouth dropped open. "*You* did *that* to make a *point*?"

"You better believe I did. I just dropped you off at your car. You promised to stay out of trouble, and now you're here? What are you thinking?"

"I have a very good explanation," I stated.

His hands were on his hips. He wore a bulletproof vest, and a gun was slung across his back. He almost looked like he was going to war. But he said nothing. He just waited.

I sighed in resignation. "I remembered a letter I received. It's in the office. It could hold the answers to this whole mess. I have to find it."

"By yourself? In the middle of riots? Have you lost your mind?" He looked outraged, and I couldn't blame him.

"Maybe I have lost my mind," I conceded. "I'm desperate."

"Where is this letter again?"

"In my desk, in one of my drawers."

He let out another sigh. "I'll get it."

I shook my head. "You won't find it. I can't give you a name or even a specific file drawer to look in. I'm the only one who can get it."

'Then you'll have to wait until the riots are over." His voice didn't leave any room for argument, but that didn't stop me.

"I can't wait that long. Someone could get hurt before then. Someone could die." The last word hung in the air. I wanted to snatch it back, but I couldn't, and it was better that way. I'd spoken the truth, no matter how painful it was to hear.

He stared at me, and I could see the tension on his features. Finally, he grasped my arm and led me away from the police line.

"I'll take you down there, but at the first sign of trouble, we're turning around. Understand?"

I nodded, both relieved and apprehensive. I was trading one anxiety for another. But there was no going back now. This whole headache could end. I could live in peace again. The people I loved could be safe.

Those things made all of this worth the risk.

Chase kept his hand on my arm as we moved down the dark street at a fast clip. Shouts from the crowds in the distance seemed like an approaching thunderstorm, rumbling closer and closer. This could no doubt be very risky. Would I regret it? Maybe. But when I'd told Chase earlier that I was desperate, I'd been telling the truth.

"You have a plan for getting to the office?" Chase asked, still unsmiling and uptight.

"Yes, there are some buildings between here and there that we can cut through. I can show you the way." I had thought all of that through.

His hand continued to grip my arm. I had no doubt he wouldn't let go unless he had to. He didn't want to do this. He probably *shouldn't* do this. But maybe he realized how dire this situation was.

I pulled open the door to an apartment complex that was under construction. Someone from church worked here, and I'd overheard him say that security here wasn't tight. Just as I expected, the door easily opened, and we slipped inside. The halls were surprisingly quiet as we started down them. Each echo of our steps in the strangely vacant space around us sent another shiver up my spine.

"How'd you know I was here?" I asked, moving closer to Chase.

"I followed you. I wanted to make sure you got home okay. You can imagine my surprise when you didn't go home."

He was aggravated, and I couldn't blame him. Maybe if I explained things a little bit more . . . "I didn't plan on this. I was on my way to work on my sister's wedding cake—"

"Why were you doing that?"

"I'm making it for her. Didn't I mention that?" We really hadn't had a chance to talk. And when we did talk, it was only about life-or-death matters. Not about the fun stuff that makes relationships unique and story worthy.

"I can't say you did."

"Well, I am. But then I remembered a letter someone associated with Arnold Pegman sent Ralph. He was begging for leniency for Arnold Pegman and asked for Ralph to step in and intervene in any way possible. What if this person is behind all this? He would know my name and be somehow associated with Arnold Pegman, and he could be trying to leverage our safety for the outcome of the court case. Other than Henry, it's the best lead I can come up with."

"It's worth a shot."

I just loved hearing his voice. I loved how he was always there, by my side, to help me when I needed it. I loved that he felt like my rock.

That's why I pulled him to a stop in the dimly lit hallway. His eyes widened with surprise when he looked at me, and, if I guessed correctly, he was worried that something was wrong. Before his thoughts went too far, I reached on my tiptoes and brushed my lips against his.

We had a thing about kissing—I didn't want our whole relationship to be about it. Way back when, I'd told myself that I would save my first kiss for my wedding day. Then I'd thought I was dying, and I'd reconnected with Chase, and things had changed.

I liked ideals, but I didn't want to be ruled by them.

So I wrapped my arms around his neck, and I kissed him again. It was tentative at first, but deepened for a moment. His chest was solid against mine, and his arms felt like steel guards around my waist. And for a moment—and just a moment—I forgot my worries.

But then the moment ended. I pulled back but hesitated to step away. Instead, I rested my head against his chest and felt his heart beat against my palm.

"What was that for?" Chase murmured.

I met his gaze, fully aware that my eyes would convey entirely too much for my comfort. Certainly, he'd see my affection for him. There'd be no doubt I was taken with him, given in fully to both my whims and my quest for finding that elusive soul mate whom I couldn't live without.

I opened my mouth, but no words came out. What did I even say? How could I possibly express everything on my heart in the brief moment we had together?

His thumb brushed my jaw. "Never mind. You don't have to say anything."

"Actually, there's one thing I do want to say. I know you always say you'll do anything for me. But I'd also do whatever it takes to keep you safe."

"I don't want you to do that, Holly." His voice was low, husky, and full of emotion. "Call me old-fashioned, but that's *my* job."

"I can't live with the thought of anything happening to you."

His eyes were dark pools of emotion. I was drawn into the swirls and on the edge of being pulled under when he leaned down and pressed his lips against mine. My heart nearly stopped when I realized I could do this all day and never grow weary.

Thankfully, Chase pulled back and took my hand. "We should probably go."

I nodded, my throat tight. My hormones were surging. It was best if we kept walking.

Gunfire exploded just as we started toward the outside door.

CHAPTER 31

Instinctively Chase pushed me behind him. "You shouldn't be here."

My heart raced even faster as danger seemed to zing through the air and leave it sizzling around us. "I don't have a choice at this point."

He peered around the corner before grabbing my hand. "Stay with me. Understand?"

"No questions."

He pulled me down the hall and out a back door. We hurried down an alley, my pulse racing with every step. This was dangerous. I felt like I was in a third world country, anywhere but America. Things like this didn't happen here.

But it was. And now I was running through a war zone, trying to protect the people I loved while putting myself in danger. I could still smell something burning. People still shouted and chanted, their voices tinged with anger. Somewhere nearby, glass shattered.

Just as we reached the building where my brother's office was located, a mob appeared in the street at the end of the alley. Moving quickly, Chase pulled me into the building. We were safer inside where we could take shelter than we were out in the open. He nearly sprinted down the hallway, and I just held on for dear life.

Finally, we reached the door leading to Ralph's office

complex. With trembling hands I pulled the keys from my pocket and attempted to jam them into the door. After three failed attempts, Chase took them from me and slid the key into the lock. The door popped open.

We hurried inside, and Chase locked the door behind us. "No lights," he instructed. "If they know you're in here, you'll be a target."

"Got it." I rushed toward my desk and opened the top drawer. Chase pulled out a penlight and shone it on the papers there. Thank goodness he had a source of illumination, because I'd never find the letter without it in this dark space.

My skin crawled as I heard the crowds outside. They were right outside the building. It would be too easy for them to bust through the windows and continue their rampage inside. Destroying a local senator's office would only help make their point, I supposed—the point that government was corrupt and unjust. At times I was inclined to agree with them, but I still didn't feel like this was the right way to express their anger. The yin and yang of compassion and logic collided inside me.

I made it through the first drawer but didn't find the letter.

"We don't have much time, Holly. I need to be out there with my guys." Chase peered out the window.

I'd been selfish in asking him to come here. Of course he had an obligation to the guys on the force.

Trying to move faster, I opened the next drawer and searched through papers and correspondence. Where was that letter? I'd know it when I saw it.

Just then, the air changed. I could feel it even from inside the office. Something had happened.

Chase must have felt it too, because his gaze was riveted on the street outside.

"Tear gas," he muttered.

"What?"

"The police are using tear gas. It was supposed to be a last resort."

"What's happening?"

"It's hard to tell, but I think the crowds are retreating. No one wants to be around that stuff, but the effects aren't permanent. It's just a deterrent."

My fingers continued to flip through folders, but in my haste I feared I was being sloppy. Finally, I found the letter. Hopefully, this held the clue we needed to solve our mystery.

"Clayton Bridges," I said as I scanned the words, written in tiny box print, on the ragged-edge paper. "That's his name."

Just as I stood, I heard a stampede of people. They were in the hallway behind us, I realized. And they were rattling the door, trying to get into Ralph's office.

I froze.

If they found Chase in here, a lone police officer, there was no telling what they might do to him. And it would be my fault.

I saw the tautness in Chase's jaw, the apprehension in his eyes. Chase was probably thinking the same thing I was.

He pulled off his vest and handed it to me. "Put this on."

I shook my head and backed away. "No way. That's yours."

"You might need it, Holly."

"I can't wear that, Chase." The words choked in my throat as I realized the implications.

Before I could argue any more, he draped the vest over my head. "We need to get you somewhere safe, just in case. You know this space better than I do. Any ideas?"

"Ralph's personal office!"

There was a closet there, which would offer two sets of locked doors. That could buy us some time. Just as we stepped into the room, the back door burst open. As crowds flooded inside, the front window broke and gas filled the room.

Tear gas.

We were in serious trouble.

CHAPTER 32

Chase pulled me into Ralph's office and slammed the door. Almost immediately, I began to cough. My eyes watered. The next thing I knew, I was in the closet.

"Pull your sweater over your mouth," he directed.

I had little choice but to listen. The next thing I knew, Chase had closed the closet door.

But he wasn't inside with me. Darkness was my only companion.

My heart lurched. Chase? What was he doing? What if this got him killed?

I sank to the floor and began praying. Praying hard. Praying with everything I had in me.

I wanted to leave, wanted to help. But I knew if I distracted Chase, then I might only get him hurt or even killed. I needed to listen to him, even if I hated myself for having to cower here.

Minutes stretched on. I could hear a scuffle outside the closet door. The shouts continued somewhere in the distance. A gun fired.

My insides felt like they died when I heard that sound.

What if Chase had been shot? What if he needed my help?

Tears rushed to my eyes. The image of Chase lying on the floor with blood around him and no one to help crushed my heart. Then I imagined the crowds kicking him in his weakness. Of them taunting him.

And I couldn't take it anymore.

I cracked the door open, fully expecting to see the scenarios that had played out in my head. Inside, I saw smoke clogging the air. I pulled my cardigan up higher over my mouth and nose, blinking as my eyes began to sting.

As the smoke began to settle, a lone figure came into view.

It was Chase.

But he wasn't lying there hurt. No, he was standing guard at the door.

"What are you doing?" he demanded.

"I thought you might be hurt." I glanced around. "Where is everyone?"

"It appears they've scattered. For now. We've got to get you out of here."

I nodded, in no position to argue. I reached his side, and he rushed me toward the door. Only halfway across the room, Chase froze.

One of the inner-city teens involved in the riots lay on the floor. He was obviously injured, based on the look of excruciating pain on his face. When he spotted Chase, he sneered.

"Don't hurt me," he warned.

Chase knelt down. "I won't. What's wrong?"

"I think my leg got broken when my friends took off."

Chase took one look at his calf and nodded. "I think you're right. You're going to need to get to the hospital."

"I ain't got no money for that."

"We'll make sure you're taken care of. You can't let this go untreated. You'll never walk normally again if you do."

The kid stared at him in contemplation. "Why are you being nice to me?"

"Why wouldn't I be?" Chase asked.

"Because cops ain't like that. You're all out for us."

"I'm sorry you think that way. But I took an oath to protect everyone in this city, not just the people like me."

If God made us, each and every one of us, then everybody is important. Everyone. Not just the ones society deems worthy. Wasn't that the lesson God had been reminding me of lately? Chase was living that out right now, and my heart couldn't help but swell with gratitude for this man.

"Holly, can you give me a hand?" Chase asked.

I nodded, and together we helped the youth to his feet.

"What's your name?" Chase asked.

"Booker."

Booker? I hadn't even recognized him. He'd been a part of the peace talks.

With an arm around each of our shoulders, we led him outside. Two other officers met us as we emerged onto the street.

"We need an ambulance," Chase told them.

While one of the officers called on his radio, Chase turned to the other. "I need you to escort her home." He nodded toward me.

"But—" I started.

"Holly, if you're here, I'm not going to be able to focus. Just go home and stay there until morning. Please."

I wanted to argue, but I didn't. Instead, I nodded. "Okay." I turned to the teen. "I hope your leg feels better, Booker."

With a final wave, I walked through the broken bottles, past cracked bricks, by smashed car windows and dented car hoods and abandoned picket signs.

It was time to go home and try to stay out of trouble.

And to get ready for Alex's wedding.

***

I fully expected Ralph to have heard a rundown on everything that had happened, and so I expected to receive a lecture the next day. But when I stopped by work for just a few minutes at lunchtime, Ralph didn't say anything to me.

I glanced around, thrown off by the rather pleasant environment around me. No one was pointing fingers or sneering or looking at me like I'd messed up.

That all seemed suspicious within itself.

One person was missing this morning. Henry. I wondered what had happened with him.

Ralph stuck his head out from his office. "Holly, can I talk to you a minute?"

I knew it! Here came the lecture. I nodded and went into his office. I shut the door and sat across from him, just waiting for the anti-fun to begin.

"Did you hear about Henry?"

I swallowed my surprise. "Henry?"

"He was caught taking a bribe," Ralph started. "Apparently, he was acting as an informant to the rioters. He'd been telling them what the police were planning after he overheard me talking to law enforcement. That's why the rioters were always one step ahead of the authorities."

"Henry? Why would he do that?" This was the last thing I'd expected to hear.

"His brother was killed by a police officer about five years ago. To talk with Henry about it, he seemed fine. But I guess deep down inside, he wasn't. He felt like his brother's death was wrong, even though his brother tried to run over an officer. The guy was drunk at the time, and the officer, by all accounts, had done the right thing. The officer would have died otherwise."

"So this was some kind of revenge?"

"Apparently. Anyway, I guess the wrong person found out what he was doing and threatened to come forward with the information that Henry had divided loyalties and was sharing sensitive information. This person blackmailed him into doing some shady things. I haven't been given the details of exactly what those things were yet, though."

"Wow. I can't believe that." So Henry, in one way, had been set up? That whole money exchange thing last night had just been part of a game that some evil mastermind had planned.

"Me neither. I try to be really careful about whom I trust, but I'm down two for two right now."

His former campaign manager had turned out to be trouble as well.

"You couldn't have known. None of us did."

He nodded. "I suppose. But at least there's good news."

"What's that??"

"Apparently, Chase saved Booker Jones during the riots last night. The kid had a broken leg and was bleeding out pretty badly. Some of the media caught everything on camera, and reporters decided to promote peace instead of inciting violence, for once. It's amazing what one little act can set in motion."

I glanced at the newspaper headline. Sure enough, there was Chase with Booker. I was on the other side of the boy, but two officers blocked me, which was fine.

"I guess one little act started all of this, and now maybe

one will end it also."

Ralph smiled. "I just wanted to share. You're not staying here today, are you? Aren't you and Alex getting your hair and nails done or something girlie like that?"

I nodded and glanced at my watch. "I have to be there in an hour. I guess I'll see you at the rehearsal dinner."

"Sounds good. I'll see you then, Holly."

At least, I hoped I'd see him then. Because, despite the good news about the riots, my gut was churning with some kind of instinctual feeling that something else bad was going to happen. Something really bad.

And I had no idea how to stop it.

CHAPTER 33

"So, what are you going to do about your dress?" Heather asked my sister as the stylist tugged on her hair.

All the food-poisoning victims still seemed a little weak, and none of them wanted to talk about food, but otherwise they seemed okay. Apparently there was nothing that a little pampering couldn't cure. The doctors had instructed them to drink water and eat a BRAT diet—bananas, rice, apples, and toast. That didn't stop most of them from sipping on some bubbly, though.

"I have a new dress that's supposed to be in by tomorrow morning," Alex said. "That's what the boutique says, at least. They put a rush on it and insisted it will even be altered on time."

"That's cutting it close, wouldn't you say?" Sarah, her snooty college friend, said.

"I'd definitely say. But what else am I supposed to do? I still can't believe the seamstress wrote down my measurements with such gross negligence. It's insane."

It was kind of crazy. Even I had to admit that.

My sister and her friends moved on to talk about senseless things as they had their hair fixed. Sometimes I participated in such mindless conversations, but not today. Today, I had too many other things to think about.

"I heard Chase may have single-handedly saved the city

from future riots." Alex's gaze zeroed on me.

I snapped back to the conversation. "Yeah, I heard that also."

"You mean that hunky police officer who was photographed and on the news this morning?" Heather's eyebrows rose with intrigue.

I nodded. "He's the one."

"You know him?" she continued.

I nodded again. "I do."

"Ooh la la. Do you think you could introduce me?" She wagged her eyebrows.

I scowled, my claws starting to come out. Claws were never ladylike, however. A quick wit was much more valuable than acting catty. But before I could formulate a reasonable response, Heather's phone rang.

She scrunched her face after a moment of talk and turned toward me. "It's for you, Holly."

She looked confused, but thankfully I knew exactly what was going on.

I took the phone and slipped away from the woman trying to smooth my hair. "Thanks."

I stepped toward the back of the spa. I'd given Heather's number to Chase. Calling my own cell phone seemed too risky, especially until I knew if my calls were being monitored.

"What's going on?" I asked.

"I just thought I'd let you know that I'm looking into this guy who sent you the letter. He's been suspiciously absent from his job the past two weeks."

Fire rushed through my veins. "Really?"

"Really. We're looking for him now. But you could be onto something, Holly. I just wanted to let you know."

"Thanks, Chase. I heard about Henry. Ralph told me."

"He has no idea who the person behind this is," Chase said. "He got anonymous calls and threats. We're running the phone numbers, but we don't expect to find anything. Whoever is behind this is smart. Maybe too smart. So be careful, okay?"

"I will."

"I wish I could be there with you tonight."

My shoulders drooped with regret. "Me too, Chase. Me too."

I hung up. Before joining the ladies again, first I ducked into the bathroom for a moment to compose myself. Just as I did, the phone in my hand buzzed.

Forgetting the phone wasn't my own, I glanced down and saw a text message. The message nearly made me have a heart attack.

Even though I shouldn't have done it, because a woman of grace was never nosy, I read the message.

Have fun being pampered. I hope the rehearsal dinner goes well tonight, and I'm really glad we've reconnected.

I knew I shouldn't do what I was about to do. But I did it anyway.

I clicked on the message feed, and the entire conversation came up.

Unlisted: **Alex still stressing out about the trial?**

Heather: **Yes. She's preoccupied with the wedding. Too much going on at once, I suppose.**

Unlisted: **Hopefully her big day will go on without a hitch from here out.**

Heather: **You can come as my date. Wouldn't that be a hoot? LOL, I'm just kidding. Exes at weddings are too awkward.**

Unlisted: **I'm glad we've been able to reconnect. It's been years since I've heard from the old college gang. By the way, how are you feeling?**

Heather: **Still reeling from food poisoning. Can you believe it?**

Unlisted: **Sounds like a classy joint. Sorry you're sick. :-/ Do you have my gift?**

Who was she talking to? Brandon?

I swallowed hard. Why would Heather be texting my sister's ex? And teasing about bringing him to the wedding? My number one duty as maid of honor was to protect my sister's big day. Heather just might be my biggest challenge.

When I had a chance, I'd ask Heather about it.

I slipped back into the room and handed her the phone. "Who was that?" she asked.

"Chase. Sorry about the mix-up. It's a long story."

"How's the hot detective?" she asked, her eyes wide and almost hungry.

Wit, Holly. Use wit.

However, nothing witty was coming to me except "Keep your claws off him."

Heather stared at me. That's when I realized I'd said the words aloud. Oh. No.

"Holly?" Alex said, looking as taken off guard as I felt.

I fanned my face. I had to recover, and fast. But I had no clue how to, so I let out a laugh instead—a laugh that sounded pretty stinkin' fake. "Just kidding! I mean, Heather already has a date to the wedding. Right?"

I was usually better than this. But I was operating on hardly any sleep and way too much stress.

Everyone stared at Heather, waiting for what she would say next. She opened her mouth but shut it again. Was she speechless now?

"Not a confirmed date." She gave me a pointed, seriously unhappy look.

"I heard everyone was going to be really shocked when you showed up with him."

"Holly, can we talk for a minute?" The next thing I knew, she'd slid off the chair and grabbed my arm.

We stepped outside. Figurative steam shot from Heather's ears. I'd practically asked for this confrontation, but that didn't mean I was happy about it.

"What are you doing?" she demanded. Her hair was half-curled and half-straight. The Shirley Temple–like roller curls on her left side made her look slightly crazy and off balance.

I placed my hand on my hip, ready to take her on. "I just happened to see a text message about Alex's wedding. It raised a few red flags."

She glared. "That was none of your business. I had no intentions of actually bringing him to the wedding."

"Who exactly is he?" This was it. The moment of truth.

Satisfaction flashed in her eyes. "You don't know?"

"Why would I know?"

"Because you think you're so smart! It's Brandon."

My mouth dropped open. I hadn't wanted to believe it, but I couldn't deny it now that I'd heard the words leave her lips. "You're hitting on my sister's ex-boyfriend?"

She sighed and stared off into the sky for a moment. "We've been talking about getting together. I didn't bring it up because I didn't want to put a damper on Alex's day. I feel fairly certain she would be fine with it, but I do try to be considerate—unlike some people."

I wasn't going to play into her guilt game right now. "But you brought Brandon up at the bachelorette party. Were you feeling her out to see if she would mind?"

She glared again, nostrils flaring this time. "Yes, are you happy now? I wanted to know if she was truly over him."

"So, is he coming to the wedding?"

She shrugged and raised her chin stubbornly. "No, he had something come up. So there's no need to mention any of this to Alex. I don't want to upset her."

I thought about it a moment and nodded. Maybe it was classless—maybe it wasn't. Either way, Heather's love life had nothing to do with the fiasco in my life.

CHAPTER 34

Overall, the rehearsal had gone well. There was only one little hiccup: Heather didn't show up.

She'd called and said she was getting a migraine and that she'd be late. We started without her and ran through the ceremony, but there was still no Heather. Everyone had fully expected she would show up by the dinner, at least.

To make matters worse, she wasn't answering her phone.

"I'm sure she's fine," I told Alex. Even as I said the words aloud, I realized they might not be true. It was one thing for Heather to be a no-show because of a migraine. It was another thing entirely for her to stop answering her phone and not to check in. That phone was practically glued to her hand.

The rehearsal dinner was held in an elegant restaurant located on the Cincinnati hillside overlooking the river. It was on the outskirts of town, away from the craziness of the busy downtown area. The place had low lights, white linen tablecloths, and a strings trio playing in the corner. The menu of ribs, chicken, and salmon seemed to appease everyone.

I'd forced my dinner down and now stood by the window, staring down at the river, my thoughts gloomy. As much as I tried to stay positive, the situation was wearing me down.

A part of me felt like I was getting so close to the

answers. In my gut, I felt like they were within my grasp. But I'd felt close before only to have any resolution slip away. This wasn't over yet; I felt sure of it. But what was the man planning next?

"You doing okay?" Ralph asked, joining me by the window.

"Yeah, just hanging out over here solo." Chase should have been here with me, which only caused my resentment to grow.

"I know what that's like."

Maybe Ralph and I were more alike than I thought. Mom was busy being a social butterfly. Alex was charming everyone and making them feel welcome. Then there were Ralph and me, choosing to be wallflowers for a minute. While everyone else was partying, we were reflective.

For a moment, I didn't feel like such an outcast in my own family.

I remembered what he'd said. *I know what that's like to be alone.* He understood not having a plus one.

I nudged him with my elbow. "Thea was asking me some questions about your love life the other day . . ."

"Thea? Really?" He pulled his face back in surprise.

I nodded. "Really. She's pretty nice."

Ralph nodded in the distance. "I heard William's best man is single. And he's a doctor."

I glanced across the room. The best man was handsome and successful. But my heart already belonged to someone. "I'm not looking."

"Because you're still in love with Chase."

"Since when did you get so insightful?" I asked, trying to lighten the moment.

"Have you told him?"

"That I love him?" I questioned in horror. That was against all my etiquette. The guy always had to say "I love you" first.

"You never know when the moment will slip away, Holly. You just never know."

His words left me with a certain heaviness. I didn't know what to say, and I couldn't begin to explain things.

"I thought you should know that Henry's indiscretions have opened up an investigation into our office," Ralph said.

"What?" I screeched.

He nodded solemnly. "I wasn't going to bring it up here, but it's weighing on me. I knew if I could tell anyone, I could tell you."

"I'm so sorry, Ralph. What's that going to mean?"

"A lot of scrutiny. Walking on eggshells. Angry voters who have even more of a reason not to trust their elected officials. You know the drill."

I shook my head. "I just can't believe that."

"It's insane, and it hits me right where it hurts—"

Before he could finish his thought, the whole restaurant shook. Everything happened at the same time. Walls crumbled. Smoke filled the air. I was knocked to the ground.

An earthquake?

We didn't have those around here.

Another bomb?

I barely had time to pull myself to my feet when I looked across the dining area and realized what had happened.

A car had crashed into the restaurant.

I coughed as dust filled my lungs; then I glanced around to survey the damage.

All the other guests seemed to be in a similar state. Dazed. Confused. Shaken.

As far as I could tell, no one was hurt, though.

I staggered as I tried to take a step. Ralph was at my side, soot covering his face, and particles—drywall or insulation, maybe?—were in his hair. We made our way toward the gaping hole in the wall across the room.

There, two headlights and a fender stared at us.

Piles of brick and glass lay scattered around the scene. The sprinkler system rained down from overhead. Panic zinged through the air as guests tried to gather their bearings.

I stepped over part of the bar area where the car had entered the building. The vehicle looked familiar, but I didn't know why.

As some of the smoke settled, I got my first glance through the broken window.

Heather was passed out behind the wheel.

"I smell gas," Ralph muttered.

With a start, I realized that this situation was even more dangerous than I thought. "Everyone, get out of here!" I yelled.

A few stared at me uncertainly. Some scrambled away at the first suggestion. Others had their loved ones pull them away from the wreckage.

I watched as William escorted Alex and my mom toward the door. Knowing they were safe, I could focus on the task at hand.

"We've got to get Heather out, Ralph," I told him, stepping over another pile of rubbish.

"We don't have much time." Ralph followed me.

I reached the car first and tugged on the door handle. "It's stuck."

I pulled harder, but nothing happened. The impact must have crunched the metal together.

"Let me try this side." He hopped over the hood.

Moving a few bricks aside, he reached the passenger door. When Ralph tugged, it opened.

Thank goodness.

I scrambled around the rubble and joined Ralph. He'd already unlatched Heather's seat belt. With both hands around her waist, he dragged her toward the opening.

The odor of gas was getting stronger, and the sense of urgency surged inside me. We were all going to be goners if we didn't get out of here soon.

Just as Ralph pulled her out, my eye caught a glimpse of something on the floor of the car.

Prescription drug bottles.

What?

I didn't have time to think about it now. I put my arm around Heather. Ralph and I rushed her away from the car.

Just as we reached the exit to the restaurant, the room behind us exploded.

CHAPTER 35

Alex threw a flower from her corsage onto the floor as we sat in the hospital waiting room with no news on Heather.

"What I am going to do?" she muttered. "She's my best friend. How could she do this to me?"

I had no answers for her. No one did, apparently. William just patted her hand. Mom was strangely quiet. Ralph paced.

"Can I even get married tomorrow with Heather in the hospital?" Alex asked, shaking her head almost neurotically.

"Of course," Mom said. "This is your big day. Don't let anyone ruin it."

"But my best friend is at death's door."

"We don't know that," William said. "Do you want me to see what I can find out?"

"I'd appreciate it."

My phone buzzed in my hands at that moment, causing my heart rate to speed. Could it be Chase? It wasn't a good idea for us to text, but maybe he'd heard what happened.

When I looked down at my screen, my hopes were dashed.

You should always expect the unexpected.

The Shadow Man. He was behind this, I realized. But

how was that possible? Had he drugged Heather and somehow sent her crashing into the restaurant?

Before I could fully formulate that thought, William came back into the room. Everyone quieted, waiting for his update.

"She's awake, and she's going to be okay. She's in a lot of pain, and I doubt she'll make the wedding tomorrow. But she'll be fine."

"Can anyone see her?" I asked.

He shrugged. "I suppose. Alex?"

Alex shook her head. Her self-pity—which I couldn't blame her for—was replaced with anger. "I don't want to see her right now. I'd give her a piece of my mind, and I don't think that would be good for her in her current physical state."

"I'll talk to her," I said, standing up.

When no one objected, I started down the hall. The door was open, so I slipped inside.

Heather was hooked up to machines and tubes and had multiple bandages. Five minutes earlier, I would have been angry with her. Driving while under the influence of drugs? Not cool.

But then I'd gotten that text. Maybe there was more to this story than met the eye. I needed to find out.

Heather couldn't turn her neck to look at me, so I stood at the foot of her bed.

She closed her eyes when she saw me, and I could sense her shame.

"It's not what it looks like," she murmured.

"What happened, Heather?"

She licked her lips. "I don't know. One minute, I had a migraine. I took one of my pills and lay down. The next thing I knew, I was in my car going down the road. It was like the car was out of my control."

"Out of your control, how?"

She sighed and rolled her eyes upward. "I don't know. I kept trying to brake, but I couldn't. I tried to turn, but I couldn't."

"Maybe it's because of the drugs."

"I honestly didn't take that many." She frowned. "Alex is never going to forgive me."

"She'll be okay. We're just glad you're still alive."

She frowned. "You and Ralph got me out. That's what I heard, at least."

I nodded.

"But you weren't hurt?"

"We got out the door just in time. A few seconds more, and it could have been a different story."

"Thank you."

I nodded. "Did they say how long you're going to be here?"

"I'm not going to make it to the wedding tomorrow." Her voice sounded monotone, almost like she was numb. "They need to observe me for longer. Even the doctor said I should be dead. No one believes my story. Do you, Holly?"

I didn't like Heather, but I had to be honest here. "I do, Heather. I want to find some answers for you."

"Thank you, Holly. That means a lot to me."

I stepped into the hallway and found Chase waiting outside the door.

"Jamie called me and filled me in," he said quietly.

I leaned against the wall a moment, glad that I'd slipped away and used the hospital phone to tell my best friend what had happened. "I had a taste of what you do, Chase—rushing toward danger instead of away. It only made me respect your career even more."

"I'm glad no one else was hurt."

"This was the work of the Shadow Man," I whispered. "I got a text from him. He said, 'You should always expect the unexpected.' What does that mean?"

"It means this isn't over yet," Chase said. "I ran the numbers he's been calling you from, but they're untraceable. This guy knows what he's doing, and he knows how to be sneaky."

I shifted. "Chase, there was one other strange thing. Heather claims she only took one pill. She said the next thing she knew, she was in the car and she felt like it was driving itself."

He squinted. "Really? Do you believe her?"

I thought about it a moment before nodding. "Yeah, I do."

"I'll mention it to the guys working the case. I'm not sure it will mean anything. Drugs can have a strange effect on people's perception." He paused. "Is the wedding still going on tomorrow?"

"It is. Last I heard, at least."

"I have a bad feeling about it."

I chomped down, not wanting to acknowledge the truth. But I had no choice. "So do I. But I can't exactly ask my sister to cancel her wedding."

"I'll keep investigating people associated with Arnold Pegman. Maybe we can figure out something and save the day."

"Not to mention saving a few lives . . ."

CHAPTER 36

I was assigned to pick up Alex's dress the next morning. I really hoped that this new one fit. Otherwise, what would Alex do? I didn't even want to think about it.

Jamie and I walked into a swanky little boutique in the Clifton area—not far from Chase's house, for that matter—and explained to the receptionist who I was. Her eyes widened, and she hurried to the back without saying a word.

Jamie and I exchanged a look at the woman's strange, almost frightened reaction.

"One word," she whispered. "Your mom."

"That's two words."

She scowled. "You know what I mean."

And I did. My mom must have put the fear of God into these people. She was as kind as a Southern belle when she needed to be, but other times that genteel charm turned into sass and attitude.

A moment later, another employee came out. She was older with tight, red curls piled high on her head, turquoise glasses perched on the end of her nose, and bright-red lipstick slathered across her lips. I could tell from looking at her that she was knit tighter than a sorority girl's sweater. The dead giveaway was the knot in between the woman's eyebrows. Something was wrong, wasn't it?

"We have the dress," she said. "It just came in this

morning."

"That's . . . great?" I ended with a question because I had the feeling something wasn't great at all. I hoped I was wrong, though.

"It came in two sizes too large." The woman threw her hands in the air and harrumphed.

My eyes widened. "How did that happen?"

The woman shook her head, her dangly earrings slapping her cheeks. "We have no idea. We entered all the information into our system just as we always do. We even double-check measurements so things like this don't happen."

"Is that where the alteration sizes were?" Jamie asked.

The woman nodded. "Everything is on computer now. It's a blessing and a curse. But we've never ever had anything like this happen to us before. We know how important weddings are."

"Well, you said the dress is too big, right?" I started, trying to think this through. "That's good news because you can take it in."

The woman let out a quick laugh. "Not in two hours we can't. There's simply no way."

"But she's getting married today. She has to have a dress."

"I don't know what to say. But the dress won't be ready. Maybe she can come in and pick out something else?" The woman's voice lilted. She was serious! How could someone who owned a bridal boutique be this clueless?

"On her wedding day? Are you crazy?"

The woman shook her head, flapping her hands in the air again. "I don't know what else to say. This is terribly unfortunate."

"You're not the one who has to tell the bride the bad

news." I sighed. "Let me have the dress. Maybe we can pin it or something."

The woman nodded and disappeared.

"You would think someone's trying to wreck Alex's wedding. First the cake, then the dress, then the bachelorette party," Jamie said with a snort. "Not to mention the rehearsal dinner. What's going to happen there? Will the bride literally break a leg?"

I froze. "What if you're right?"

"I was just kidding," she started.

I shook my head. "No, you could totally be onto something. I mean, the number of things that have happened with this wedding are truly strange. What if someone connected with the Arnold Pegman trial is trying to ruin Alex's big day?"

"Why would they do that? What purpose would it serve?"

"Maybe this person is messing with her head."

"He's going to extremes just to mess with her mind. There are easier ways to ruin a wedding."

I shook my head, trying to sift the decent thoughts from the outrageous ones. "The woman said the numbers in the computer had been changed. What if someone hacked into the computer? If Alex is distracted by all these problems, then she can't give her full attention to the case."

"It still sounds extreme. What about the other prosecutors? Have they been affected by any of this?"

"I have no idea. Alex hasn't said anything, but I've been keeping quiet about these threats, for more than one reason." My thoughts were still racing. "Jamie, get the dress. I need to make a phone call."

I stepped outside and found the number in my contacts for the baker who'd canceled on Alex. To my surprise, someone answered. "Happy Hills Catering. How can I help you?"

"Happy Hills Catering?" I repeated.

"That's right. How can I help you?"

"I thought you were going out of business?"

"Going out of business? Well, no. Business has never been better. We're even going to be featured on the Food Network."

My suspicions continued to rise. The pieces just weren't fitting together here. "Then why did you tell my sister you couldn't make her cake because you were closing?"

The woman on the line remained silent. "I don't know what you're talking about."

"Does the name Alex Paladin ring any bells?"

The woman remained quiet a little too long. "Alex Paladin? I can't say it does."

"You need to stop playing games. You know good and well who she is. You lied to her. Why?"

"Really, ma'am. I don't know what you're talking about."

"The quiver in your voice tells me you do," I told her.

"I don't want any trouble."

"Then start talking. Otherwise, I'll begin a campaign to expose the truth, and when I discover it, I'll post it all over the Internet for everyone to see. Do you know what bad word of mouth does for a business nowadays? Terrible, terrible things. Terrible, no-more-business type of things. The excuse you told my sister might become reality."

"Please, don't do that. I can explain." Her voice broke with desperation.

"I'm listening." Wow, I was talking tough. Sometimes I didn't think I had it in me. But when push came to shove, no one was going to walk on me, even if I had to roll up my sleeves and get dirty.

"A man called me. He said he'd give me ten thousand dollars if I wouldn't do your sister's cake. I wanted to refuse on principle. But my family could really use the money. My husband was injured on the job—he was a contractor—and since then he's been out of work. That money could pay major bills. And your sister could find someone else to make her wedding cake. It wasn't a matter of life or death. I knew it wasn't right, but I did it. I don't know what else to say."

Compassion squeezed my heart. That pesky compassion. It always seemed to get in the way at the worst possible times. "Do you have any idea who this man was?"

"No idea."

"Did he pay you?"

The woman's voice had gone from light and hopeful to downright scared. "I found cash in a bag outside my back door one morning. There was no note, no anything. Just money. Ten thousand, just like he'd promised. I really don't want trouble. I'm just trying to do what's best for my family."

I could think of a hundred lectures I could give her right now about lying and blackmail and standing on principle. But this wasn't the time or place. Besides, even though I'd like to say if I were in her shoes, I'd behave differently, I knew from experience how desperate situations could lead you to the brink of compromise. I'd been there one too many times before.

I hung up and walked back inside. Jamie was handling the bridal dress like a groom carrying his bride over the threshold on their wedding day. Only she was scowling. "Do you have any idea how heavy this is?"

"Pretty heavy. Sorry about that. But, boy, did I find out something interesting . . ."

CHAPTER 37

My perfect sister, Alex, bawled like a baby as she stared at herself in the floor-length mirror in Mom's bedroom.

"This is just horrible," she whined. "I can't possibly wear this. I look like a big, fat, white powder puff!"

I squirmed. That did not sound like something my composed sister would say. I patted her shoulder, remembering again that it was my duty to make things go smoothly. "It's not that bad."

"Are you looking at the same catastrophe I am?" she exclaimed, going all Bridezilla on me. Her eyes were wide, her mascara smeared, and her nostrils flared.

Scary was the best word to describe her. Not flattering, but highly accurate.

I backed away ever so slowly in an attempt to get out of the line of fire. The dress *was* horrible on her. It was too large at the chest, and it sagged downward, too revealing to be classy. It was too long, even with the three-inch heels she wore. The waist puckered out, and the sleeves kept slipping down in a sloppy, trashy kind of way.

"With a few more pins . . ." I started. I'd already used about fifty safety pins, trying to make the dress presentable. It hadn't worked.

"If I have one more pin on me, I might as well be a donkey at a child's birthday party." She managed to say the words without moving her jaw.

Again, way scary. I didn't even bother to respond. But we were supposed to be at the church in an hour—an hour! That's when the organist would play "Here Comes the Bride." Alex couldn't walk down the aisle like this.

Mom frowned in the background. "I might have an idea. Wait right here."

I watched Mom walk off, wondering exactly what she was planning. Maybe superglue could fix this mess. Was it possible to use that on a wedding dress? Or duct tape, maybe? I had no idea.

"Why is everything going wrong?" Alex stomped over to a chair and plopped down with a pouty frown. Again, very unlike my sister.

I didn't want to be the one to tell her that a psycho connected with the Arnold Pegman trial might be trying to sabotage her wedding, as well as my life. She wasn't in the right mental state to accept that news.

A moment later, Mom returned holding something in her hands.

It was . . . her own wedding gown.

The dress that I, Holly Anna Paladin, the official sentimental one in the family, was supposed to wear on my wedding day. The white one with a simple lace brocade along the front. Sleeveless. Gently gathered at the waist. Delicate beads sewn on the skirt.

"I took the liberty of having it altered earlier this week, just in case. It should fit you." Mom held it against Alex, her eyes beaming with delight.

My mouth dropped opened. *Keep it all good for Alex*, I told myself. But inwardly, I was fuming. If that dress had been altered for Alex, then it would never fit me. Alex was tall and had curves in all the right places. I was petite and slender, with a girlish figure.

"I know old things aren't your first choice," Mom said. "But don't you at least want to try it on?"

Alex stood and wiped the tears from her eyes. "I was so mean about this dress. I said it looked outdated."

I turned away as Alex slipped the ruined wedding dress off and put Mom's on. I heard them gasp behind me and couldn't stop myself from turning. I blinked in surprise. The dress fit Alex perfectly. Even with its lacy brocade and simple lines, Alex made it look like a million bucks.

"This is perfect, Mom," she said. New tears shone in her eyes now. But these were tears of joy instead of sorrow. She kissed Mom's cheeks. "Thank you so much for being so considerate."

Considerate? What about being considerate of *me*? I knew this was no time for a tirade, but really? That dress had been promised to me. For the past eight years, I'd been planning on wearing it on my wedding day. In every single one of my fantasies, that dress was there.

"What do you think, Holly?" Alex asked.

I looked over, fighting my own tears this time. "It's lovely," I finally croaked out.

She smiled. "Well, I guess I should get my makeup fixed and get going. It's time for me to get married!"

Mom was positively glowing. I supposed she'd forgotten that promise to me. I kept trying to push aside my own feelings and desires, but they kept popping to the surface again, as feelings were prone to do.

I primped my hair once more and adjusted the black, sleeveless gown I wore. I just had to get today over with. After Alex was married, then I could concentrate on everything else.

"Holly, are you okay?" my sister asked as we started toward the front door. "You look a little pale."

I forced a smile and turned toward her. "Of course. You look beautiful, Alex."

She gave me a hug. "Thanks, Holly. I couldn't have done any of this without you. You're the best maid of honor ever."

A sob got caught in my throat.

Before it escaped, my cell phone beeped. It was Chase.

If he was calling my cell phone, then it must be important. I still had fears this one was bugged.

"Holly, I have some news for you."

I stepped away from the crowds. "What's that?"

"Arnold Pegman's friend? The one you got the letter from?"

"Yes, what about him?"

"He's been in London the past two weeks with an old friend of his. He definitely wasn't the one threatening you."

My blood went cold. "Really? You're sure?"

"Positive."

"But where does that leave me?"

"It leaves you in a very dangerous position still. Whoever this man is who's been threatening you . . . we still have no idea who he is. Be careful, Holly. I'm not sure any of this is over yet, and that's what scares me the most."

***

I could hardly concentrate as Alex, the rest of the bridesmaids, and I were sequestered in a room before the ceremony. All the other ladies were clucking like hens, but worry stained my every thought. If someone truly wanted to ruin the wedding, this was the perfect time to do it.

All my leads had fizzled, and I had no clue whom to watch out for anymore.

Meanwhile, Alex had gone from Bridezilla to being as happy as a clam.

While everyone else seemed content, I sat down in the corner and opened a box Snooty Sarah had brought in. Pictures filled it.

Sarah must have spotted me because she beelined toward me. "Everything okay?"

I nodded, way too melancholy for this day. "What are these?"

"Alex wanted some pictures for the slide show during the reception—I was in charge of putting it together, so I collected pictures from your mom, and I had some of my own from back in the day as well. She said she wanted more than just pictures of her and William. They're starting from when they were babies and leading up to when they met, or something. Anyway, those are the leftovers."

I picked up the first one and smiled. It was a picture of Alex with Dad. Again, hot moisture filled my gaze. I was turning into a weepy, sobbing mess. What was wrong with me?

But I knew what had caused this reaction. Dad should have been here. He should be glowing when he saw Alex waiting to be walked down the aisle. He should have pictures from this day that he could place in his wallet and show people with pride. I *needed* him to be here. I needed him to be on my side through the thick and thin of life.

But that wasn't going to happen.

Before I let my emotions get the best of me, I put the picture down and picked up the next one. It was of Alex and her friends from college, partying hard in an Ivy League type of way. They all looked preppy and pretty but with a glimmer of trouble in their eyes.

I continued to flip, but I stopped on one of the photos. It was a group of guys, their arms around each other, and the mountains in the background. Based on the backpacks at their feet, they'd just been hiking.

One of the men in the picture looked familiar, but I couldn't remember why. There was just something about him that struck a chord with me, that made me think I'd talked to him before. Was it . . . ? No, it couldn't be.

"Who is this?" I asked Sarah.

She laughed, looked at me like I was testing her, and then sobered. "You really don't remember?"

I shook my head. "No, I really don't."

She smirked. "That's Brandon."

I stared at the picture again. That's when I realized with a quick and sudden start who was behind all this chaos. If I closed my eyes and added about twenty pounds to the man in the photos. If I gave him different hair and clothes. A different personality. Maybe even a different nose.

How could I not have seen it earlier? Was I that dense?

Apparently I was, because he'd pulled this off flawlessly.

I stood, ready to take some kind of action. Before I could, the door opened and the wedding coordinator stepped inside with a wide flourish of her arms.

"It's time!" she exclaimed.

Tension rose in me. What was I supposed to do? Stop the wedding? That wouldn't go over well, especially since all of this was just a hunch. I hadn't had a chance to think everything through. But I knew who the bad guy was. I knew he wanted to ruin this wedding. I wasn't sure why or what he was planning. But this could all turn out very ugly.

We all lined up. I actually felt like I was kind of shoved in place. As I took my position, I grabbed my cell phone and stuck it in my bouquet of roses. I glanced around. No one had seen me.

Before I could say anything or warn anyone, we were ushered out the door and into the foyer by the sanctuary. My brother joined Alex at the back of the procession. He was going to give her away. Did either of them have any clue what kind of madness might ensue in the next few minutes?

Mom hurried toward me, which was odd considering she was supposed to be seated soon. The ushers were waiting for her at the door, but instead she leaned toward me with a glimmer of worry in her eyes. "Guess who's here."

An impending feeling of doom surfaced in my gut, and I gasped for air. "Who?"

"Brandon Gordon," she whispered, her lips forming a perfect O. "Can you believe it? I hardly recognized him."

My blood pressure ratcheted into the sky.

My worst fears were confirmed.

Brandon had been right under my nose this whole time. And I'd failed to see him, even hiding in plain sight.

CHAPTER 38

I held my bouquet closer and slipped my hand inside. Trying to be subtle, I typed in the name of Segreto, the dating service, and waited for the page to load. This was supposed to be their launch day, after all. Certainly they had a site up by now.

I blinked in surprise when I saw the pictures of the company's founders.

"Holly, move!" Alex urged behind me.

I looked up and saw the other bridesmaids had already started down the aisle. I raised my chin and tried to pretend I was happy and relaxed. But my phone was staring at me from my bouquet. This was breaking every etiquette rule I'd ever subscribed to. Mary Manners would not approve. Nor would my mom. Not even jailbird Martha Stewart.

I glanced down, knowing the page I needed to see was just a few clicks away. Then I could confirm whether or not my theory was crazy. I suspected it wasn't.

I grinned at the people around me as I attempted to look composed. I tried to concentrate on the classic architecture of the sanctuary with its steepled ceiling and massive wooden beams. I saw stained-glass windows, intricate arches near the choir loft, and a perfect center aisle that was decorated elegantly with a red runner and white rose petals.

I wished I could say I cared. But, at the moment, I didn't.

Finally, I reached the front of the sanctuary, took my

position, and turned to face the guests in attendance.

All of their attention riveted toward the back as "Wedding March" began playing. This was my chance.

I glanced at the screen and blinked twice. I saw the two men I'd talked to in the office that day. Al K. Duh and Toaster. Then my gaze traveled to the third founder of the dating service. Benjamin Radcliff.

The Benjamin listed on their website was not the same Benjamin Radcliff I'd met, however.

The Benjamin I'd met looked an awful lot like Brandon Gordon.

I gasped at the confirmation.

When I did, my phone tumbled out of my bouquet and scattered onto the floor. People looked away from Alex during her Big Walk Down the Aisle and stared at me.

I glanced up. My sister's smile slipped and a scowl replaced it. A scowl directed toward me.

My phone was right where Alex was supposed to stand in the center of the stage. I let out a feeble, airy—hopefully nearly silent—laugh before reaching down and grabbing the device. As I did, William caught my eye. His eyes should have been on Alex, but instead I'd caused a scene at the worst possible moment.

My cheeks flushed at the thought. This was not my style, nor did I enjoy stealing other people's spotlights.

I jammed the phone back into my bouquet and acted like nothing had happened. It was the best way to defuse the situation. Inwardly I wanted to crawl under a rock, though.

As I surveyed the chapel—and as people turned back to Alex in her big moment—I spotted someone in the back.

Chase.

Why had he shown up here? I mean, I was thrilled to

see him. But I thought he'd agreed not to come until this whole fiasco was over. He knew the risks.

It was more than that, though. The look in his eyes told me that something was wrong. And he wasn't standing in the back of the room out of respect. Well, maybe partially. But I had a feeling he was keeping an eye on something. Could he know?

Jamie also stared at me from her fourth-row seat. Her eyes narrowed, and she silently asked me what was going on. I tilted my head and widened my eyes, trying to confirm her suspicions that something was seriously wrong.

Somehow, our silent communication seemed to work, because her eyes widened also, and she glanced around. She seemed to sense that the trial had never been the reason behind this whole ordeal. No, the wedding was. And the bad guy was here and waiting to make his move, most likely.

I still didn't know Brandon's motive. Was he simply vengeful? Was he having an "If I can't have you, no one can" moment? I didn't know. But right now that didn't matter as much as keeping everyone safe did.

Ralph agreed to give Alex to William, he kissed her cheek, and she sauntered up the steps. I rushed to straighten the train of her heirloom dress, weighing my options in my head but reaching no firm conclusions as to the right thing to do.

Just then my phone buzzed in my bouquet. I glanced down as my screen lit. It was a text message.

I have a bomb.

I gasped. As my sister cut her gaze toward me, I offered a weak smile and tried to play it off—something I was never good at doing.

"You look so beautiful," I whispered instead.

That seemed to pacify her temporarily, and she turned back to William. The minister began his opening remarks, talking about the beauty and sacredness of marriage. Any other time, I'd love to listen. But not right now.

I glanced around. I knew Brandon was here, and he was watching. But where? Why couldn't I spot him? There were probably three hundred guests here, but still.

Sweat beaded across my forehead.

"Holly," Alex whispered.

I looked over and saw her trying to hand me her bouquet. I took it from her as she and William turned to face each other for their vows.

I glanced out again and saw both Ralph and Mom giving me odd looks. They had no idea.

Where would Brandon have hidden a bomb? Under a pew? In the choir loft? In one of the presents?

That last possibility seemed to make the most sense. Those gifts were all sitting right out in the lobby, just waiting to be opened. Plus there was that text message I'd seen on Heather's phone. *Do you have my gift?*

As I scanned the guests again, I spotted him. Brandon. He was here. And he was gloating at me.

My phone buzzed again.

"Really?" Sarah whispered behind me, her voice lilting self-righteously.

Thankfully I didn't think anyone but the people onstage could hear anything. I glanced down, but a rose blocked the message on my phone. It was tricky because now I had Alex's flowers also. But I carefully reached over and shoved the flower aside.

Object to this wedding or I'll blow the whole place up.

My mouth dropped open. He had to be kidding.

I looked over at Brandon and saw him smirk. He wasn't kidding. He really would blow this place up.

CHAPTER 39

Hadn't Brandon worked for a private defense contractor? And he was a genius. That must be how he had his knowledge of bombs and technology. My own father might have taught him a thing or two about being a locksmith. In fact, I vaguely remembered Brandon filling in on some weekends and in the summer. I'd been away at summer camp and would have been gone for most of that time.

There was no way I was objecting to Alex's wedding. She'd never forgive me. Of course, if she were dead, then none of this would matter.

What was I going to do?

Someone stood up and began to sing "I Choose You."

Oh no. I felt it. The nausea that began in my gut. Stress always made me want to throw up. And now vomit was rearing its ugly little head.

Not here. Not now. Not in the middle of all this.

I handed Alex's bouquet to Sarah, mumbled an apology, and hurried off the stage amongst the gasps of the crowd.

I kept walking until I reached the back of the sanctuary and entered the foyer. Chase was by my side in a heartbeat.

"He's here, Chase," I said, my voice trembling. "He has a bomb. He wants me to object to the wedding. If I don't play along, he's going to blow this place up."

"How do you know?"

I pulled my phone out. "He's been texting me."

"We've got to get everyone out of there, Holly."

"I can't ruin her wedding." My words sounded lame. I mean, I knew the implications. But what a mess. "But there is one thing I can do."

"What's that?"

I reached beside me and pulled down the fire alarm. "That," I muttered as sirens filled the air. "I'm so sorry, Alex."

People began rushing through the doors. Chase and I stood near the presents, watching everyone hurry by. Panic tinged the air and made us nearly invisible to everyone. Well, almost everyone.

Mom stopped beside me, her cheeks flushed.

"What is going on?" She sounded exasperated, and rightfully so. Only a jerk would ruin someone's wedding . . . or someone who was desperate to save the people she loved.

"Hopefully the fire department can tell us." I patted her shoulder.

She shook her head and wagged her index finger at me. "You and I need to have a long talk when we get home, young lady."

And, at once, I was ten years old again. "Yes, Mother."

"Well, are you coming?" She took a step away.

I nodded. "I'll be there in a minute."

Ralph gave me an odd look before leading Mom away.

Most of the crowds had scrambled outside. But I looked behind me and saw Alex standing there. She shook her head, her claws out, and her teeth close to being bared.

"How could you?" she seethed.

"Alex—"

"No, don't try to explain this." Her eyes were crazy wide as she stared at me. "You're mad because I'm wearing this dress, aren't you? That's why you're acting like this."

My eyebrows shot up. "You think this is because of the dress?"

"I know you've always wanted to wear it. That obviously won't be happening unless your measurements change between now and whenever."

"Alex, you're being irrational." I tried to calm her, but I wasn't sure how successful I'd be at this point.

"My wedding is ruined!" Alex continued. William tried to nudge her away, but she wouldn't budge.

"Alex, you should get out of here," I encouraged.

"There's no fire, is there?"

"I can explain—"

"There might be," a new voice said.

I slowly turned. Brandon stood behind me, an oddly vacant look in his eyes. Gone was the clueless man who'd intruded into my life, acting under the assumed identity of Benjamin Radcliff. All of that had been an act—and a good one at that. He'd obviously even had a fake driver's license made. This man looked calculating, too smart for his own good, and like he was coming unhinged.

He had something in his hand. Probably a detonator, I realized with fear.

"Brandon?" Alex whispered. Her disbelief was evident in her parted lips, her wide eyes, and her hoarse voice.

"Who's Brandon?" William asked, looking earnestly confused.

Alex ignored the question and stepped back, her hand going over her heart, before glancing quickly at William, as if Brandon's presence betrayed him. "I didn't invite you."

"I noticed."

"What is that?" Alex nodded at his hand and took

another step back.

I glanced around me. Thankfully, Mom had gotten out. But William, Alex, Chase, and I still remained.

"It's a bomb. It's going to explode in"—he glanced at his watch—"eight minutes and twenty-one seconds. Sooner if you upset me."

"Why . . . why would you do that?" Alex stuttered.

"If I can't have you, no one can."

Everyone was silent when Brandon started laughing—a cackling, maddening laugh.

"You don't think I'm serious, do you? That would be pathetic. This is about justice, about an eye for an eye, about people who couldn't care less about the lives they ruin."

"What are you talking about?" Alex said.

I peeked at Chase and saw him surveying the area, trying to formulate a plan to get us all out of this. He could tackle Brandon, but that act could set the detonator off.

Things clicked in my mind, the pieces fitting together more and more easily. "You moved here for a job, didn't you?" I asked. "That's where you met Tom Picket. The cameras that were found in his place sounded just like the ones you hid in my house."

"There were cameras hidden in your house?" Alex asked.

"And yours, and Ralph's, and Chase's."

"Why would you do that, Brandon?" Alex asked.

"You wouldn't understand. You destroy lives all the time without a thought about how your decisions will affect other people."

"You wanted a job with the government," I said. "Tom Picket told everyone you were crazy, so you didn't get the position. You have a record of instability. You decided to get revenge on him by murdering his wife and framing him. But Alex didn't buy it that Tom was guilty, and that brought back all the hard feelings you've been trying to swallow. You wanted Tom to pay for what he did to you. So you killed him yourself."

Brandon glared. "I'd spent my life developing these products, and then one person ruined it all. I came back here, and I was going to really make a name for myself. Maybe win Alex back in the process. But she was already engaged, and I didn't get the job. The government had no faith in my projects. In fact, they're now trying to copy what I created."

"You mean the ability to remotely control cars while someone else is supposedly driving?" Chase said. That must have been what he'd discovered, which had brought him to the wedding.

Pride glimmered in Brandon's eyes. "Exactly. Heather was the perfect test dummy. And she kept me informed of all the bridal activities so I could wreak my havoc."

I shook my head. "You're the friend who invented a way of tapping into cell phones and using them to eavesdrop, aren't you?"

His smile deepened. "How do you think I overheard so much? Isn't it brilliant? Can you believe the CIA didn't want to use that kind of technology?"

"That's . . . amazingly invasive."

"No more invasive than all these people who spy on others via the cameras on their computers. It's just smart business in today's world."

"Why did you murder Mark Reynolds?" I asked. I really hoped Chase was formulating a plan as I kept the man talking.

"Murder?" Alex said with a gasp. William pulled her closer.

"If you had talked to him, you would have gotten too

many answers, and I would never have been able to pull this off. I needed all of you in one place. I had the whole plan worked out, and I couldn't let you ruin it."

"Why in the world did you tell me I had to break up with Chase?" Maybe my timing wasn't right, but I wanted to know. I *needed* to know.

"You had to break up with him so you could bring me as your date to the wedding. But that fell apart, and that's led me to this moment." Sweat lined his upper lip. His hair was standing on end, and he had a strange scent, some kind of pheromone or something. He looked like he was coming undone. But his eyes brightened with pride. "I fooled you good, didn't I? That whole bumbling, no-social-graces routine? You fell for it. You had no idea it was me."

"I didn't." *Because you're a psychopath.*

"I knew you were the best way to get to Alex," he continued. "I played on your loyalty, and it almost worked. I didn't quite anticipate that you'd follow me to my fake office. It was a good thing I did my research and took on a real person's name. It bought me a little more time."

"This is a little drastic, don't you think?" Chase asked. "There are better ways to try and get revenge on an ex-girlfriend and someone who lost you a job."

"That's part of the fun." He cackled before coughing and turning practically demonic again. "Don't you see? I have nothing else to lose."

"You need help, Brandon," Alex said. "You're not yourself. You're a brilliant man. Maybe your brilliance has driven you off the deep end."

"I've never seen life so clearly!" His eyes held a dangerous gleam.

Facts continued to collide and solidify in my mind.

"You're targeting all of us, Brandon. Why?" I asked.

Brandon's gaze swung toward me. "Very good, Holly. You always were the unassuming one. You used to look so innocent as you apologized for kicking my shins. Everyone else bought your little act, but I knew the truth. You hated me."

"*Hated* is such a strong word. But that's not enough reason to pull me into this. What did I have to do with this?"

"Don't you see? This wasn't just about you. It was about your whole family. You all ruined my life by keeping Alex and me apart. The years since then have been difficult. Yet I look at all of you, and my heartache hasn't even affected you at all. You've all gone on your merry way."

"So you wanted to get revenge on all of us?" I repeated.

"Exactly! I knew I had to hit you each where it would hurt the most. Holly, it's always been about relationships with you, so making you deceive the people you love was an easy choice. With Alex, I knew all I had to do was distract her so she wouldn't be on her game during one of the biggest trials of her career. For Ralph, it was about his reputation. Henry was such a willing and easy participant."

"And my mom?" I asked.

"It was the pain of seeing her children hurt, of course."

The man was almost diabolical in his actions. He'd planned every moment of our suffering, and he'd enjoyed it.

"There's no need to let a bomb explode, Brandon," Chase said. "You need to think this all through."

Something flickered in his eyes, and my stomach dropped. He didn't care anymore, I realized. He was beyond reason.

I glanced at the clock on the wall behind us. We were down to three minutes. We needed people to clear out of the parking lot. Who knew how big this bomb was? How much damage it could do?

Sirens sounded outside, and I glanced back. Sure enough, I could see the crowds in the parking lot through the glass doors.

Somehow, we had to think of a way to get out of this, but how?

"You've always been the one I wanted to marry, Brandon." Alex stepped toward him.

What?

Brandon let his guard down for a moment. His shoulders relaxed, and he flinched with surprise.

"I always knew you were the one. My family didn't want us to get married, though."

I glanced toward the door and saw Jamie standing there. I motioned at her to go, praying my gestures would somehow communicate that everyone should move far away from the fiasco.

She stared another moment, and I waved my hand behind my back even harder. Brandon seemed distracted by Alex and didn't notice. Thankfully, Jamie seemed to get the message, and she began ushering people away from the building.

"I've always loved you, Alex," Brandon said.

Just then, Chase tackled him. The detonator flew from his hands. I lunged across the room and grabbed it while Chase pinned Brandon to the floor.

"We have only two minutes!" I shouted.

"You'll never get out in time," Brandon shouted. "You won't get far enough away."

William scooped Alex into his arms and dashed toward the door.

Chase pulled Brandon to his feet. "Let's get out of

here."

As soon as Brandon had the chance, he darted toward the sanctuary. Chase started to go after him, but I grabbed his arm.

"We've got to go, Chase."

He took one more glance at the double doors leading inside. Finally, he nodded. He grabbed my hand, and we sprinted outside. Just as we reached the grass beyond the parking lot, a loud explosion boomed behind us. Chase threw himself over me as debris rained around us.

When I felt Chase shift on top of me, I lifted my head and looked around. It appeared all the guests were safe across the street. Flames darted from the church's roof and windows. Brandon . . . had he died inside?

I looked at Chase. Neither of us had to say a word to express our thoughts at the moment. We'd survived. Thank God, we'd survived.

EPILOGUE

Alex and William didn't have the wedding of their dreams. Most of the guests had rushed home. But the few who'd remained were able to enjoy a simple ceremony held in the garden in the backyard of Mom's house.

The afternoon wedding had turned into an evening wedding, thanks to the intensive investigation and interrogation by the police.

Alex had ditched her veil and her high heels. I'd long since lost my bridal bouquet. There were no flowers draped down the aisle or fancy music. I thought the insects chirping around us and the scent of honeysuckle were a nice replacement, though.

The reception band had stuck around, and they played unplugged on the deck.

Sarah and Mom had strung up some lights to give the area some atmosphere, and the caterer had mercifully scrounged up some finger foods.

All in all, I thought this version of Alex's wedding was much better than the stressful, overly fancy version she'd planned.

Best of all, for me at least, was the fact that Chase was here.

In fact, I was in his arms right now, and we swayed back and forth to "I Only Have Eyes for You" by The Flamingos. The patio wasn't the best dance floor, but it would do. The evening had turned chilly, so Chase draped his coat over my shoulders. It drowned me, but I didn't care.

"It's a good thing you pulled that fire alarm. If you hadn't, I can't imagine everyone would have gotten out in time."

"A girl's gotta do what a girl's gotta do," I said. "I even think Alex has forgiven me. She did some pretty quick thinking there at the end also, distracting Brandon and all."

Investigators had found his body in the church. He'd also left a note at his house explaining where Deborah Picket's body was and taking credit for all his devious deeds. He'd obviously planned on dying today. It made me sad to think someone was that desperate.

"You keep finding yourself in these precarious situations," Chase said. "How is that?"

I shook my head, craning my neck up so I could look into his eyes. "I'm not sure. I seem to have a knack for it."

"Well, I wish you had a knack for other things, like staying safe."

"Even when we pass through the waters, God is with us. If nothing else, this whole ordeal has confirmed to me that God is beside me, whatever's happening."

"There you go again, always looking on the bright side. It's just one more thing to love about you."

"Being positive doesn't always change our situations, but sometimes it changes us, you know?"

His arms tightened around me, so I rested my head against his chest as we swayed to the music.

Somehow, I knew that everything was going to work out. Alex had gotten her wedding. She'd eventually get her honeymoon, and now she wouldn't be so distracted during the trial. With this new evidence, Ralph's name should be cleared in the whole Henry-gate fiasco. I was back with Chase. And because all her kids were happy, Mom was happy.

"Holly?" Chase murmured.

"Yes?"

"I love you," he whispered.

I froze and jerked my gaze toward him. "What?"

"I love you," he repeated with a soft smile. "I've known that I loved you for a while, but then you broke up with me and everything." His lip curled upward as his grin widened.

"Oh, Chase."

He paused. "Is that a good 'oh, Chase' or a bad 'oh, Chase'?"

I laughed. "It's a great 'oh, Chase.' If this ordeal has proven nothing else, it's shown me beyond a doubt that I'm totally, completely, and 100 percent in love with you also."

He pulled me closer. "Now, those are words that can make a guy's day. You have no idea what it does to me to hear that, Holly. When I thought I'd lost you, I realized I'd lost the best thing in my life. You make me a better person."

"I think you're already a pretty great person." I shrugged innocently.

"You just did that thing again."

"What thing?"

"That thing you do. Your hip bumps out and your head tilts and you look coy."

I grinned. "You bring out a sassy side of me. What can I say?"

"I look forward to the adventures that life will hand us in the future," Chase said. "Everything's more bearable with you by my side."

My heart swelled with love for this man. I nestled my

head against his chest again and fully engaged in enjoying each moment, because sometimes the moment was all we had.

###

Christy Barritt

Did you miss *Random Acts of Murder*, the first book in the Holly Anna Paladin Mystery series?

When Holly Anna Paladin is given a year to live, she embraces her final days doing what she loves most—random acts of kindness. But one of her extreme good deeds goes horribly wrong, implicating Holly in a string of murders. Holly is suddenly in a different kind of fight for her life.

Only two other people know Holly was at the site of the murder, and one of them is the killer. Making matters stickier is the fact that the detective assigned to the case is her old high school crush and present day nemesis.

The clock is ticking as Holly is forced to play a dangerous game. Will Holly find the killer before he ruins what's left of her life? Or will she spend her final days alone and behind bars?

Random Acts of Malice

When Holly Anna Paladin's boyfriend, police detective Chase Dexter, says he's leaving for two weeks and can't give any details, she wants to trust him. But when she discovers Chase may be involved in some unwise and dangerous pursuits, she's compelled to intervene.

Holly gets a run for her money as she's swept into the world of horseracing. The stakes turn deadly when a dead body surfaces and suspicion is cast on Chase. At every turn, more trouble emerges, making Holly question what she holds true about her relationship and her future.

Just when she thinks she's on the homestretch, a dark horse arises. Holly might lose everything in a nail-biting fight to the finish.

Random Acts of Scrooge

Christmas is supposed to be the most wonderful time of the year, but a real-life Scrooge is threatening to ruin the season's good will.

Holly Anna Paladin can't wait to celebrate Christmas with family and friends. She loves everything about the season—celebrating the birth of Jesus, singing carols, and baking Christmas treats, just to name a few. But when a local family needs help, how can she say no?

Holly's community has come together to help raise funds to save the home of Greg and Babette Sullivan, but a Bah-Humburgler has snatched the canisters of cash. Holly and her boyfriend, police detective Chase Dexter, team up to catch the Christmas crook.

Will they succeed in collecting enough cash to cover the Sullivans' overdue bills? Or will someone succeed in ruining Christmas for all those involved?

If you enjoyed this book, you might also enjoy the Squeaky Clean series:

Hazardous Duty (Book 1)
On her way to completing a degree in forensic science, Gabby St. Claire drops out of school and starts her own crime-scene cleaning business. "Yeah, that's me," she says, "a crime-scene cleaner. People waiting in line behind me who strike up conversations always regret it."

When a routine cleaning job uncovers a murder weapon the police overlooked, she realizes that the wrong person is in jail. But the owner of the weapon is a powerful foe . . . and willing to do anything to keep Gabby quiet.

With the help of her new neighbor, Riley Thomas, a man whose life and faith fascinate her, Gabby plays the detective to make sure the right person is put behind bars. Can Riley help her before another murder occurs?

Suspicious Minds (Book 2)
In this smart and suspenseful sequel to *Hazardous Duty*, crime-scene cleaner Gabby St. Claire finds herself stuck doing mold remediation to pay the bills. But her first day on the job, she uncovers a surprise in the crawlspace of a dilapidated home: Elvis, dead as a doornail and still wearing his blue-suede shoes. How could she possibly keep her nose out of a case like this?

It Came Upon a Midnight Crime (Book 2.5, a Novella)
Someone is intent on destroying the true meaning of

Christmas—at least, destroying anything that hints of it. All around crime-scene cleaner Gabby St. Claire's hometown, anything pointing to Jesus as the "reason for the season" is being sabotaged. The crimes become more twisted as dismembered body parts are found at the vandalisms. Who would go to such great lengths to dampen the joy and hope of Christ's birthday? Someone is determined to destroy Christmas . . . but Gabby St. Claire is just as determined to find the Grinch and let peace on earth and goodwill to men prevail.

Organized Grime (Book 3)
Gabby St. Claire knows her best friend, Sierra, isn't guilty of killing three people in what appears to be an eco-terrorist attack. But Sierra has disappeared, her only contact a frantic phone call to Gabby proclaiming she's being hunted. Gabby is determined to prove her friend is innocent and to keep her alive. While trying to track down the real perpetrator, Gabby notices a disturbing trend at the crime scenes she's cleaning, one that ties random crimes together—and points to Sierra as the guilty party. Just what has her friend gotten herself into?

Dirty Deeds (Book 4)
"Promise me one thing. No snooping. Just for one week."

Gabby St. Claire knows that her fiancé's request is a simple one that she should be able to honor. After all, Riley's law school reunion and attorneys' conference at a hoity-toity resort is a chance for them to get away from the mysteries Gabby often finds herself involved in as a crime-scene cleaner. The weeklong trip is a chance for them to be "normal," a word that leaves a bad taste in Gabby's mouth.

But Gabby finds herself alone for endless hours while Riley is busy with legal workshops. Then one of Riley's old friends goes missing, and Gabby suspects one of Riley's buddies might be behind the disappearance. When the missing woman's mom asks Gabby for help, how can she say no?

Secrets abound. Frankly, Gabby even has some of her own. When the dirty truth comes out, the revelations put everything in jeopardy—relationships, trusts, and even lives.

The Scum of All Fears **(Book 5)**
Gabby St. Claire is back to crime-scene cleaning, at least temporarily. With her business partner on his honeymoon, she needs help after a weekend killing spree fills up her work docket. She quickly realizes she has bigger problems than finding temporary help.

A serial killer that her fiancé, a former prosecutor, put behind bars has escaped. His last words to Riley were: *I'll get out, and I'll get even.* Pictures of Gabby are found in the man's prison cell, and Riley fears the sadistic madman has Gabby in his sights.

Gabby tells herself there's no way the Scum River Killer will make it across the country from California to Virginia without being caught. But then messages are left for Gabby at crime scenes, and someone keeps slipping in and out of her apartment.

When Gabby's temporary assistant disappears, Gabby must figure out who's behind these crimes. The search for answers becomes darker when Gabby realizes she's dealing with a criminal who is more than evil. He's truly the scum of the earth, and he'll do anything to make Gabby and Riley's lives a living nightmare.

To Love, Honor, and Perish (Book 6)

How could God let this happen?

Crime-scene cleaner Gabby St. Claire can't stop asking the question. Just when her life is on the right track, the unthinkable happens. Gabby's fiancé, Riley Thomas, is shot and remains in life-threatening condition only a week before their wedding.

Gabby is determined to figure out who pulled the trigger, even if investigating puts her own life at risk. But as she digs deeper into the facts surrounding the case, she discovers secrets better left alone. Doubts arise in her mind, and the one man with answers is on death's doorstep.

An old foe from the past returns and tests everything Gabby is made of—physically, mentally, and spiritually. Will her soul survive the challenges ahead? Or will everything she's worked for be destroyed?

Mucky Streak (Book 7)
After her last encounter with a serial killer, Gabby St. Claire feels her life is smeared with the stain of tragedy. Between the exhaustion of trying to get her fiancé back on his feet, routine night terrors, and potential changes looming on the horizon, she needs a respite from the mire of life.

At the encouragement of her friends, she takes on a short-term gig as a private investigator: a cold case that's eluded investigators for ten years. The mass murder of a wealthy family seems impossible to solve but quickly gets interesting as Gabby brings more clues to light. Add to the mix a flirtatious client, travels to an exciting new city, and some quirky—albeit temporary—new sidekicks, and things get really complicated.

With every new development, Gabby prays that what she's calling her "mucky streak" will end and the future will become clear. But every answer she uncovers leads her closer to danger—both for her life and for her heart.

Foul Play (Book 8)
Gabby St. Claire is crying "foul play" in every sense of the phrase.

When crime-scene cleaner Gabby St. Claire agrees to go undercover at a local community theater, she discovers more than backstage bickering, atrocious acting, and rotten writing. The female lead is dead, and an old classmate who's staked everything on the musical production's success is about to go under.

In her dual role of investigator and star of the show, Gabby finds the stakes rising faster than the opening-night curtain. She comes face-to-face with her past and must make monumental decisions, not just about the play but also concerning her future relationships and career.

Will Gabby find the killer before the curtain goes down—not only on the play, but also on life as she knows it?

Broom and Gloom (Book 9)
Gabby St. Claire is determined to get back in the saddle again.

While in Oklahoma for a forensic conference, she meets her soon-to-be stepbrother Trace Ryan, an up-and-coming country singer. Trace shares that a woman he was dating went missing a month ago, and he suspects a crazy fan girl may be behind her disappearance.

Gabby can't pass up the opportunity to investigate. But her schedule is tricky as she tries to juggle her conference, navigate being alone in a new place, and locate a woman who may not want to be found.

She discovers that sometimes taking life by the horns means staring danger in the face, no matter the consequences.

Dust and Obey (Book 10)

When Gabby St. Claire's ex-fiancé, Riley Thomas, asks for her help in investigating a possible murder at a couples retreat, she knows she should say no. She knows she should run far, far away from the danger of both being around Riley and the crime.

But her nosy instincts and determination take precedence over her logic. At the retreat center she feels like she's stepped into the pages of a creepy gothic novel: an isolated island that's often foggy, an old lodge with a dark history, and a small pool of suspects who each have either motive, means, or opportunity for murder. When another life is threatened, the risk intensifies.

Gabby and Riley must work together to find the killer. In the process, they have to confront demons from their past and deal with their present relationship. If they don't learn to trust each other, they could both end up as fodder for the supposedly cursed island's folklore.

The Sierra Files

***Pounced* (Book 1)**
Animal-rights activist Sierra Nakamura never expected to stumble upon the dead body of a coworker while out filming a project. She definitely never expected to get involved in the investigation. But when someone threatens to kill her cats unless she hands over the "information," she becomes more bristly than an angry feline.

Making matters worse is the fact that her cats—and the investigation—are driving a wedge between her and her boyfriend, Chad. With every answer she uncovers, old hurts rise to the surface and test her beliefs.

Saving her cats just might mean ruining everything else in her life. In the fight for survival, one thing is certain: It's either pounce or be pounced.

***Hunted* (Book 2)**
Who knew a stray dog could lead to so much trouble?

Newlywed animal-rights activist Sierra Nakamura Davis is coming face-to-face with her worst nightmare: breaking the news she eloped to her ultra-opinionated tiger mom.

Her perfectionist parents have planned a vow-renewal ceremony at Sierra's lush childhood home, but a neighborhood dog ruins the rehearsal dinner when he shows up toting what appears to be a fresh human bone.

Between the dog, a nosy neighbor, and an old flame turning up at all the wrong times, Sierra hunts for answers. Surprises abound at every turn as Sierra embarks on a journey of discovery that leads to more than just who committed the crime.

***Pranced** **(Book 2.5, a Christmas novella)**
Sierra Nakamura Davis thinks that spending Christmas with her husband's relatives will be a real Yuletide treat. But when the animal-rights activist finds out that his family has a reindeer farm, she begins to feel more like the Grinch.

Even worse, when Sierra arrives, she discovers that those very reindeer are missing. The community is depending on the creatures to spread holiday cheer at the annual light show. Plus, Sierra fears the animals might be suffering a far worst fate than being used for entertainment purposes.

Can Sierra set aside her dogmatic opinions to help get the reindeer home in time for the holidays? Or will secrets tear the family apart and ruin Sierra's dream of the perfect Christmas?

Other Books by Christy Barritt:

Dubiosity
Savannah Harris vowed to leave behind her old life as an intrepid investigative reporter. But when a friend raises suspicions about two migrant workers who've gone missing from the sleepy coastal town Savannah calls home, her curiosity spikes.

As ever more eerie incidents begin afflicting the area, each works to draw Savannah out of her seclusion and raise the stakes—for both Savannah and the surrounding community. Even as Savannah's new boarder, Clive Miller, makes her feel things she thought long forgotten, she suspects he's hiding something too, and he's not the only one. Doubts collide in Savannah's mind: Who can she really trust?

As secrets emerge and danger closes in, Savannah must choose between faith and uncertainty. One wrong decision might spell the end…not just for her, but for everyone around her.

Will she unravel the mystery in time, or will doubt get the best of her?

The Good Girl
Tara Lancaster can sing "Amazing Grace" in three harmonies, two languages, and interpret it for the hearing impaired. She can list the Bible canon backward, forward, and alphabetized. And the only time she ever missed church was at seventeen because she had pneumonia and her mom made her stay home. But when her life shatters around her and her

reputation is left in ruins, Tara decides escape is the only option. She flees halfway across the country to dog-sit, but the quiet anonymity she needs isn't waiting in her sister's house. Instead, she finds a knife with a threatening message, a fame-hungry friend, a too-hunky neighbor, and evidence of ... a ghost? Following all the rules has gotten her nowhere. And nothing she learned in Sunday School can tell her where to go from there.

Death of the Couch Potato's Wife (Suburban Sleuth Mysteries)

You haven't seen desperate until you've met Laura Berry, a career-oriented city slicker turned suburbanite housewife. Well-trained in the big city commandment, "mind your own business," Laura is persuaded by her spunky seventy-year-old neighbor, Babe, to check on another neighbor who hasn't been seen in days. She finds her neighbor, Candace Flynn, wife of the infamous "Couch King," dead, and at last has a reason to get up in the morning in suburbia: murder. Someone is determined to stop her from digging deeper into the death of her neighbor, but Laura is just as determined to figure out who's behind the death-by-poisoned-pork-rinds.

The Trouble with Perfect

Since the death of her fiancé two years ago, novelist Morgan Blake's life has been in a holding pattern. She has a major case of writer's block, and a book signing in the small mountain town of Perfect sounds like just the solution to help her clear her head. Her trip takes a wrong turn when, on her way there, she's involved in a hit-and-run—She has hit a man, and he has run from the scene. Before fleeing, he mouthed the word, "Help." She plans to give him that help, but first she must find him. In Perfect, she finds a town that offers everything she ever wanted. But is something sinister going on behind the town's cheery exterior? Was she invited as a guest of honor simply to do a book signing? Or was she lured to town for another purpose—a deadly purpose?

Home Before Dark (Carolina Moon Series, Book 1)

Nothing good ever happens after dark. Those were the words country singer Daleigh McDermott's father always repeated. Now, her father is dead, and Daleigh fears she returned home too late to make things right. As she's about to flee back to Nashville, she finds a hidden journal belonging to her father. His words hint that his death was no accident.

Small-town mechanic Ryan Shields is the only one who seems to believe that Daleigh may be on to something. Her father trusted the man, but Daleigh's instant attraction to Ryan scares her. She knows her life and career, however dwindling it might be, are back in Nashville and that her time in the sleepy North Carolina town is only temporary. As Daleigh and Ryan work to unravel the mystery, it becomes obvious that someone wants them dead. They must rely on each other—and on God—if they hope to make it home before the darkness swallows them whole.

Home Before Dark offers a blend of Nicholas Sparks meets Mary Higgins Clark, a mix of charming small-town life in North Carolina tangled in a gripping suspense.

Gone By Dark (Carolina Moon, Book 2)

Charity White can't forget the horrific crime that happened ten years ago when she and her best friend, Andrea, spontaneously cut through the woods on their way home from high school. In the middle of their trek, a man abducted

Andrea, who hasn't been seen since.

Since that fateful day, Charity has tried to outrun the memories and guilt of that one hasty decision. What if she and her friend hadn't taken that shortcut? Why wasn't Charity taken instead of Andrea? And why weren't the police ever able to track down the bad guy?

When Charity receives a mysterious letter that promises answers, she decides to face her worst nightmare. She returns home to North Carolina in search of closure and a touch of the peace that has eluded her for the past decade. With the help of her new neighbor, Police Officer Joshua Haven, Charity begins to track down mysterious clues. They soon discover that they must work together or both of them will be swallowed by the looming darkness.

About the Author:

USA Today has called Christy Barritt's books "scary, funny, passionate, and quirky."

Christy writes both mystery and romantic suspense novels that are clean with underlying messages of faith. Her books have won the Daphne du Maurier Award for Excellence in Suspense and Mystery, have been twice nominated for the Romantic Times Reviewers' Choice Award, and have finaled for both a Carol Award and *Foreword Magazine*'s Book of the Year.

Christy is married to her Prince Charming, a man who thinks she's hilarious—but only when she's not trying to be. She is a self-proclaimed klutz, an avid music lover who's known for spontaneously bursting into song, and a road-trip aficionado. When she's not working or spending time with her family, she enjoys singing, playing the guitar, and exploring small, unsuspecting towns where people have no idea how accident-prone she is.

Find Christy online at:
www.christybarritt.com
www.facebook.com/christybarritt
www.twitter.com/cbarritt

Sign up for Christy's newsletter to get information on all of her latest releases here:
www.christybarritt.com/newsletter-sign-up/

If you enjoyed this book, please consider leaving a review.

Random Acts of Deceit

Made in the USA
Middletown, DE
16 August 2019